"Molly, wait!"

I froze in place for a moment. It was definitely a man under the tree though I couldn't see his face...and he knew my name.

"Do I know you?" I called in an unsteady voice. It seemed, though, as if my words were taken by the wind. Who was this man? And how did he know my name?

He moved away from the tree with a tentative step. His clothing was formal—a dark suit and white shirt—as if he had just been to a funeral. I hadn't remembered seeing a canopy for a funeral on the grounds, but I wasn't about to take my eyes off the stranger for one instant to confirm that suspicion.

I thought I saw a flash of white teeth from under his dark mustache, but he was still some distance away. Golden highlights in his chestnut hair caught the sunlight, and my mouth dropped open. He was undoubtedly one of the most handsome men I had ever seen in my life. My stomach rolled over at the sight of him, though not exclusively with admiration of his good looks. Cold sweat broke out on my forehead, and I put my hand to my mouth as if to hold back the morning's breakfast...if I'd had any.

For here—in the flesh—was the man of my dreams. Not just any dreams. More specifically, my dreams of the previous evening. Yet I couldn't for the life of me remember ever seeing him before until this moment.

"Be careful what you wish for," I muttered behind the hand that covered my convulsing mouth.

"Molly, do not be frightened. I can see that you are. I do not want to scare you." He took another step forward and held his hands up palms out...as if to show me he wasn't armed, I thought hysterically, or to calm me down. Either way, it wasn't working.

What They're Saying About *Across the Winds in Time*

"I have to say that Ms. McBride has outdone herself yet again. I love her creative storylines and her well-developed characters. She created such an engrossing story that I found myself hanging onto her every word and I eagerly couldn't wait to see what happened next for Molly, Sara and Darius. The author knows what readers look for in a great story and she surely delivers it each and every time.

~Diana, Night Owl Reviews

"Across The Winds of Time is an exciting, amazing time travel that kept me on the edge of my seat. Ms. McBride does a wonderful job at solving the many mysteries, and subplots in this impressive story. The characters are vibrant and kept me anxious to see what would happen next. There is also humor hidden in the pages that made me smile. It is a charming story and one I would definitely suggest you read. I am looking forward to many more stories from this author." *~Mariah, The Romance Studio*

"Ms. McBride writes with her usual flair and unique spin on time travel. The reader is genuinely satisfied with the quirks and awkwardness expected with the 100 year age time difference and varied customs and clothing. The scenes range from comedic to romantic to frantic and back again. The attention to detail when the author describes the Victorian home, the surrounding land and the scenery in both time periods is phenomenal." *~Laura, You Gotta Read Reviews*

Across the Winds of Time

Bess McBride

ACROSS THE WINDS OF TIME

Contact information: bessmcbride@gmail.com

Cover Art by *Tamra Westberry*

Formatted by IRONHORSE Formatting

Published in the United States of America

ISBN: 1491218002
ISBN-13: 978-1491218006

OTHER BOOKS BY BESS MCBRIDE

Time Travel Romance
Forever Beside You in Time
Moonlight Wishes in Time
(Book One of the Moonlight Wishes in Time series)
A Smile in Time
(Book Three of the Train Through Time series)
Together Forever in Time
(Book Two of the Train Through Time series)
A Train Through Time
(Book One of the Train Through Time series)
Love of My Heart

Contemporary/Romantic Suspense
Will Travel for Romance Boxed Set Books 1-5
A Penny for Your Thoughts
A Shy Woman in Love
A Sigh of Love
A Trail of Love
A Penny for Your Thoughts
Jenny Cussler's Last Stand

Contemporary/Ghost Story
Caribbean Dreams of Love
On a Warm Sea of Love

Dedication

For Les, who patiently wandered cemeteries with me in search of my ancestors' tombstones on my genealogical odyssey through the Midwest.

For Cinnamon, Mike and Lily, as always.

And for all my relations...

Dear Reader,

Thank you for purchasing *Across the Winds in Time.* This edition of *Across the Winds in Time* is a re-release of the book previously published in September 2011. I acquired the rights back to the book and have republished the book. New cover! Same story! If you have already purchased *Across the Winds of Time*, you don't need to purchase the new version unless you just like the cover! The story hasn't changed.

Across the Winds in Time was inspired by my love for genealogy and the joy—and frustrations—often inherent in searching for my ancestors.

I recently spent several years working and living in Lincoln, Nebraska, where I had an opportunity to search for the final resting place of my great-great grandparents somewhere across the state line in Iowa. During that search, I found a wonderful cemetery on a hill in a lovely little town, and I hoped an ancestor of mine was buried there. Any ancestor! I loved that cemetery so much. The wind... I also came across a delightful little rundown Victorian house in the same town, and a time travel romance was born. I didn't find my ancestors there, but I did find a story!

You know I always enjoy hearing from you, so please feel free to contact me at bessmcbride@gmail.com, through my website at www.BessMcBride.com, or my blog Will Travel for Romance.

Thanks for reading!

Bess

Chapter One

I never believed in time travel...or in ghosts, for that matter. Until I fell in love, that is.

I first heard the voice that would haunt my dreams late in the afternoon on one of those dog days of August in the Midwest when cicadas sang and warm winds blew across the prairies.

I paused at the top of the cemetery hill with my arms outstretched, willing the wild wind to catch me and send me soaring into the air. The brisk breeze coming in off the valley below blew my hair from my face, and I reveled in the feel of it streaming behind me. Rolling fields of corn in the valley below the hill swayed gently, seemingly escaping the strong current by virtue of their seclusion amongst the small hills and knolls.

I turned my head slightly to focus on the unrelenting sound of the rustling leaves in the huge oak trees dotting the old burial grounds behind me. Warm sunshine beamed down around me, chasing away any notions of doom and gloom one might otherwise have in the old cemetery. Although I'd never been to that particular cemetery before and knew nothing of the lives of the people laid to rest on the grounds, the old burial grounds felt like a happy place—its residents well cared for and loved.

Words could not express the joy I felt in that moment, and I could not understand the bliss which literally seemed to warm my heart. There I stood in an unfamiliar cemetery on a windy hilltop in a small town in the Midwestern farming state of Iowa, far from where I'd ever lived, and yet an inexplicable "connection" to my surroundings seemed to embrace me—to welcome me, as if I'd "come home." Yet, I'd never been to Iowa before...at least not to my knowledge. My lungs expanded as I widened my arms, and I drew in deep breaths.

With a fervent desire to share my strange sense of elation, I looked around for my sister. Where was she? I squinted and searched the length of the cemetery for the small figure in a white blouse and blue jeans, and spotted Sara on the other side of the cemetery, intently studying the rows of tombstones as she walked. She was too far away to hear my call—especially over the loud hum of the trees in the steady wind.

I cupped my hands to my mouth and tried calling her anyway.

"Sara!"

She didn't look up.

"Yoooohooooo!!! Saaarrraaa! Come here and feel this wind! It's great!"

The wind carried my voice away, and Sara moseyed on among the tombstones, head bent, her back to me.

I dropped my hands and shrugged. With an apologetic glance toward the nearest dearly departed residents for my inappropriate screeching in their final resting place, I turned to face the valley of crops below once again.

It was just as well. I wasn't certain I wanted to share this experience with anyone else. How could I explain the vibrancy I felt as the wind simultaneously pushed and pulled at me, whipping around my body, encircling me in its warm embrace? How could I explain the connection I felt to this place? I wasn't sure Sara would understand my reactions to the wind...to the cemetery. I felt suddenly...*alive*—an ironic sensation in the middle of a cemetery.

How long had the wind blown like this here on the hill? Days? Weeks? Centuries? I wished I knew more about geology and meteorology than I did.

And what a strange place for a cemetery! A beautiful place no doubt, but the unruly wind must certainly have forced the ladies to clutch their hats during graveside funeral services over the years. I stifled a chuckle at the image and pressed my lips together in proper reverential form.

Perhaps the town had selected this site as a cemetery because the top of the hill was least likely to sustain crops given wind and erosion? I shrugged. I had no idea. As a city girl, I knew nothing about farming except that I liked vegetables.

Guilt nudged me, albeit gently, and I sighed and glanced over my shoulder once again to survey nearby tombstones. I was supposed to be looking for the names of ancestors who might not even be buried here...as Sara was so diligently doing on my behalf. But this cemetery had been a long shot...just a small patch of ground in a small town in mid America.

I had convinced Sara to stop at this quaint little cemetery for a quick "run" through the stones in the seemingly fruitless search for the final resting place of our dearly departed great-great-grandparents. Sara and I had driven through the small town of Lilium in a roundabout fashion on our way back to Council Bluffs, Iowa from visiting our great-grandparents' graves in Missouri Valley.

And here I stood, not even participating in the search, but merely pretending to be a bird who wanted nothing more than to soar in the exhilarating wind, while my sister dutifully trudged up and down the rows of tombstones looking for any familiar names.

"Molly, my love."

I turned, expecting to see Sara close behind me. But no one was there. I could see the back of Sara's small form still far away on the opposite side of the cemetery. At any rate, the voice had a distinctive baritone to it. Was someone else here?

A quick visual sweep of my surroundings revealed I was alone. And in a cemetery with no other living people about, alone was a good thing. I cupped my hands and tried yelling over the wind once again in Sara's direction.

"Did you call me?"

She didn't look up. I couldn't face another shout. Bellowing over the sleepy stones seemed so disrespectful.

I gave myself a quick shake. Must have been my imagination. Turning back to the valley, I checked my watch, fearing it was growing late. 5 p.m.

I sighed, reluctantly accepting that Sara and I should leave soon. We had a 45-minute drive back to our hotel in Council Bluffs, and the day had been long. But I didn't want to go. I had the oddest desire to linger at the cemetery. I supposed it was that sense of connection I still felt. For the first time on our "cemetery hopping" journey in search of ancestors, I felt a kinship to a place, though it bore no resemblance to the familiar cloudy skies and wet forests of my home in the Evergreen State of Washington.

I relaxed again and beamed as I surveyed the cemetery and listened to the rustling leaves of the trees. The unexplained peace and contentment continued to keep me company in this new bond I had formed with the Midwest—here in this cemetery, where it seemed likely no single relative of mine actually even resided for all eternity.

The wind continued to whip around me, pushing the hair from my face. There was no sense trying to drag my bangs back down over my impossibly high forehead. I'd given up the day before when I first encountered the incessant winds of the prairies bordering the Missouri River of Iowa and Nebraska.

"I have missed you so much, Molly."

I jerked my head around again.

"Sara?"

But Sara had moved off even further, lost in her explorations. I cocked my head to the left to hear better. I could have sworn it was a man's voice. Was it a trick of the wind? A sigh from one of the grand old oak trees protecting the cemetery from the winds?

"Is someone there?" I whispered. I truly hoped no one was. There was no answer...thankfully.

I gave myself a shake and dropped my gaze to scan the surrounding stones, one bright white stone catching my eye for an instant before I allowed my gaze to move on.

"Please come back to me, Molly." The poignant sadness in the deep voice took my breath away. I swung around, scanning the surrounding area in a 360 degree panorama. My pulse pounded against my throat, and I raised a hand to my neck as if to soothe it.

"This is ridiculous," I squeaked as I crushed my arms across my chest and turned to hurry toward Sara. It was definitely time to leave the cemetery if I had begun to hear things. I didn't believe in ghosts, and I wasn't about to start now...here in the cemetery. We were only on day three of our "ancestor hunting" trip, and we still had several more cemeteries to visit in the coming days. Hearing voices in the graveyards could certainly become an impediment to the rest of the trip. Especially if those voices seemed to know my name.

I thought I heard the elusive sound one more time as I scurried along the graveled path toward the other side of the cemetery...and the sanctuary of Sara. I quickened my step. The wind at my back helped propel me forward, and I reached my sister's side in minimal time, albeit slightly out of breath.

"Did you find something?" Sara straightened from an examination of a tombstone and looked up at me with vivid blue eyes...so like our mother's.

I threw an embarrassingly furtive glance over my shoulder before replying with a shake of my head. I hesitated telling Sara about hearing a voice, certain she would think my imagination was in overdrive...as usual. It would be just like me to be the only person around hearing voices. And if word got back to my parents, they would chuckle and say, "That Molly! You never know what she's going to come up with." They would exchange knowing looks. "Molly! Such a vivid imagination, you can't take her too seriously."

"No, nothing," I replied. "I don't see any familiar names on the tombstones. This was a long shot, but I'm glad we stopped by." I gestured expansively, though I noticed my hands shook a bit. "What a beautiful cemetery!"

Sara rested her hands on slim blue-jeaned hips and surveyed the grounds.

"It is beautiful, isn't it? And you thought for sure some long lost relative would be here when we drove by. I'm sorry we couldn't find anyone."

Now that I was within the sphere of my practical, no-nonsense sister and out of the spell of the captivating wind, I felt a sudden urge to leave as soon as possible. I linked my arm in Sara's and pulled her toward the dark green rental car parked just inside the entrance of the cemetery as I chattered inconsequentially.

"I'd say I'm sorry I dragged us on a wild goose chase to this cemetery, except that I really like it. I don't know why I wanted to come in here. I thought we might find some relatives buried here, that's all. Just a weird feeling, you know? I can't really explain it."

And if I kept talking, I wouldn't hear the voice again, would I?

"Well, some of the stones are so old, I can't even read them. The lettering has worn away," Sara said as she allowed me to pull her along without complaint.

"Yeah, I noticed that over there as well." I nodded in the direction of the top of the hill. "The wind blows so steadily, it must have done some damage over the years. For all we know, we might have a whole family of ancestors buried here."

"Let's call the town clerk tomorrow and see if they have a listing of the names of people who are interred here," Sara said with renewed enthusiasm. "If we don't recognize any names, we'll move on to the cemetery in Council Bluffs. At least we know our great-great-grandparents on the Hamilton side are there."

Sara hopped in the driver's seat while I pulled open the door on the passenger side. I didn't hold out much hope that we'd have luck with the town clerk, and I felt a bit guilty allowing Sara to expend energy pursuing any further links to Lilium. But Sara was in her element. The practical sister...the one who made phone calls to town clerks during office hours to eliminate wasted time. I, on the other hand, was the dreamer...the impractical sister...who'd rather just stumble into a cemetery and search for ancestors by "intuition" or a "feeling." Sara had been more than patient with my half-baked way of finding ancestors.

"Gee, Sara, I really don't think we have anyone here," I sighed. I was aware of an irrational desire to have a relative buried in the cemetery on the hilltop. I saw myself popping in to visit my dear ancestor on occasion, blithely ignoring the fact that I lived 2000 miles away in

Seattle. But there was no way Sara could understand my whimsy...at least I didn't think so. I turned to give Sara my best "I'm over this fad" smile. Hopefully, though, my dear relative wouldn't decide she...or he...had to actually talk to me.

Sara eyed me quizzically for a moment and nodded before she turned the ignition key.

"Well, we'll call anyway," she said with a knowing smile. I hadn't fooled her. She knew I was drawn to the cemetery. "It can't hurt...just in case."

Anxious to leave and yet reluctant to do so, I turned to take one last look at the top of the hill. Inexplicable longing brought a sudden, sharp ache to my chest, and I couldn't breathe for a moment.

The late afternoon sun crowned the hill with a blaze of fiery gold. A distinctively white stone gleamed and basked under the light—maybe the same stone I had noticed earlier. I couldn't remember if I'd looked at the marker closely to see the name. I put my hand to my chest as if to soothe the sharp pain, but the ache seemed too deeply embedded to touch. I swallowed hard, fighting against a profound and overwhelming sense of loss as we drove away.

****

That night, I tossed and turned in bed. The hotel sported large comfortable queen-size mattresses, so I knew my restlessness wasn't the discomfort of strange sleeping accommodations. In fact, the bed was much more comfortable than my plain no-frills mattress at home.

A man's face drifted in and out of my dreams. I couldn't really remember the substance of the dreams...something about the cemetery in Lilium...the wind...the bright white stone. He looked familiar, but I couldn't remember how. Surprisingly, the image was in black and white. Did I always dream in black and white? I hadn't noticed before.

He kneeled before a tombstone, his head bent as he rested one tanned sturdy hand along the top of the stone. The white stone?

"Molly," he whispered. "Please come back to me."

He raised his head and kissed the tips of his fingers before transferring his hand to the stone. Finally, I could see his face.

His face was long and angular with light-colored eyes under heavy, sensuous lids. His jaw line seemed to be carved out of stone, ending in a distinctively masculine chin. A full, well-groomed mustache draped over his upper lip and ran down past the corners of his mouth in an old-fashioned style. His thick hair appeared to be light brown with a soft wave that swept away from a side part and settled just over both ears with a slight lift at the ends. I could just see where it settled on the bottom edge of his stiff high-collared white shirt. Long sideburns framed his face, again in the style of another time. I couldn't make out the color of his eyes, but it wasn't for lack of trying. Were they blue? Green?

He turned as if he saw me and sprang to his feet. His wide smile welcomed me as he opened his arms. I melted against him and he folded me in a loving embrace.

I opened my eyes in the dark. The room was quiet. Sara wasn't a snorer, thank goodness. A faint light from the bottom edge of the closed bathroom door kept the room from total blackness. I'd left the bathroom light on as a nightlight in a strange place to avoid stubbing my toe should I need to get up in the night.

That bittersweet moment came upon me in the semi-dark room...that moment when we realize our handsome lover existed only in a dream. I sighed in the dark.

Why did this man's face seem so familiar? Had I watched some historical movie recently with a Rhett Butler-type character? The man in my dreams looked as if he stepped straight out of the nineteenth century. If his unexpectedly handsome sideburns and mustache weren't enough of a clue, the thin satin string tie around the squared color of his white shirt certainly screamed, "I don't own a flannel shirt."

I turned on my side toward the wall, closing my eyes once again and willing myself to return to my dream at the exact spot where I left off. I had no idea what my handsome man was doing in the dream, but I wanted to see him again and delight in the twinkle of his eyes as he looked at me.

****

I awakened in the morning, unaware of any further visitations from my handsome historical man, but I felt energized and determined to return to the cemetery I'd visited the day before in the little town of Lilium, though I had no plan and no coherent thought other than a sense of something left behind. I wasn't sure I had explored the cemetery as thoroughly as I should. The bright morning erased my anxiety of the day before. The memory of the voice in the cemetery seemed distant...and rather absurd. It seemed likely that what I'd heard was the wind whistling in the trees. And it was the memory of that wind that drew me back to the cemetery again...that and a nagging sense that I'd missed something. I just didn't know what. But I had a nagging suspicion that if I didn't go back, I would always wonder what I had missed.

"Sara..." I paused in the act of brushing my shoulder-length ash brown hair in front of the dresser mirror. I watched Sara in the mirror as she looked up from the phone where she was apparently on hold with the Lilium town clerk's office.

"Hmmm?" she said.

"No matter what they say at the clerk's office, I'm going back to that cemetery today." My gaze flickered away from her and back to my reflection where I watched my face redden. I brushed a few curls over my cheeks to cover my heightened color. I honestly couldn't justify returning to the cemetery, and I didn't want to try. I just wanted to go back.

Sara narrowed her eyes but was interrupted by the return of the town clerk. I watched her in the mirror.

"No Peters then? How about Hamiltons? No? Okay then, thank you very much for your time."

Sara closed the phone and leaned back against the headboard of her neatly made bed, eyeing me with a crease between her dainty dark eyebrows.

"Well, that's it then. There's no one in the Lilium Cemetery that we're related to. You don't still want to return, do you? It's almost an hour drive from here...in the wrong direction. We need to hit the old cemetery here in Council Bluffs today." She looked down at the silver watch on her slim wrist. "If we're going to stay on schedule."

I chewed my lower lip and turned slowly, moving over to sit on the edge of my bed. I lowered my gaze to the hairbrush that I twisted in my hand.

"I do need to go back. I'm not sure why, but I need to."

"Well, that's just weird, Sis."

I looked up to catch Sara watching me with narrowed eyes and a twitch at the corner of her lips. I could hear her thoughts now. "That Molly, always marching to the beat of a different drummer." She and our mother might look at each other. "You try talking some sense into her. I can't," Mother would say. Ultimately though, Sara was much more tolerant of my flighty ways than my parents. She'd come to my defense more than once when my head had been "in the clouds."

"What do you hope to find there?" Sara asked with a lift of her right eyebrow.

"I don't know." I shrugged helplessly. "Maybe a connection we missed. Something. I just have a feeling about the place." I grinned at my foolishness and stood to return the hairbrush to my cosmetics bag. "Maybe I just like the wind."

"I did notice how windy it was out there. I can't imagine how those old oak trees managed to get a foothold on that hill back in the day."

I stood up and faced the mirror once again, running some lipstick across my lips for a bit of color on my fairly pale face. Coffee-colored brown eyes, thanks to my father's genes, stared back at me.

"Someone must have planted them," I ventured as I closed my lipstick and returned it to the cosmetics bag. I'd wondered that myself the day before. I turned away from the mirror and faced Sara once again.

"So, what do you think? Are you coming with me?" I asked, hoping she would say no. I was conflicted about Sara's presence at the cemetery. I had a compelling desire to return there alone, so I wouldn't have to explain what...or who...or what I was looking for.

Sara shook her head. "No, I don't think so. You know what I will do though? I'm going to call Debbie and see if we can meet today. I told you about her, remember? We went to school together. She lives here in Council Bluffs. I was going to find time to see her anyway. She said to call her anytime." Sara picked up her cell phone to dial. "If she's free, this will work out great!"

I breathed a sigh of relief. That had gone well. And if Debbie would pick Sara up, I could take the rental car. I waited while Sara made her call. Luckily, Debbie was available, and Sara made arrangements with her for an early lunch and a day of sight seeing.

"So, I can take the car, right?" I asked when she hung up the phone. The words "ungrateful" and "disloyal" popped into my head as I contemplated abandoning my sister this way.

"Sure. Debbie is picking me up." She dropped her phone on the bed, gave me a "don't worry" grin and rose to walk into the bathroom. I heard the sound of running water.

I grabbed my purse and the keys to the car and headed to the door where I paused...with a continuing edge of guilt over my self-absorbed interruption of our plans.

"You're sure this is all right?" I asked.

Sara stepped out of the bathroom with a face towel pressed against her wet pink cheeks.

"Well, I think it's pretty strange, but I'll be fine today, if that's what you're asking. Lilium seems a long way to go without any real plan in mind, especially since we were just there yesterday and apparently don't have any relatives buried there."

"I know," I sighed, always susceptible to the voice of reason but unable to understand how practical people thought. "I'm not too sure why I'm going either."

Hearing the wavering doubt in my voice and fearing Sara's common sense might sway me from my as yet undetermined goal in Lilium, I squared my shoulders, did my best to ignore Sara's questioning look and sailed past her out the door with an airy wave. Why, this was nothing more than an off-schedule repeat genealogical exploration, I told myself. Nothing more.

"Be back later," I breezed. "Have a good time with Debbie."

Forty-five minutes later, I left the exhilarating speed of the interstate and slowed down to twenty-five miles an hour as I entered tiny Lilium. Destination near at hand, I finally relaxed from what had suddenly turned into a pell-mell return run toward Lilium. I studied the houses as I drove along Main Street where a line of majestic oaks draped gracefully over the road to create a leafy canopy of shade. The massive trees had overgrown their original plantings, dwarfing many of the older houses along the street. Sara and I really hadn't seen much of the town the day before as we'd been focused on finding the cemetery.

I turned right to head for the cemetery on the outskirts of town. The small grouping of houses of the town thinned out. Approximately a mile down the road, a flash of color on the left caught my eye, and I tapped on the brakes to slow the car. An old, decrepit and seemingly abandoned Victorian house peeked out of the thick line of trees, its faded colors of pale turquoise and salmon pink begging a bystander to admire its once fine beauty.

With a glance in the rearview mirror to see if I was holding up traffic—an unlikely event on this quiet road—I put the car in motion again, eased it over to the edge of the dirt road and came to a stop.

The house absolutely begged me to take its picture. And who was I to resist such a request? I loved Victorian houses anyway. There were so many beautiful specimens in the Pacific Northwest, and I never tired of looking at them. With a grin, I grabbed my pocket-sized digital camera from my handbag and climbed out of the car. I leaned against the closed door and took several shots from the opposite side of the road to encompass as much of the oddly appealing house as possible.

Though my view of the surrounding property was partially obscured by the thickness of the massive oak trees in the front yard, I could see the property appeared large—perhaps five acres or so. However, I was no expert at judging acreage given my current apartment lifestyle in the city.

I snapped a few quick photos before lowering the camera to examine the house in depth, as if something might prevent me from securing its likeness and immortalizing it in a photograph—something avoidable like the camera battery dying or something bizarre like darkness suddenly descending. I wasn't quite sure what I was thinking. I only knew an avid desire to get some quick pictures before the magic of the house disappeared, though I really had no idea what that meant.

Satisfied with several quick shots from across the street and anxious for a better look at the house, I pocketed the camera in my jeans and crossed the quiet road.

An old, rusted, wrought iron fence surrounded the property, though sections of it appeared in danger of toppling over. The gray and weathered railing surrounding the front porch must have once been a thing of beauty. Some of the dainty and elegant scrollwork reminiscent of other Victorian homes I had seen remained intact, and I sighed at its delicate beauty.

A brisk breeze lifted my bangs from my forehead. Ah, the wind. So, it wasn't just limited to the cemetery. What a wonderful life the owners of this house must have once had, swinging on the porch or rocking in a chair as the steady breeze kept pesky bugs from landing long enough to become a nuisance.

I walked along the edge of the fencing and turned into what was probably a driveway though it had never been paved as far as I could tell. Grass covered what could have once been a gravel surface. I could see ruts where cars—or wagons—might have once parked. I paused midway up the drive to study my surroundings.

The house was set back fifty yards from the road and presided over several acres of overgrown grass. The rutted drive led to a small garage at the side of the house, which I suspected had probably been added after the house was built. The house looked too old to have come with a garage.

A marmalade cat lazed about on the grass of the drive. I noticed a rusted for sale sign on the front lawn. A fixer upper opportunity without a doubt, I mused. The sign wasn't really in the best location. It should have been posted on the street so passersby could see it readily. As with the house, the front lawn-overgrown and unkempt as it seemed to be-was hardly visible from the street given the wide trunks of the trees and dense cover of leaves.

I returned my attention to the cat.

"Hi, kitty. Do you live here?"

Kitty licked one paw and proceeded to clean its face, apparently taking no notice of me.

I turned to study the house again. Did someone live here? It appeared to be abandoned and looked as if it hadn't been lived in for some time. Surely, that was a several-year accumulation of oak leaves from the surrounding trees on the front porch steps, I thought. Though perhaps not. The monumental trees promised to bring some owner the unmitigated joy—or horror—of raking leaves for weeks during the fall season.

The turquoise and pink pastel paint on the outer walls of the house was weathered and faded, and the white trim around the windows and on the porch cracked and peeled away from the wood underneath. I cocked my head to the side and contemplated a new color scheme. A soft gray for the walls and a fresh coat of white paint on all the trim seemed a better fit. Many of the Victorian houses in Seattle were colorfully decorated in pastel schemes, but this house seemed too...dignified...for anything so fanciful. It wanted a soft neutral color to show off its classic lines—much like a handsome man knew when neutral-colored clothing accented the firm lines of his jaw or the broad set of his shoulders.

What the—? I blinked and raised my hands to my cheeks where a flash of heat spread across my face. Where had that come from? The face of the man from my dreams tantalized me for a moment—the firm lines of his jaw and the broad set of his shoulders. My heart skipped several beats. He certainly looked like he could have lived in a house like this. I imagined us on the porch, hand in hand, on a loveseat...

I grinned foolishly and glanced at my watch. It was already 11 a.m. If I was going to wander through that entire cemetery again in a quest to make sense of my inexplicable attachment to it, I'd better get moving.

I hated to leave the once lovely house, and I promised myself I would take another peek at it on my way out of town—a guarantee that made it easier for me to cross the street once again and return to my car. I finished the short drive to the cemetery, noting with surprise that the Victorian house was much closer to the cemetery than I'd realized. I pulled in under the black iron arched gate and brought the car to a stop under a tree. Probably once designed for horses and buggies, there was really no parking lot in the older cemetery.

As soon as I stepped out of the car, the wind greeted me, and I welcomed the fresh breeze on my face. I tucked the camera back into my jeans pocket and trudged up the gentle slope to the top of the hill...where I remembered the late afternoon sunlight playing on a stone the day before. I wanted a picture of it. If only I could remember which one it was.

What would I do if I found it? Take a picture and then what? Was I expecting to recognize the name? Was that the reason I'd felt this strong compulsion to return to the cemetery?

I twisted my lips into a wry grin and shook my head. Who knew? Sometimes, I was just too fanciful to suit even myself. No doubt I was just under the spell of too much ancestral gravesite hunting. All the family names and relationships were overlapping each other.

I reached the top of the hill and made my way to the edge of the cemetery—my favorite spot—where the wind had seemingly whispered my name. It blew as it had the previous day—and probably as it had for hundreds of years—creating the luscious loess hills of fertile soil along the Missouri Valley.

I scanned the stones in the surrounding area—some of chiseled gray granite, some in a lovely rose granite, while others seemed to be made of a soft white material such as sandstone. It was one of those that brought me to a standstill. The tombstone was about three feet high, as bright white as the day it was carved out in a quarry somewhere. To my bemusement, it actually seemed to glow brighter as sunlight beamed directly down on it.

The inscription was difficult to read, and heedless of grass stains to my blue jeans, I knelt to examine it more closely. With tender fingers, I reached out to trace the lettering. I caught my breath at the unexpected warmth of the stone, so unlike other cold headstones we had examined over the past week. It seemed to hold the sun's heat as if its porous nature acted as a sponge.

I flattened my hand across the stone to better absorb the warmth, to draw from the imagined energy reverberating from it. I pulled back to study the inscription once again.

***** ******, aged 28 ****, 2 mos, 4 ****

My age! I reared back for a moment and checked the date on my watch. I swallowed hard as I realized that I was, in fact, born 28 years, 2 months and 4 days ago. We shared the same birthday...my new friend and I! Though I suspected years apart. The stone was not new. Time and weather had worn the carving smooth, and I couldn't make out the letters of the name, nor could I see any dates. I sat back on my heels, longing to know the name of my "twin." Was he a man? A woman? How had he or she died? Twenty eight was far too young to die. I made a mental note to see my doctor when I got back to Seattle for a physical.

I resisted the urge to give the stone a sisterly hug of compassion and instead, pulled out my camera.

I positioned the camera and took several close-up photos of the tombstone. When I viewed them on the camera, they seemed overexposed, and I tried taking them again—this time at a different angle. Another check revealed that the shots continued to come out too bright, and the inscription—worn away as it was on the weathered sandstone—simply could not be read. Now what, I wondered?

I wished I had paper and thick crayon for an etching, but neither Sara nor I had had the foresight to come prepared with such equipment.

I straightened and backed up to adjust the camera in the hope I could bring the lettering of the stone into some relief in the photo. Still no success. The sun shone too brightly on the stone at this time of day to get a good shot.

"Molly..."

I froze. The breeze blew in from the valley below, but I knew this voice wasn't a trick of the wind. And Sara wasn't with me this time. My heart pounded in my chest as I twisted around to survey the deserted cemetery. I was alone, and someone spoke my name.

Chapter Two

Instinctively, I took a step backward, though I wasn't sure which direction the voice had come from.

"Who's here?" I called out. "Is someone here?" I scanned the cemetery once more. Nothing moved but the rippling leaves of the sun-dappled trees.

"Molly."

I clutched the camera to my chest, genuine fear setting in now. My heart seemed to have jumped into my throat, pounding even louder if that were possible.

"Who is it?" I screeched. "This is nuts. Sara, if that's you, I swear..."

I took a hasty step in the direction of the car, but a movement underneath one of the massive oak trees caught my eye. A figure stood there, in the shadow beneath the canopy of the tree.

"Who are you? Did you call me? What do you want?" I tried to speak in a calm voice, but anxiety continued to bring a shrill note to my words. I resumed backing away toward the direction of the car.

"Molly, wait!"

I froze in place for a moment. It was definitely a man under the tree though I couldn't see his face...and he knew my name.

"Do I know you?" I called in an unsteady voice. It seemed, though, as if my words were taken by the wind. Who was this man? And how did he know my name?

He moved away from the tree with a tentative step. His clothing was formal—a dark suit and white shirt—as if he had just been to a funeral. I hadn't remembered seeing a canopy for a funeral on the grounds, but I wasn't about to take my eyes off the stranger for one instant to confirm that suspicion.

I thought I saw a flash of white teeth from under his dark mustache, but he was still some distance away. Golden highlights in his chestnut hair caught the sunlight, and my mouth dropped open. He was undoubtedly one of the most handsome men I had ever seen in my life. My stomach rolled over at the sight of him, though not exclusively with admiration of his good looks. Cold sweat broke out on my forehead, and I put my hand to my mouth as if to hold back the morning's breakfast...if I'd had any.

For here—in the flesh—was the man of my dreams. Not just any dreams. More specifically, my dreams of the previous evening. Yet I couldn't for the life of me remember ever seeing him before until this moment.

"Be careful what you wish for," I muttered behind the hand that covered my convulsing mouth.

"Molly, do not be frightened. I can see that you are. I do not want to scare you." He took another step forward and held his hands up palms out...as if to show me he wasn't armed, I thought hysterically, or to calm me down. Either way, it wasn't working.

I threw a hurried glance over my shoulder to locate the car. It was so, so far away across the cemetery. I swung my head around to face the "man of my dreams" once again. I put my hands out as he did, but as a defensive gesture to keep him from continuing to approach me. He stopped at once and dropped his hands to his sides. He was still about thirty feet away, and I couldn't see the color of his eyes. Somehow, that knowledge seemed important to me.

"Look," I began to rattle. "Something is seriously wrong here. I don't know you. I think I've seen you before, and I don't know where. Well, actually, I do know where, but that doesn't count, and I don't think I know you...at all. So..." I ran out of voice for my incoherent thoughts.

His shoulders lifted and fell as if he took a deep breath. He put his hands behind his back and tilted his head to the side. Another charismatic flash of teeth threatened to disarm me.

"Molly, I can see that you are frightened—" he began, but I cut him off.

"Who are you? How do you know my name?" My voice continued to betray my anxiety, and I took yet another step back.

He held out a pleading hand, palm up.

"Wait, Molly, do not leave. Please let me talk to you. I do not mean to frighten you."

He took another step forward.

"Well, you're doing a good job of it. This is a cemetery, for Pete's sake. Why wouldn't I be terrified of some strange man calling my name?" I was helpless against the nervous babble of words erupting from my mouth. "Stop right there and tell me how you know my name. Were you here yesterday? I heard a voice here yesterday. Did you hear my sister call me? Is that how you know my name?" I lowered my voice and shook my head. "Did I see you yesterday? How could I have dream—" I stopped abruptly and stared at him.

He cocked his head in my direction with what seemed like a frown on his face, but I couldn't see his expression clearly across the expanse of the cemetery lawn. He took another step forward. I suspected that he couldn't hear me. The leaves in the trees rustled loudly in the wind. I thrust out my hand in the universal signal for stop, and he stilled.

I scanned the cemetery quickly again, wishing someone else were there with us. I couldn't calm the rapid beating of my heart or the anxiety which robbed me of air. I was too far from the car to make a run for it, and I found myself remarkably reluctant to do so at any rate.

Who was this man? What should I do? There was no way I was leaving without some answers. No way.

I gritted my teeth and took several hesitant steps forward to make myself heard.

"Who are you? How do you know my name?" I repeated in a louder voice, albeit with that irritating squeak.

"Do you want me to shout over the wind...or shall I approach?"

A shiver ran up my spine at his words—a shiver of anticipation, I realized, co-mingled with fear. Irrationally, I wanted him to come to me...a strange man in an isolated cemetery.

I stared at him for a moment—the tanned skin of his handsome face, the impossibly long length of his trousered legs, the chestnut hair which rolled in thick waves away from his face when the wind wasn't playing with it. And I nodded. Yes, I wanted him to approach me, most definitely.

He moved toward me slowly, obviously aware of how frightened I was, and I had all I could do to keep breathing—though from fear or anticipation, I couldn't say.

A feminine voice seemed to whisper his name on the wind. *Darius*. I knew his name was Darius as sure as I knew the wind would always blow on this hill.

"Darius," I whispered as he came near. The turquoise blue of his eyes mesmerized me, the downward tilt at the corners at once charming and sincere. In some strange way, I trusted him implicitly, without question.

"You are here. You have come back to me," he murmured as he pulled me into his arms.

I tilted my head back to meet his mouth. Without hesitation, I closed my eyes and leaned into him, knowing his strong arms would steady me as my knees seemed incapable of holding me up. I wrapped my arms around his neck as if I'd been doing it all my life.

"I have missed you so much, my love," Darius whispered against my lips. I suppressed the sudden ache in my heart and held him tighter. I don't think I had ever realized that I'd never, ever been in love in my entire life...because I'd always been in love. With Darius. No one had ever come close to touching my heart. And now I knew why.

Darius! I knew that I had loved him and lost him, but I couldn't remember anything else.

I was vaguely aware of questions that needed to be asked and answered, but at the moment, all I wanted...all I needed was to be in his arms.

His lips caressed mine with a gentleness which spoke of restrained passion. I melted into him, heedless of where I was. He kissed my cheeks, my neck, my ears and my forehead, and I lost myself in his touch, craving the strength of his tall body against mine.

He raised his head to gaze at me for a moment, and I unwrapped my hands from his neck to cup his face. Under the spell of some mysterious force beyond my comprehension, I asked him the obvious.

"How can I be in love with you, Darius? How do I know you?" I could only whisper. "I don't know if I've ever even met you, but I know I love you."

Darius smiled, even white teeth against the tan skin of his face.

"Because you are the love of my life, Molly," he said simply. "You always have been. We can never be parted."

I stretched back in his arms to study his face, the mosaic blue of his eyes holding me captive.

"Were you here yesterday? You called my name, didn't you? I didn't see you. Where were you?"

He shook his head, and then he nodded. Dark eyebrows pulled together in an expression of confusion.

"I was here...and yet not, I think." A slight almost apologetic smile played on his lips.

I shook my head. "I don't understand." I looked around. "*Where* were you? Why didn't you come when I called out?"

"I-I do not understand either, Molly. I came to see you..." He paused and studied my face. "But not here...not like this."

"I don't understand," I repeated again, seemingly incapable of articulate speech. "Were you here or not?"

He raised his head to look around as if in disbelief, then he looked at me again.

"I was here, Molly, but not as you think."

"What are you talking about? Not as I think?" I surprised myself by grabbing the lapels of his dark jacket to give him a small shake as if he were some beloved, but exasperating lover. He tilted his head and regarded me with glowing blue eyes as he leaned in to kiss my forehead.

"I have missed you so much, Molly." His tender smile brought tears to my eyes. My dream lover had come to life.

"I do not understand what is happening here. I am afraid to lose you again. I must think. I need time."

"Time for what? What do you mean?" The warm feel of his arms around me felt safe and secure, yet the loud pounding of my heart reminded me of the bizarre situation I found myself in.

"It had to be you here yesterday," I continued. "You're saying the exact same things I heard."

Darius hesitated and shook his head slowly. He bit a corner of his lower lip for a moment before answering, and my heart skipped a loud beat at the charming boyishness of his gesture.

"I know you have many questions, my love, and I do not have the answers for you. I have many questions myself."

Part of my besotted mind did have tons of questions. For instance, what was I doing in the arms of a man I had never met...yet loved. Oh, yes, there were plenty of questions. But it seemed as if Darius was short on answers as well. I tried to bring a sense of reality into the situation by asking a more practical question.

"Okay, let's start with the basics then. The easy stuff. The beginning, I suppose," I said weakly. "Where do you live, Darius? Do you live in Lilium?" I nodded in the direction of the town. By now, I realized I should have gathered my wits and stepped out of this strange man's arms, but against my better judgment, I delayed.

He lifted his head to look in the direction of Lilium.

"Yes, I live here. At least...at one time, I lived near here, yes."

"At one time?" Would this man never give me a simple answer?

"Yes...many years ago, it would seem."

I shook my head in confusion and ran a fingertip across the line of his firm jaw. Who knew when I would get the chance to touch him again? This dream would have to end soon.

Really, Molly! Feel free to slide out of his arms at any time. This is nuts!

"So, you don't still live here? Where do you live now?"

He bent to kiss me again. What small shred was left of my common sense told me the kiss was meant to silence my questions, but I didn't care at the moment. His lips moved against mine with such familiar intimacy that my head swam. When I thought my weak legs would support me no longer, I broke off the kiss. Blue eyes sparkled at me.

A question. I asked him a question. What was it?

"You're stalling, Darius, aren't you?" My lips twitched involuntarily. My enigmatic stranger seemed at a loss. I almost felt I had the upper hand...just for a split second. "Where do you live?" I pressed.

He hesitated again and took a deep breath before answering.

"I am not certain. It would seem that I now live here...where you see me."

I followed his gaze as he scanned the cemetery. A dizzying feeling swept through me and sucked the air from my lungs. He couldn't be serious! I stiffened in his arms, and with a quick look at my face, Darius slowly lowered his arms to his sides. Sickeningly aware of a sense of loss as he let me go, I backed up a step to stare at him.

"Are you saying you live here? In the cemetery?" I squeaked.

Darius dropped his gaze to the ground, slipped his hands in the pockets of his trousers and shifted on his feet. He inclined his head in assent.

"Perhaps...I am not certain. Perhaps," he murmured.

My knees wobbled for a moment, and I took another step back...if only to keep my balance. I opened my mouth to speak, but my brain simply would not allow me to come up with a single coherent word. I turned to survey the grounds once again, knowing deep in my soul that he wasn't as crazy as he sounded.

In fact, he probably wasn't crazy at all.

Maybe I was.

The sunny day turned suddenly dark and swirled around me. I couldn't breathe...

****

I heard the comforting sound of a rhythmic beating heart against my ear, and I opened my eyes slowly. I was lying in Darius's lap where he held me against his chest. His chin must have rested on the top of my head, and I tried to keep my breathing steady to pretend continued unconsciousness, but I could not control the stiffening of my body.

"Molly? Are you awake?" Darius lifted his chin and looked down into my eyes. I straightened quickly and slid out of his lap in an effort to jump up. He dropped his arms to let me go, but a wobble on my part brought him to his feet to steady me.

"You always did faint at the slightest shock, my love. That certainly has not changed over the years. However, the smell of your lovely silky hair has changed to a...fruity fragrance, not the lavender I have always known. That is new. I like it," he grinned.

I stared at him as if he was insane, and I tried to ignore the warmth in the pit of my stomach when he spoke of my hair or called me his "love." The man was definitely psychotic—or I was—and I much preferred that it was not I.

He reached for me, and I backed away.

"Stay back," I thrust out a hand. "I don't know what I was thinking before, but I don't know you. I can't even...I don't...I just don't know you. This is nuts." I scanned the cemetery with wild eyes, looking for help, but no one else was around. I could run, I thought, turning back to throw a wild glance at his face. He bit his lower lip, giving him a crestfallen look that tore at my heart.

"Molly, please." He reached out a hand toward me again, but I backed further away. My widened eyes must have shown my fear and confusion.

His sigh made me catch my breath. His broad shoulders slumped. I didn't want to hurt him.

"Molly, please do not be afraid of me. I am not going to harm you. I understand your fear, but it is I, Darius. I love you. You love me. I saw it in your eyes. I felt it on your lips. Please do not run from me."

I had half-turned away to flee, but his words made me hesitate. I turned back to look at him. He watched me carefully for a moment. I suspected he could see the indecision in my face. But could he also tell how desperate I was to stay with him, though I feared for both his sanity and mine? I hoped not. At the moment, I was pretty sure I was the one with the addled brain.

"I-I..." I struggled for words. "I don't believe this is happening. I can't believe I kis—I-I don't know who you are. I don't even know who *I* am right now."

I must have looked as pitiful as I felt because he stepped forward as if to take me in his arms again. I jumped back and put up a hand to ward him off. He stilled and clasped his hands behind his back like a small schoolboy who'd just been lectured. His eyes clouded, and I felt like crying at the sight.

"I do not understand what is happening, either, Molly." He dropped his head to study the ground for an instant before raising his face to look at me with a troubled expression on his brow. I'm sure my forehead mirrored the same lines of confusion.

"It seems likely that I have memory and you do not. You remembered me for a moment. You remembered my name." He gave me a hopeful look. "Do you remember anything else?"

I shook my head in mute silence.

Darius sighed. "I do not understand how you have come to be here—in this time. When is this time...exactly? I have been studying the dates on the headstones since yesterday when I first...em...arrived," he gestured toward the cemetery in general, "and I presume we are in the second millennia?"

I gave him a dubious look but provided the current date. He blinked and raised an unsteady hand to his forehead as if to brush away cobwebs...or confusion.

"It doesn't seem possible. I buri—" He stopped abruptly and stared hard at me.

"I'm sorry?" I wondered whom it was that he had buried.

Darius shifted his gaze to the ground and shook his head again.

"Nothing," he murmured. "I meant to say that I do not understand how you can be as you are." He looked up again and gestured toward me with a tanned hand. "How it is that you can look so young? So many years have passed." He turned and looked toward the white stone that had caught my attention earlier. "It seems so difficult to believe this was only a meadow once. You must remember that?" He returned his gaze to me, and all I could do was shake my head.

"I have no idea what you're talking about. What years have passed? Where did you come from? And when? You said you 'arrived' yesterday? Arrived from where? Are you suggesting that you're a—a ghost?" My voice rose to a squeak, reminiscent of a mouse.

Darius's grave expression broke into a grin.

"Don't smirk at me! Do you think this is funny? Are you nuts? You *are* nuts, aren't you? Because if you're not, then I am!" I jabbed a thumb toward my chest. My cheeks flamed.

Darius sobered his expression and pressed his lips together firmly before clearing his throat.

"By nuts, do you mean crazy?" He shook his head firmly. "No, I do not think I am insane. Neither do I think you are. But for some reason, we have been brought together again, and I, for one, am deeply grateful."

I shook my head in disbelief. What was he talking about?

"Molly, my love, I do not know what to say. I am at a loss as to how to convince you of something that I do not fully understand myself. I do not believe we are insane, but I am certain that something beyond our control has happened—a miracle that I dare not examine too much lest it disappear."

That he was miraculously handsome, I could not deny. And that something beyond my control was occurring also seemed too real to dispute. But I had to fight the spell he had apparently cast over me. Because if he hadn't, why hadn't I hightailed it out of there at once? I decided to bring the mysticism of the situation under some sort of control. My practical Sara would have known how to handle this situation. But then, this wouldn't have happened to her at any rate.

"Where do you live?" I remained obsessed with the simple question. One eyebrow raised, I crossed my arms and waited for his answer. Although how he was going to stand there and try to be serious in that museum piece of a suit, even as well tailored to his long and lean figure as it appeared to be, was beyond me.

I watched him scan the cemetery, his face showing the same desperation I'd felt myself all too often in the last half hour.

"I am afraid my answer remains the same. It would appear that I live here at the moment," he murmured in a bemused tone as he returned his blue gaze to my face.

I winced at his answer. Definitely insane. So handsome and so totally off his rocker.

I must have recoiled more visibly than I thought, because he reached a tentative hand in my direction.

"Don't touch me," I whispered as I backed up a step. I ached as I fought against that tender familiarity I felt with Darius, but I couldn't allow myself to continue in this strange dream...or nightmare. Could I?

"Molly, I will not hurt you. Please believe me."

"I don't know what to believe. I don't believe in ghosts, I know that." I was so near to tears that my voice shook against my will.

Darius looked around. "Sit with me a while, Molly, and we will try to understand what has happened...together. You knew my name. You know we are intertwined in some way. I am not a stranger to you."

I looked into his turquoise eyes. No one with eyes that clear and beautiful could harm me, it just didn't seem possible. I dragged in some air, dropped my gaze and allowed my tightened lips to curl into a small half-smile as I nodded.

"All right," I murmured.

Darius's quick intake of breath brought my head up.

"Good!" he murmured with a broad smile. The lines of his forehead smoothed and he gestured to a bench under the shade of one of the large oak trees. He reached to put his arm under my elbow in a distinctly old-fashioned manner, and I jerked.

"Forgive me," he murmured and clasped his hands behind his back once more. "I am not used to...not touching you."

"What?" I came to a standstill. The intimacy of his words shocked me. Though I had only moments before kissed him with a passion I didn't know I was capable of, that had been some sort of temporary aberration...and best forgotten.

"No matter what just happened between us, Darius, I do not know you. We have never met. And we have never...um...touched." I reddened at my inarticulate phrasing.

Darius tilted his head in the most charming way and searched my face for what seemed like an hour but must have only been a few seconds. I fought to keep my gaze on his.

"I understand, Molly. Or at least I am trying to." He ran a harried hand through his hair. "It would appear that you and I have different memories, and I must go slowly with you. I cannot bear to lose you again, and I will do anything to keep you."

I cannot bear to lose you again, and I will do anything to keep you.

He spoke the words every woman wanted to hear from a tall, dark and handsome man. I was no exception. So, I did what all women confronted with such declarations of love would do. I clenched my fists and stomped my foot in response.

"Now, listen! I am going to walk away this instant if you don't stop talking that way. I don't know what you're talking about. And you're scaring me. I'm just too morbidly curious about this whole thing to walk away right now, but if you don't stop making these vague references to some great romance that I don't remember, I'm leaving." I slammed my arms across my chest and squinted at him with my best steely-eyed look. "I mean it," I added for good measure.

Darius's lips twitched, but to his credit, he did not laugh though he looked as if he wanted to. He pressed his lips together.

"Yes, Molly, my dear." He inclined his head. "I shall behave." He kept one hand behind his back in a courtly gesture and extended the other in the direction of the bench. "Shall we?"

I swept ahead of him as if I had transported myself back in time and wore a fabulous silk dress that swished angrily as I stormed ahead. Less than a minute brought me to the wrought iron bench which graced the foot of the oak tree where I'd first seen Darius. I was acutely aware of him close behind me as I dropped onto the bench in a most unladylike fashion, silk dress forgotten.

Darius did not sit immediately but looked up at the tree, which hummed loudly as the leaves rustled in the wind.

"This tree was just a small seedling when last I saw it. It has grown into a magnificent oak, has it not? I did not know if it would withstand the winds on this hill."

I followed his gaze upward. The grand tree was indeed beautiful, massive...I guessed about 48 feet in height, and appeared to be quite sturdy. There was no doubt it had been there a long time. The wide trunk hinted at longevity. I had no earthly idea if I believed that Darius planted it or not. He certainly believed it.

I lowered my gaze to study his face and found him looking at me with a smile of...affection.

"I know that you and I are at some sort of impasse, Molly. We do not understand what has happened. And you do not believe much of what I say."

I started to protest, but he held up a hand.

"Your face is very easy to read, my lov—Molly."

His eyes seemed to twinkle...or maybe it was just my imagination.

He placed his hand lightly over his heart and grinned. "Observe even now how impossible it is for me to refrain from endearments. I trust you will forgive me a few indiscretions."

I tried to give him a hard stare, though my heart wasn't in it. In fact, my heart wanted desperately to hear his endearments, though my brain told me I should probably schedule a visit to a mental health therapist as soon as I returned to Seattle.

"Perhaps we could come to some form of understanding between us? I know you think I am...em...insane. If you could suspend disbelief for a while and grant me the benefit of doubt? I know my appearance here in the cemetery seems...unusual." He rubbed his jaw as he paused. My gaze focused on his broad, tanned hand, and I found myself wishing he would touch my face again. He sighed and continued.

"I believe that I am not in my own time, and I have no idea how I arrived in yours." His face tightened and he looked away toward the valley for an instant. "Nor do I understand how it is that you are here—in this time."

At this, I couldn't stay quiet. "Where else would I be? Are...are you suggesting that I..." I grimaced "...*lived* in your time? And I don't even know when that was, by the way," I pointed out.

Darius brought his gaze to mine as I spoke. The crisp blue of his eyes softened as he looked at me, and my heart skipped a wayward beat.

"May I sit?" he asked.

"Oh, sure," I mumbled. I made a pretense of scooting over to the edge of the bench, but I already huddled at the far end of the bench, and he had plenty of room to sit. His formal question evoked an improbably old-fashioned set of manners that wasn't common in this day and age. It was almost easy to believe he was from a different time.

He lowered himself to the seat with graceful ease and clasped his hands together on his lap as he turned to look at me. He searched my face for a moment. Under his scrutiny, I willed my features into a blank expression, and I hoped he didn't notice I wasn't breathing. He sighed and turned his face forward to survey the cemetery. I gulped for air.

"I did not realize the cemetery would grow so large when I donated the land to the town." He seemed lost in thought, and I wondered if he was going to answer my question. I wasn't going to let it drop. I pounced... verbally speaking, that is.

"When was that?"

He turned toward me, chewing on a corner of his lower lip for a moment before answering.

"1880."

I heard myself gasp as if from a long way off and felt the blood drain from my face. I knew what he'd been hinting at, but to hear him say it out loud was...surreal.

He began to speak quickly, and I struggled to focus on his exact words.

"I wish you could remember, Molly. You loved to walk up to this hill, raise your arms in the wind and pretend you could fly. You would come up here often while I worked on the house—the house that I hoped would be our home."

I shook my head soundlessly, unsure if the weak gesture was meant to tell him I couldn't understand what he was saying or that I didn't believe anything he was saying. I hardly knew which.

Darius kept his gaze on me while he spoke. He reached for my hand once but hesitated and then pulled back. He dragged in a deep breath. The pounding in my ears told me I was holding mine again. He cleared his throat and continued.

"In the early days, when I came out from Virginia, these hills and valleys were wild and fertile. Forests and thick foliage abounded along the edge of the Missouri River. The land was difficult to tame." He looked past my shoulder, toward the valley. "But it seems heavily farmed now. I wonder how many men work this land. And how many horses and plows they must own!"

An unexpected giggle escaped my throat, and I clamped my hand over my mouth. Oh, surely I wasn't going to break out into hysterics!

Darius turned to me with a tentative smile.

"I am pleased to hear you laugh at long last. And what have I said to amuse you?" he murmured with a sparkle in his eyes.

I dropped my hand from my mouth to gesture toward the valley. "I don't think anyone uses horses to farm anymore, Darius. It's all done by heavy equipment like tractors."

"Ah, yes... Tractors. Of course."

I threw him a sharp glance. Did they have tractors in the late 1800s? He sounded as if he knew what I was talking about, but I wasn't entirely convinced. He looked away toward the valley again. I still needed some answers from him. I ignored the small voice in my head which demanded answers to the question, *"Why are you still sitting here with this delusional man?"*

"Darius, what are you doing here?" I tried to face him directly, but a sudden gust of wind blew a handful of hair across my face. I brought shaky hands to my head to restrain the hair. . "I mean...are you really...?" I let my gaze wander toward the stones. I couldn't say the words. "If you're really..." I winced. No, I really could not say the words. I could only nod in the direction of the stones.

"What are you doing here?" I repeated helplessly. I realized with horror that some part of me had actually begun to believe him...some *very* small part.

Darius dropped his eyes to the hands clasped in his lap.

"I don't know, Molly." He dragged in a ragged breath, his smile shaky. "I have little experience with this myself. In fact...none. I am not certain what has happened." He shook his head and turned his palms up in an empty gesture.

"Can you...? Will you...um...disappear again?"

I crossed and re-crossed my legs anxiously. His gaze followed my movements, lingering on my legs before he looked away quickly. I looked down at my jean-clad legs for a moment, awaiting his answer.

"I do not know," he shook his head. "I am not sure I want to disappear, as you say, for fear of losing you again. I would much rather stay with you."

I heard those wonderfully poignant words of love again and had the same awful reaction. I jumped up and began to pace before him, my arms barricaded across my chest. Jumbled thoughts erupted into a barrage of chaotic sentences.

"Listen, buddy, I'm just barely hanging on here. I don't really think I believe this...ghost thing you're trying to hand me, Darius, so please don't push it. You can't *stay* with me. How would that work? I can't *stay* here at the cemetery. Don't tell me you're going to follow me back to the hotel...back home, that is?" I stilled for a moment and buried my face in my hands. A high-pitched laugh forced its way from my constricted throat.

"Oh, my sister would love that. Someone following me home from a cemetery. Sara is going to love that!"

I watched him open his mouth and close it again. Hah! Well, that had certainly silenced him, hadn't it? So, why did I want to throw myself in his arms and cry? I hugged myself even tighter and stared at him through narrowed eyes. He sagged and dropped his elbows to his knees as he lowered his head to run unsteady hands through his thick sandy brown hair. He looked defeated, and I hated that I had taken the sparkle from his eyes. But I had to know more.

"So? What do you do when you're not...? Well, you know...hanging around in cemeteries?"

He rose quickly, and I jumped back.

He stiffened.

"Do not worry. For pity's sake, Molly, I am not going to attack you." He locked his hands behind his back and began his own pacing, long legs striding across the grass in front of the bench. I watched and held my breath.

"I do not know what is happening," Darius began. "I do not know why I am here. The last thing I remember is coming up here to visit your—" He stopped abruptly and stared at me. "I do not know how I came to be here," he said with a frown. "Nor do I understand why you seem to have no memory of me."

I stomped my foot again in frustration.

"Because I've never met you before, that's why!"

He shook his head as if to repudiate my words.

"If that is true, my dear, then, how did you know my name? Why did you return my kiss as you did? Surely, you do not suffer the embraces of strangers easily, do you? You remembered me, Molly! You remembered me." He jabbed a thumb toward his chest.

My mouth dropped at his vehemence. Aware I was holding my breath again, I exhaled, and my rubbery legs gave out on me. I moved over to sink down onto the bench. Darius's expression softened as he watched me. He lowered himself to the bench once again, taking the far opposite end, and folded his arms across his chest as he thrust his legs out in front with crossed ankles. Even in the midst of this chaos, I couldn't help but admire the muscular tone of the impossibly long legs visible through the wool of his dark trousers.

I dragged my gaze to his face and tried to choose my words with care. I couldn't bear to hurt his feelings, but it seemed I was capable of doing nothing else at the moment.

"I don't know what that was about, I'm afraid, Darius. I felt like I knew you at that moment. That's all I can say. I dreamt..." I bit my tongue. No, I would not tell him about my dream. We would end up with adjoining cells at the institution.

I shrugged. "I have no other explanation. But I don't remember anything about you. How could I? I've never met you before." I raised my hands in a helpless gesture.

"You have the same mannerisms, you know." He smiled tenderly. His voice held that affectionate note that sent my heart racing.

"What?"

"Your hands. You used to do that often...raise your hands just so." He nodded toward my upturned hands.

I dropped my hands and locked my fingers in my lap.

The sound of wheels on gravel caught my attention, and I turned toward the entrance. A large black sedan pulled past the cemetery arch and came to rest behind my car.

"Someone comes," he murmured with the voice of one doomed. "The arrival of this large black conveyance does not bode well for me, I think."

I caught my breath. Someone was here! A real live person was here! Sanity! Reality! Panic, never far away over the last hour, seemed to set in, and I didn't know if I wanted to run to the new arrival or stay with the mesmerizing and enigmatic stranger beside me.

"I have to go, Darius. I-I think I have to go. Can they see you?" That I had to ask that question told me I had fallen under his paranormal spell.

Darius shrugged helplessly. "I do not know." He gave me an unexpectedly playful look and grinned. "Shall we find out?" He made as if to rise.

"Don't you dare!" I grabbed his arm and held him down. He looked down at my hand and covered it with his own. His hand felt warm, strong, sturdy, alive...Hardly ghostly material. There had to be another explanation for these strange events.

"No? Admit it, my girl. You want to know if they can see me as well, don't you? You want to know if I am really a ghost."

I pulled my hand out from under his and shook my head, wondering if allowing myself that hysterical shriek of laughter might just make me feel better. I opted to choke down any such silliness and turned to stare at the car.

"They're blocking my car. I can't get out anyway."

"Your car? Is that what you call it?" Darius tilted his head as he looked toward the parked vehicles. "I think there have been many new inventions."

"Well, why don't they get out of the car? What are they waiting for?" Even as I fussed, two silver-haired women slowly worked their way out of the large black vehicle. One maneuvered a walker on which she leaned heavily. The other ambled around the car to offer her a solicitous arm.

"What is this object she leans against?" Darius pointed to the women.

"It's called a walker." I sighed, feeling a bit guilty for my impatience with the women. "That explains why they had such a hard time getting out of the car."

"And why does she use it? Is it some sort of enlarged cane?"

"I think she has probably had hip surgery and needs it for balance. My grandmother used one after her hip replacement."

"Replacing hips," Darius repeated in a thoughtful tone. He watched the women with interest, though they were some yards off in the distance.

"Have you seen them here before?" I asked.

Darius swung his head to look at me.

"I beg your pardon?" he asked with a frown.

I reared back as if stung. "I-I was just asking if you'd seen them here in the cemetery before. It's not a big deal."

"Woman! Do you think I have been lurking about in this cemetery for over a hundred years...prancing about on the stones and scaring the townspeople...on the hope that someday you would come?" He jumped up and turned away from me, settling one rigid hand on his hip and running the other impatiently across his jaw.

I watched him in stunned silence for a second before I stood briskly.

"Well, I was *just* asking. No need to get in a huff, Mister... What *is* your last name anyway?"

"Ferguson. Darius Ferguson." He turned back to face me, the anger leaving his face.

A horrible thought struck me. What if...what if my dream had all the right characters, but the roles were reversed. What if...he hadn't been visiting my tombstone? What if I was the one visiting his? I couldn't make the name out, but what if it was Darius's tombstone?

"Is...is that your stone?" I blurted out.

"Where? What stone?" His eyes narrowed, and he turned in the direction I pointed. The tombstone I'd touched earlier basked lazily under the sun's warmth.

"I couldn't make out the name. I tried, but the lettering is worn away," I mumbled. Horror didn't describe my feelings at the moment. It seemed more like...pain. Pain for his possible death. I wrapped my arms around my chest to distract myself from the ache inside. He stood before me, so tall, so handsome, so...vibrant. This couldn't be happening, I thought with dread.

"How old are you?" I remembered the age on the tombstone.

He turned from contemplation of the stone and faced me, the muscles in his jaw working.

"If I tell you that I am twenty-eight, will you run screaming from me?"

I shuddered, though the August wind was warm. And I stood my ground, not because I wasn't tempted to run screaming to my car, but because his troubled blue eyes begged me to stay.

"The age on the stone is twenty-eight. Whoever is buried there died when they were twenty-eight." My voice shook, and I avoided looking into the eyes which pulled at my heart.

"Of course," he muttered. "Of course, the age is the same. I do not suppose there is a year of death on the stone...anything that could salvage this day."

I shook my head. "No, most of it is worn off. Come see for yourself." I took a step forward, but his words stopped me.

"I think not," he sighed. "I would have you believe that I am here—in this time—in some capacity other than as a dead man."

I shivered again. I looked up at him from under my lashes to see dejection and confusion on his face. Once again, I'd taken the twinkle from his beautiful blue eyes.

"You know? Maybe that's not your tombstone anyway. Maybe, you did...um...," I searched for the right words in such an indescribable situation, "...come here some other way. Maybe, you're not really from the late 1800s." I warmed to my rationalizations. "What if you... um... were... oh, say... an actor, and you got in some sort of accident and had amnesia?"

The look he gave me wasn't exactly withering, but it could have been without the softening effect of his twitching lips. His thick mustache covered most of his upper lip, and I couldn't tell if he was laughing or not.

"Just so," he murmured. "Amnesia...Yes, of course. Except that I have very strong memories of you...of us."

"Oh, yes, there's that," I mumbled. Out of the corner of my eye, I spotted the ladies standing near some stones on the other side of the cemetery. The sight of them tugged at the last vestiges of rational thought in my brain.

I turned back to Darius.

"I think I should go," I mumbled. I didn't want to leave him, but I didn't think I could stay either. Nothing made sense, and I needed to clear my head. I simply could not think rationally in his intoxicating presence.

Darius took a step forward, and I retreated.

"Please do not leave, Molly. Will I see you again? Will you come back?"

I shook my head.

"I don't know. I don't think so. We have to move on. My sister..."

I looked up into his face, and realized I made a mistake. His eyes, full of a love I had never known, pleaded with me.

I tore my gaze from his and shook my head.

"I have to go now. I can't stay here."

Darius grabbed my arm, albeit gently. I looked down at his hand but did not pull away. How do you tear yourself away from someone you desperately want to be with? I looked up at him, knowing that I needed to get away from him...for my own sanity.

"Molly! I cannot lose you again. Please do not go. Stay with me. How will I find you again?" He searched my face for a moment, then shook his head and gave a short mirthless laugh. "No, that is unfair to you. Forgive me, my love. Of course, you must do as you wish. Will you come back? Will I see you again?" With his free hand, he brushed hair tenderly back from my face.

"I don't know," I answered in a small voice. "None of this makes any sense to me. I have to get out of here and think straight." I shook my head again, my entire body quivering with tension as I tried to break free... emotionally. I jerked my arm, and he let me go. He locked his hands behind his back in that endearingly vulnerable pose of his.

"I understand," Darius murmured. His suddenly controlled face gave no hint of his thoughts. He seemed distant—the stranger that he was.

"Well, I don't! This is bizarre. I resisted the urge to stomp my foot again...or dive back into the surreal loving embrace of his strong arms.

"Goodbye," I whispered as tears welled in my eyes. I turned and hurried away toward the car, wondering why on earth I felt like I was running headlong into a vast emptiness rather than escaping from a lunatic.

"Molly," his voice whispered behind me. It cost me every ounce of strength I had to keep going.

Chapter Three

The tears burst forth as I hurried away from the stranger named Darius. It was as if I couldn't get away from the insanity of the situation fast enough...and yet, I couldn't seem to bear the thought of walking away from him. The logical part of my brain told me he was a disturbed man who wandered cemeteries in search of lonely women. The emotional part of my brain-some sort of primal instinct—told me that somehow I had loved him all my life...and before. It had to be the dream! The dream I'd had the night before...of the handsome man kneeling by my grave. Had I seen him the day before and not realized it? It had to be the dream.

With shaking hands, I wiped at my wet face and stumbled on the path. I threw a frenzied glance over my shoulder, terrified that he might be following, but he was nowhere in sight. Where did he go?

I hurried on toward the car. When I reached it, I saw with despair that I really wasn't going to be able to get out, as the large black town car blocked my retreat. There seemed to be no way to drive forward or turn around. I could see the ladies further out among the tombstones, but I didn't think I had the strength to drag myself over and ask them to move their car. I turned to search the cemetery again with blurry eyes, but Darius seemed well and truly gone. What if I never saw him again? What if he'd just been a figment of my lonely imagination?

And why, oh why, did these ladies have to block my car? I needed to get out of there!

A sob of frustration forced its way out, and despite my best efforts at self-control, I began to shake and sob. I wrenched the car door open and threw myself into the driver's seat, slamming the door shut behind me. I fumbled with the lock as a wave of grief I could not understand shook me. I wrapped my arms around the steering wheel, dropped my head on my arms and bawled my eyes out for what seemed like hours.

A gentle tapping on the driver's side window broke through my wails, and I froze at the sound. Oh, please, no, not Darius! The man had to leave me alone. I really couldn't take any more. I held my breath and peeked over one arm toward the driver's side window. A white face surrounded by black filled my window. I shrieked and buried my face in my arms again.

"Miss. Are you all right? Miss?"

Several more taps followed. I heard the fairly normal, albeit concerned words, and I uncovered my face to look at the window again. The pale face belonged to that of a very senior lady who wore a black dress and black pillbox hat with a froth of net, reminiscent of Jacqueline Kennedy. An old-fashioned outfit to be sure, but smacking of this century. I loosened my grip on the steering wheel.

"Are you all right, miss?"

I swiped at my wet face with embarrassment. Next to the woman stood another older female, also in black, though she eschewed a hat over her short silver curls.

"Is there anything we can do for you, miss?"

I threw a quick searching look in the direction of the bench under the giant oak tree, but Darius seemed to have vanished. Or maybe I just couldn't see him anymore. I shivered again, bit back a cry of despair, and unrolled the window.

"I'm fine. I'm sorry." I forced a watery smile. "I'm just crying. You know how it is." I attempted a light shrug, but the weight of grief made it difficult.

The first lady, leaning on the walker, straightened just a bit as if it pained her to bend.

"Yes, of course, dear. We've just been visiting our husbands ourselves. Do you have someone dear here?"

Her words brought me to the verge of a new round of sobs, and I coughed to stem the imminent flow of tears.

"No, no. I'm just doing some genealogy research, that's all." Feeling somehow trapped in my car, I popped the lock, opened the door and stepped out. Drained of energy, I leaned against the car with self-consciousness as the older women examined me from head to toe...though I sensed more with a sense of concern than judgment. "My sister and I have been visiting cemeteries in the Midwest, looking up some of our ancestors," I murmured weakly.

The older women nodded sagely.

"I see," said the shorter of the two. "We've done that as well, though

I'm afraid we didn't have to look very far. All our ancestors are here." She gave a throaty chuckle and spread her arms to encompass the cemetery.

"I'm Cynthia Dawson, and this is my sister, Laura Hale." The smaller of the two women reached out a white, blue-veined hand which Molly took gently. "Our families have been here for generations. Is there someone we can help you find?"

I stole another glance over my shoulder toward the bench, but Darius seemed to have vanished. Still, I felt the hairs on the back of my neck stand on end. Was he watching from somewhere? Did he even exist?

I blinked to stop a new flood of tears.

"No, not really," I replied. "I don't think we have any ancestors here at this cemetery. It's a beautiful cemetery though. I love the wind here."

Cynthia gave a short titter. "Oh yes, the wind. It never stops blowing. I'm glad you like it."

"Don't mind her, Miss..." I supplied my name to Laura. "She'd rather move down to a condo in Florida. Always did like the big city."

"I can't wait," Cynthia hooted, a twinkle lighting up her otherwise faded blue eyes. "All we have to do is get that museum piece of ours rented or sold, and away we go."

I relaxed for the first time in over an hour. The normality of the two women seemed to ground me into some sense of reality. *He'd just been a figment of my imagination, hadn't he?*

I caught Cynthia eyeing me with a speculative gaze.

"You wouldn't be looking for a house to buy, would you? An old broken down Victorian house?" A suggestive tilt of one eyebrow and an infectious lift of her lips brought a responding grin from me. Could they be talking about the old Victorian house I'd fallen in love with just this morning? Somehow, that seemed like a lifetime ago. I perked up.

"As a matter of fact, I did see one in town that caught my eye. Well, actually it's not that far. Down the road here."

"That's our place!" Cynthia squealed. "It's been in our family for over a hundred years, but our children have all moved away and none of our other relatives want to buy it. We have no idea what to do with the thing. We haven't lived in it since we got married. Our parents passed about twenty years ago. Since then, we've tried to keep the grass mowed and plumbing running, but the house is getting kind of old and lonely."

"So, you liked it, huh?" Laura grinned.

I saw the gleam in their eyes and warded them off with raised hands. "Now, wait a minute, ladies. I said I liked it, not that I wanted to buy it. I had no idea it was that old. And I don't even live here in Iowa. What would I do with a house in a strange town where I don't even live?"

"You could fix it up and rent it?" Cynthia reached out to pat my arm. "It would give you some extra income."

I stared at the women with rounded eyes. "Who would rent a huge house way out here? It's kind of isolated, isn't it?" I remembered wondering that very thing when Sara and I first drove through the town yesterday.

Laura nodded and sighed. "Yup, that's the problem. We don't know anyone who wants to live out in the country either. Everyone wants to live in the cities."

"Including both of us, I might add, Sis," Cynthia chimed in. She shifted her large black pocketbook to her other arm while balancing precariously on her walker. "Well, Molly, even if you don't want to buy the old house, why don't you come by for a tour? As you say, it's just down the road...and I can see the gleam in your eye."

Anxious to leave the cemetery and avoid the possibility of a reappearance by the strange man named Darius, I willingly agreed. And I did so want to see the inside of the house.

"I've never been inside a Victorian-era home. That sounds wonderful."

"Great," murmured Laura. "Let me back this big car out, because I can see I've been blocking you. No wonder you were crying."

"Oh, no, I wasn't crying about that," I demurred as I climbed back into my car. I watched the older women totter over to the car, Cynthia on her walker with her huge handbag draped over her arm.

While I waited, I pulled down the rearview mirror and stared at my pale and strained face. My eyes were swollen. What was I doing? Going to look at an old house with two ladies who were obviously bent on talking me into buying it? Near a cemetery that held, at best, a deranged man? At worst...a ghost? At the very worst...a figment of my imagination, a lover from a dream? I slid my gaze in the direction of the swaying oak tree. Or maybe I was the one who was deranged.

It seemed as if half an hour passed before Laura managed to get the big black town car out of the cemetery, and I worked on my patience while I waited for them. I pulled out behind them with a last glance toward the bench beneath the tree. Nothing. He was gone.

Less than half a mile down the road, Laura slowed—if that were possible—and turned into the driveway of the house. I followed and pulled in behind them. I edged my smaller car next to Laura's vehicle, which had stopped just short of the front porch. I climbed out of the car and walked around to the right side of the town car to help Cynthia out while Laura hoisted the walker out of the back seat.

"Hell, orange kitty," Cynthia called as the marmalade cat I'd seen earlier jumped on top of the railing of the front porch to greet them. "He's not our cat. I'm allergic, but he just appeared recently and hangs out around the house all the time. Seems happy enough."

I held out my arm while Cynthia leaned on it heavily. As we moved, I eyed the cat whose tail jutted skyward as he began an enthusiastic prance up and down the railing. "He looks healthy. Someone must be feeding him," I murmured.

"Oh, we do. Laura and I put some food out for him once a week when we go to the cemetery. I think he gets his water from the pond at the side of the house. We'll have to get someone to take over for us when we finally do sell the place and move down to Florida."

Walker in tow, Laura joined them at the foot of the wooden stairs leading to the front porch. She helped me pull Cynthia up the three wide wooden steps. On closer inspection, the porch was much bigger than I had originally thought. The paint, once white, was indeed cracked and peeling. Laura opened up Cynthia's walker, and we followed the shuffling Cynthia down the length of the porch to the front door. She braced her hip against the walker while she rummaged about in her handbag for the key.

"Now, where is that thing? It's an older key, not hard to find," Cynthia grumbled.

"Here, let me," said Laura. "I don't know how you find anything in that suitcase of yours." Laura chuckled as she took the purse from Cynthia and fished out the skeleton key, which appeared to be of brass. I eyed the antique key with admiration bordering on reverence.

Laura inserted the key in the keyhole of the old varnished oak door. She rattled and shook it until it finally turned.

"It's old," she murmured unnecessarily with a rueful glance in my direction.

"I know. That's what is so great about it," I breathed.

"Our parents actually never locked the door when we were young," Laura said. "There really wasn't much call to lock things up in those days."

"Not like today," muttered Cynthia as she put her walker in gear and pushed in through the front door. Laura gave way and let her enter, urging me to follow Cynthia in. We paused just inside.

Sunlight from the open door behind us spilled onto the old oak floors, highlighting the shine where the remnants of a high varnish still remained in a large square pattern in the middle. It seemed obvious a small carpet had covered much of the floor just inside the door, protecting it from wear and tear. We stood just to the right of a steep wooden staircase, which bore remnants of the same highly polished varnish as the floor.

"That's the living room off to the right there. The dining room is through there," Cynthia pointed past the staircase to an open doorway to the far end of short hallway. "And the kitchen is to the right of that. You can get to the kitchen from the dining room, the living room and from another door leading to the porch on the other side of the house."

I dropped my jaw at the sight of the massive fireplace on the south wall of the living room. The white paint on the wooden mantel was now grimy and cracked with age, but the hearth still held court over the room.

"What a huge fireplace! It's gorgeous."

"Kept us warm many a night, I'll tell you that. There were a couple of blizzards where we all huddled down here together and slept on the floor. Kind of like a family slumber party!" Cynthia crowed.

"No central heating?" I gulped.

"Not in those days." Laura sighed. "I know we should have had some put in over the years, but neither one of us lived here as adults...so it didn't seem worth the effort. We tried to talk my parents into central heating...but they saw no need for it after so many years of living here."

Suddenly, an orange shape darted past us and ran down the hall into the dining room, leaving small footprints on the dusty floor.

"Bad kitty!" Cynthia scolded as she took a halting step forward. "I guess we should have shut the door."

"I'll go after him," I offered, no stranger to cats as my next door neighbor was taking care of my own calico, Sassy, who was more than aptly named.

I moved quickly and hurried down the hall, which led into an empty room with large windows on two sides, which I assumed to be the dining room. The kitchen opened to the right, and orange kitty eyed me from a door that presumably led to the outside. I approached him slowly, and the cat bolted, heading toward the living room.

I raced through the living room just in time to see the cat running up the stairs while Cynthia and Laura watched me with a suspicion of laughter on their faces, though they did their best to control themselves.

"I'll get him, I swear," I panted as I grabbed the large oak newel and poised on the first step to see the cat sitting at the top of the landing. He bent to lick his tail once and meowed loudly while he watched with interest.

"Come here, kitty. Kitty, kitty, kitty," I coaxed. I eyed the old wooden stairs with suspicion, but they looked remarkably sturdy. Tentatively testing the first one, I pulled myself up by the newel. The steps felt solid—as if they had just been built.

"Come on, kitty," I urged with some impatience. I followed him up the stairs at a slow pace, wondering if the twitter I heard behind me at the bottom of the stairs came from Laura or Cynthia.

I reached the landing and began the next ascent. "If I don't get you out of here, you're going to get locked in. Forever. I'm not kidding."

I watched him run just past my head on the second floor as I moved up the stairs. When I reached the top, I turned to see that he'd run into another open doorway—probably a bedroom just to the right of the staircase. Several open doors along the hallway enticed me, but I was determined to catch the cat. The oak floors on the second floor also appeared to have had a lustrous shine at one time, though they were now scratched and dulled. Nothing a good sanding and another coat of varnish wouldn't take care of.

I followed the cat into the room and came to a halt. Orange kitty sat on the large sill of a huge bay window situated on the south side of the room. A white-painted wooden window seat nestled below it.

Forgetting about my pursuit of the cat for a moment, I crossed over to the window to peer out, driven by an excitement I did not understand. Down below in the garden, a small pond sparkled under the rays of dappled sunlight that were allowed in by a huge oak tree, which shaded the right side of the house. Beyond the garden, I could see the rolling hills and dales of the nearby farmlands, with seemingly endless fields of corn. And occasionally, the oak tree parted just enough to allow me a glimpse of white stones on the hill of the cemetery beyond.

I sank down on the window seat and unconsciously reached out a hand to pet the cat as I stared out the window. The view was mesmerizing—at once tranquil and scenic, charming and beautiful—everything a gal could want from a bay window.

The cat purred as he looked out the window alongside me, seemingly content to soak up the midday sun streaming through the window.

"I don't know if Sassy's going to like you, Marmaduke. She likes to rule the roost." I scratched the newly named cat's ears and watched the sun highlight the tombstones in the distance. "Just give her some space when she gets here, buddy. You'll be fine."

Because I knew in that instant when I saw the view of the hill from the window that I would buy the house.

CHAPTER FOUR

"What?" Sara swung around from the mirror, brush frozen in midair. "You did what?"

I rested on the bed, exhausted from the excitement of the day, massaging my right ear, which ached from spending half the day with the cell phone pressed up against it.

"I bought a house."

Sara dropped the brush with a thud on the oak veneer dresser.

"Where?"

"Here," I murmured, suspecting that a mere fifty years before, my sister would have had me committed to an asylum for the insane. I kept my eyes on my aching elevated feet, wiggling my toes now and again.

"Here?" Sara shrieked. There were no other words to describe the sound. She really shrieked, and I didn't blame her one little bit.

"Why on earth would you buy a house here?" she continued. "I mean...I know you've been saving for one, but here?" She held up her hands and looked around the room. "This is so far away from Seattle. What's here?"

"A house I want."

Sara moved over to the opposite bed and dropped down to gape at me.

"Where? I thought you went to the cemetery in Lilium today. When did you decide to go house hunting?"

I grinned and closed my eyes for a moment, trying to recall the whirlwind sequence of events. I elected to skip telling her about Darius. At this point, I decided he must have been a figment of my overactive imagination. I subdued a surge of grief at the thought.

"It all seemed to happen at the same time. I met these two little ladies at the cemetery and...well...they sold me a house." I smiled widely as I recalled Laura and Cynthia's not so subtle maneuvers to entice me to buy the house. Now they were happily planning their move to Florida. And I had inherited a house with no central heating and a marmalade cat.

Sara narrowed her eyes and cocked her head as she regarded me. I got the distinct impression that my sister was planning on having me committed anyway...modern day notwithstanding.

"You're wondering if I'm insane," I mumbled, wishing only for sleep, and not at all certain that I didn't want to use sleep as an escape from my bizarre choices of the day.

"Well, yes, as a matter of fact, I am," Sara muttered. "So, exactly where *is* this house?"

"Just down the road from the cemetery. In fact, just about right next door." I closed my eyes again, fully expecting an animated response.

"To a cemetery?" Sara's shriek tapered off to a whisper. "Now, I know you're nuts. Who buys a house near a cemetery?"

I opened one eye and focused it on Sara. With a lift of my eyebrow, I asked, "And what have *we* been doing for the last week?"

"Yeah, well, that's different. We've been looking for our ancestors—at your instigation, I might add. This genealogy thing was always your thing. I'm just along for the ride."

I grinned. "And I thank you very much, Sis. I couldn't have gotten this far without you."

Sara crossed her arms and arched her own brow in response to mine.

"This far...as in buying a house?"

"Exactly."

"Okay, so the darn house is just about sitting on a cemetery. What else?"

"It's a Victorian."

Sara nodded. "Well, I'm not surprised about that with all the oohing and aahing you've been doing over those silly houses ever since you were little." She shook her head with a lift of her lips. "How many of those weird Victorian house Christmas ornaments do you own now, anyway?"

I chuckled. "Five, so far. Don't forget to get me one for this year."

"Do you have a picture of the house? Did you take any pictures? You know...most people do that when they buy a house?" Sara shook her head again. "I can't believe you just bought a house."

I nodded. "I did take pictures. The camera is in my bag over there." I wriggled my toes once again, trying to bring life back into my feet after being on them all day. Sara got up to search my bag for the camera.

"By the time I'd met with the realtor, and we called the bank and started on the financing and the ladies finished telling me their plans for Florida, it was almost dusk. I was so exhausted, I just wanted to get back here and put my feet up." I didn't mention that I'd driven back to the cemetery one more time but could see nothing in the dark and opted not to get out of the car.

Camera in hand, Sara sat down on her bed once again and began to fidget with the buttons of the camera.

"I'll have to go back with you tomorrow to check out this house," she said as she peered closely at the photos on the camera.

I watched her face carefully to see if I could tell when she saw the pictures of the house. Maybe the photographs would be too small on the camera screen to do the house "justice."

"I warn you. It's a fixer upper," I said with a shaky smile.

"Of course it's a fixer upper," Sara snorted, pursing her lips together as she viewed the camera. "What Victorian house isn't?"

Was that a good reaction or a bad reaction, I wondered? What were my parents going to think? Sara's report to them on the house would be influential in having them accept my impulsive decision with a minimum of recrimination.

She raised her head and stared at me like a newly discovered specimen under a microscope.

"Oh, yes, that definitely looks like a fixer upper. I'm just trying to figure out who would build a Victorian house on the prairies and cornfields of Iowa?"

"Oh, come on, Sara! You know how beautiful it is over there in Harrison County! Those rolling hills? The beautiful trees? The wind!" I sighed. "At any rate, the house belonged to Cynthia and Laura's family. They grew up in it. They say it's always been in their family."

"Good gravy, how old are these gals? A hundred and ten? Because they'd have to be to live at the turn of the century when this house was probably built." She peered down at the camera once again.

"No, silly. They're in their 70s, I think. Both widows. I'm sure it belonged to their grandparents or something."

"Whose tombstone is this?" Sara glanced up.

I blinked. I knew which photo she meant.

"I don't know. It was in the Lilium cemetery. I just thought it was interesting."

"But no one we're related to, right?"

I shook my head. "No, I can't even read the name."

Sara gave me a quizzical look and shrugged. She put her hands on her blue-jeaned knees to rise.

"Well, let's go get something to eat to...uh... celebrate. Something is bound to be open this late."

"I'm too tired," I whined.

Sara reached down to pull me to my feet. "Get up. We're going out amongst your peeps now. You're going to be a resident of Iowa! Do you have any idea what the tax laws are here in the state? State income tax? Property taxes?"

"No," I mumbled. "Should I?"

"Geez, you're naïve," Sara chuckled as she found my shoes and set them in front of me.

****

Two weeks later, I was back in Iowa, thanking my lucky stars that the Indian summer nights had not yet turned cold because the heating and cooling guys weren't going to be able to get on the project for another week.

I could have waited in my apartment in Seattle for the comfort of upgraded wiring and plumbing in my new house, but Sassy asked me daily when we were moving. I rocked in my white wicker porch chair and grinned. Not really.

Sassy had traveled from Washington State to Iowa in my small hybrid car, caterwauling and screaming for the first two days. On the third day, she settled into a depressed resignation and hung like a limp rag doll in my arms when I took her out of her cage that night in the motel room.

Now, Sassy sat on the inside window sill of the large bay window on the first floor and threw resentful looks in my direction as her human enjoyed the wind on the front porch of her new house—her newly purchased house, that is.

Sassy was a born and bred indoor city cat and it was too dangerous to let her out on the town, so to speak. I had no idea what critters roamed the nearby fields looking for naïve kitties. The cornfield-wise Marmaduke took full advantage of the situation by preening with tail held high as he freely marched up and down the railing of the front porch. Little did he know that I had already set up an appointment to have him neutered the following week.

I reveled in the first purchase for my new home—a white wicker porch set that smacked of Victorian décor—or at least I thought it did. I adored the fluffy bright yellow and rose-flowered seat cushions. With a bottle of lemonade on a dainty glass-topped table by my side, I waited for the movers to bring the rest of my furniture, which, in its entirety, wouldn't even fill up the living room.

My funds were limited, and I would have to furnish the bedrooms and formal living room of the house slowly. The cable company was scheduled to set up my satellite service within the week, so I would be fully wired and online with my graphic design work—a great job with a wonderful company that allowed me to pick up and move halfway across the country just as I had done.

The wind I loved blew gently across the porch from the south. I turned my head in that direction, but of course I couldn't see the cemetery through the trees of my garden.

My garden! I hugged myself with glee. A garden. Who would have thought I would ever have a garden of my own? Admittedly, it was overgrown and not much to look at, but I hoped to have that fixed soon. I would have to hire someone to re-sod the front lawn as weeds had taken over the grass.

I straightened in anticipation as a car pulled into the driveway. It wasn't the movers, but Laura and Cynthia. I jumped up and made my way down to the car to help Cynthia alight.

"Hello, my dear. So, here you are, your first day in your new home. How do you feel?" Cynthia leaned on me while Laura retrieved her walker from the back seat of the town car.

"Great, Cynthia. Just great. Broke, but great!"

Cynthia laughed. No...she snickered.

"And I feel very well off, thank you," she hooted.

Laura came around to meet us, and we hauled Cynthia up the steps.

"I'm afraid I don't have anything to offer you," I sighed. "I just arrived this morning myself. The appliances aren't being delivered till tomorrow."

"Oh, you're getting new things? How lovely for you!" Cynthia was settled into the wicker love seat, and Laura took up one of the chairs.

"Did you just get this furniture? It looks new!" Cynthia patted the arm of the love seat.

I preened, just as Marmaduke continued to do on the porch railing.

"Yes, I did. The store delivered it this morning, just about an hour ago. I ordered it online last week, with the express plan to have it here first thing. What do you think?"

"It's lovely, dear. Just lovely. My parents would have loved to own such a set." Cynthia sighed. "But they really couldn't afford nice things, as poor as they were."

"Poor? With this beautiful house?"

"Oh, they didn't buy the house. Our dad inherited the house from his grandmother, and she really didn't have any money either. It seems her husband, my great-grandfather, a scholarly type from Virginia, inherited it from some brother who died young. I think he was left some money by the brother, but bad investments..." She smiled with a small shrug. "Something like that."

"So, even though my family owned the place, they never really had the money to actually buy it or maintain it." Laura grimaced as she looked around. "And neither of our husbands wanted to live here. I'm afraid we let it go."

"I wouldn't worry about it, Laura," I patted her arm. "The house has good bones. That's what the inspector said. In fact, he said it had been built by a master craftsman. Did you know that?" I couldn't contain my pride.

Cynthia and Laura turned bemused faces on me. "No, we didn't. That would be that great-great uncle I just told you about. I don't remember what his name was. He built the house himself."

Laura added, "I'm glad to see it in good hands—like yours, Molly. We had to let it go, but I'm glad it went to you. You seem very...I don't know...comfortable here. Like you fit in."

I beamed. "I feel very much at home here. It's strange really. I don't think my family has any ancestors in this particular town, but somehow, this place just captivates me. It feels familiar in some way...like home." I blushed at my whimsy. And I wondered how long before I would be able to get to the cemetery. I hadn't been back since the day I bought the house. Sara and I had cut our trip short and returned to Seattle so I could make arrangements to relocate.

Cynthia leaned over to pat my blue-jeaned knee. "Well, it *is* your home now, dear, and we're your new family now—even though we'll be in Florida for most of the year."

A round of chuckles accompanied Cynthia's quip, and they moved onto a discussion of their plans for buying a condominium in Tampa Bay, Florida.

When the moving truck pulled in a short while later, Laura and Cynthia thought it wisest to get out of the way. After some discussion, the truck driver backed out into the road to allow Laura to pull out. I said goodbye to my first visitors while the truck driver patiently pulled back into the driveway.

Two hours later, my furniture was settled into the living room, kitchen, and the upstairs bedroom that had the view of the cemetery, and my new appliances had been delivered, although the only thing that could be hooked up was the refrigerator. The stove, washer, and dryer would have to wait for a wiring upgrade, scheduled for later in the week.

Hands on hips, I surveyed my modern bright orange microfiber sofa with its angular lines and geometrically patterned sage green pillows, and I shuddered. Sassy, finding something that smelled like home, jumped up onto the couch and took the opportunity to clean one of her paws.

"This is awful, Sass. Our furniture really looks hideous in here. And I need a carpet for the floor. I'm not sure I have enough money to get any more stuff. The electrical work and heating and cooling are going to put me in the poorhouse as it is." I scrunched my face, and my lips twitched. "Did you hear that, Sass? Poorhouse? That's what this is." I waved a hand to encompass the house. "The poorhouse. Everyone's been too poor to afford the darn thing. Now, I know what they meant."

Sass ignored me completely and moved on to capturing the end of her tail and cleaning it as if this was once-a-week Saturday bath day.

"Well, that's it for visitors today, Sass. I'm just going to take a quick walk. Up the road."

At this, my black and orange speckled calico cat fixed me with a reproving stare. At least, that's how I interpreted it.

"What?" I challenged the pint-sized dynamo with a matching glare. "What? So, I've got work to do...unpacking boxes. Is that your point?"

Holding her own, Sass continued to eye me with an unwavering gaze.

"Oh, I see. It's because I'm thinking about going up to the cemetery. Well, what would you know about it, missie? By the way, Marmaduke is going to be coming in and out of the house, but you aren't going to be going outside. I hope you're okay with that!"

I turned my back on the silly cat and walked out the door. Marmaduke jumped down from the railing and followed me down the driveway to the road.

"Oh, no, pal. You're not going with me. That's all I need is to be seen wandering around a cemetery with my familiar. They'll burn me at the stake for sure. You stay here. Besides, you don't want to get hit by a car, do you?"

I interpreted the marmalade cat's look to mean "What cars?" And he was right. Few cars seemed to use this country lane which led only to the cemetery.

"Okay, no cars. You're right. It doesn't matter. Stay here!"

I stepped out onto the road and turned left. A glance over my shoulder reassured me that Marmaduke did as he was told. I clasped my hands behind my back, and instead of briskly striding up the road, I found myself taking tense, hesitant steps—unsure of what I would find at the cemetery. At the base of the hill, the loud humming of cicadas in the nearby trees and bushes caught my attention, and I paused to listen with fascinated absorption. One might call the noise a "racket" if the buzzing sound didn't have such a steady rhythm to it.

No swarm descended on me, and I was oddly comforted by the presence of the vibrating cicadas. Life pulsed all around me. The vivid green of the trees and bushes delighted the eye. Lush crops of corn across the road sprung from obviously fertile earth. I inhaled deeply—the sweet country air itself a celebration of life.

Feeling somewhat fortified, I pushed myself forward and marched up the hill. I reached the entrance with its iron arch all too soon and stopped one foot short of entering the cemetery.

My heart pounded as I scanned the grounds from my limited vantage point. The base of the majestic oak tree where I'd seen Darius several weeks ago appeared barren, the bench empty. Nothing moved except the graceful oak trees as they swayed in the stiff breeze, stronger now on the top of the hill. The late afternoon sun danced across those tombstones that weren't directly in the shadow of the massive evergreen trees, warming them to a light golden hue.

I took several wary steps into the cemetery, stopping often to scan the area. The constant humming of the wind blowing through the pine needles of the trees provided a loud backdrop of noise, and I realized I wouldn't be able to hear any approaching footsteps—a realization that gave me an uneasy vulnerability.

I swallowed hard and moved on through the cemetery, coming to a stop near the massive oak tree where the wind blew the hardest, half expecting to see Darius materialize, half hoping he wouldn't. But he wasn't there. He didn't "appear."

I turned to look at the wrought iron bench—the one we had shared. It was empty. Darius had never really been there, had he? And I'd never been fortunate enough to have another dream of him, try though I might. A heaviness descended on me, and the once bright and hopeful day seemed to grow dark, though the sun still shone. I dropped down onto the bench and crossed my arms over my chest.

I had imagined him. The handsome man of my dreams. What had I done? What insanity had I gotten myself into? I was dangerously close to admitting a humiliating truth—even to myself.

I had bought the house to be near Darius. I hadn't wanted to admit it to anyone, least of all to myself, but I knew the moment I saw the cemetery in the distance from the bedroom window of the house, that I was destined to live in the Victorian.

And now, it seemed likely that Darius—a man I knew I loved with every fiber of my being, whom I'd always loved though I could not remember when or how—had been a fantasy lover...a romantic creation from my lonely subconscious.

I pulled my legs up to my chest and rested my face on my knees. I wanted to cry, but tears failed to come. I mourned the loss of a dream I'd lived with for two weeks—perhaps all my life. I grieved for the loss of all that was familiar in Seattle when I'd left the city to move to an out-of-the-way town in the Midwest. I worried that I had suffered a mental breakdown of some sort.

"Stupid ancestors," I muttered. "This whole thing has put me over the edge. Living in the past like this. It's nuts. Unhealthy. No one should do it." I felt better for hearing a human voice—even if it was my own.

I thought I heard a sound. With a muffled gasp, I peeked over the edge of my hands. I held my breath and listened intently for a repeat of the sound.

Still...nothing moved. My imagination was running away with me. Again. I looked down at the rest of the empty and cold iron bench, wondering if I could just lie down and sleep there awhile. I hadn't slept much in the last few weeks, and not at all last night in the generic motel as I anticipated my return to Lilium and the house...and Darius. The bench looked uncomfortable, but it was where I wanted to be. Perhaps if I waited long enough...perhaps if I dreamt...Darius might return.

I started to stretch out when the whimsical tune of my cell phone broke the empty silence. I cursed the intrusive sound of the foolish ring. It jarred me out of my reverie, my desire to sleep.

I dragged it from my jeans pocket.

"Yes!" I snapped.

"Oh, my dear, did we catch you at a bad time?"

"Laura? Cynthia?" My muddled brain couldn't quite make out the voice.

"It's Cynthia, dear. Are you all right? You sound so..."

"Oh, I'm fine. I'm sorry I answered so sharply."

"Have the movers gone then?"

"Yes, they're gone. Everything I own is in the house. Thanks for asking."

"Well, I actually called because Laura and I are packing up our things as well, and we realized we're missing some of our old family pictures—the ones of our family when we were growing up."

I absentmindedly stared at the light playing on the stone that caught my attention on my last visit to the cemetery.

"So, I was wondering if you could run up to the attic and see if there are any boxes up there. Do you remember seeing any during the inspection, dear?"

I straightened. I couldn't exactly run upstairs at the moment, but I already had the answer.

"Oh, shoot! I'm glad you said something. Yes, the inspector took me up there and showed me several cardboard boxes in the attic. I meant to tell you about those. I'm not at the house right now, but I can dash home, get them and drop them off at your place."

"No, no, dear. Laura and I can stop by to pick them up ourselves. Is 6 p.m. okay with you? Will that give you enough time to return from where you are?"

"Oh, sure. I'm not far away."

"Laura and I are on our way to the cemetery in about 30 minutes to visit our husbands and then we'll stop by."

"Oh!" I swallowed hard. I wasn't quite sure why I was so reluctant to tell Cynthia where I was. All of a sudden, cemetery hunting had taken on a whole new meaning when one wasn't looking for deceased ancestors but instead wandering around looking for some sort of undead.

"Sounds good, Cynthia. I'll see you at six then."

"See you later, dear."

As if Cynthia and Laura were pulling into the gates of the cemetery at that very moment, I snapped the phone shut, jumped up and hurried across the cemetery to the arched entrance. I jogged back to the house, arriving at the driveway out of breath, clutching my aching ribs, and bemoaning my poor physical condition. The life of a sedentary computer geek did nothing to promote good physical fitness. And I had been away from the gym for over a month.

Marmaduke waited for me at the entrance to the driveway—as if he'd never left his sentry post.

"Out of breath...can't talk now," I gasped as I bent over, bracing my hands on my knees. "Ladies coming... Box..."

He continued to regard me with an unblinking stare.

"Okay," I wheezed. "Thanks for listening. Let's go into the house."

Marmaduke jumped into action and led the way back to the house, his tail jutting high like a rudder of a miniscule orange airplane. I followed at a slower pace, eyeing the lovely lines of the Victorian house in front of me and marveling once again that such an elegant house belonged to me—regardless of why I bought it. My spirits lifted.

I entered the house with Marmaduke at my heels. He and Sass, sprawled on the sofa in the living room, hissed a greeting toward one another and promptly ignored each other. He followed me as I climbed the stairs, past the second floor and up a narrow set of stairs to the tiny door leading to the small attic. The door opened with a creak, and I stepped into the low-ceiling room. Had I been any taller than 5 feet 3 inches, I might have had to bend. A small dusty window graced the end of the room and provided the only available light.

The boxes lay on the dusty unvarnished wooden floor just inside the door. As I lifted the first box with a handwritten "Photos" on it, I scanned the small room and wondered how I could best utilize it during future renovations. It was too intriguing a spot not to convert into a small reading room or something.

Huffing and puffing, I hauled both boxes of photos down to the second floor with absolutely no help from Marmaduke who imperiously led the way. I paused for a breath and then maneuvered my way down the stairs to the living room with the boxes. I dropped onto the couch with the boxes at my feet, heedless of the dust on the front of my jeans, and rested my head against the back of the couch while I caught my breath. A shower was definitely in order to wash off the dust from the attic, but a check of my watch showed I had only 15 minutes before Cynthia and Laura came. At any rate, I didn't even have a shower yet. The only bathing would be done in the clawfoot tub in the single bathroom on the second floor.

I closed my eyes for a moment, trying to remember when the plumbing guy was coming. Dates and tasks ran across my brain like the pages of a calendar lifting in a breeze. Tuesday?

A soft scratching sound near my feet caught my attention, and I opened my eyes and leaned forward. Sassy, the cat who had thus far managed to survive her curious nature, stood on her hind legs, poking and prodding the opening of the box with a delicate paw.

"Sassy! Stop! That's not yours...or mine. Besides, you're going to get dirty and dusty, and you'll be miserable. I know you!"

The small cat gave me a look that some might describe as withering, and returned to her efforts of trying to lift a corner of the box with her tiny paws.

"Sassy! I'm warning you!" I slid off the couch and sat down on the floor next to Sassy who paused as if curiously awaiting her human's next move.

"All right. So, what's in there? I can see a picture already."

Hoping Cynthia and Laura wouldn't mind, I pulled open the first box and peered inside. Pictures of smiling people standing on the front steps of the porch looked out at me. Feeling not a little guilty for snooping into someone else's property, I slid the photos around with a delicate finger to see as many as I could without having to confess that I'd actually taken them out of the box.

Some of the photos appeared to be older—the sort of photos one would wish were kept in some sort of proper preservation container. I had no idea what sorts of materials were available in that department.

One photo lay face down, and I peered closely at the date handwritten on the back. 1880. The age of the photo quite took my breath away.

I glanced up at the front door, half expecting Cynthia and Laura to ring the bell at the very moment that I decided to pick up their century-plus-old photograph with the tips of my unprotected fingers and turn it over to see the front.

I suppose I should have known.

How could I not have suspected? Did he not say that he'd donated some of his land to the town for a cemetery?

As I gazed at the photo, I stopped breathing, I was certain of that. The pounding in my ears warned me that I wasn't breathing, but I couldn't exhale for fear I might breathe on the old sepia-toned photograph—the photograph of the man of my dreams. Darius Ferguson looked up at me with a sparkle in his light-colored eyes and a half smile on his devastatingly handsome face.

Chapter Five

My head began to swim, and I forced myself to open my mouth mechanically and gasp for air. The hand holding the photo shook uncontrollably, and I steadied it with my other hand.

I had dreamed of Darius's face exactly as it was in this picture, posed at a slight angle, but still looking directly at the camera. His gaze seemed so intimate that I involuntarily pulled back. I had seen that expression in his eyes when he looked at me, and it still made my toes curl with exhilaration.

He wasn't a dream! He wasn't a dream. I wanted to dance with joy. I almost jumped up to do just that until I remembered that I was looking at a photograph of a man taken in 1880. However, such was my insanity that I hardly let that small detail dampen my joy at "finding" Darius once again.

The photograph was in good condition for the historical period, the edges of the framed backing firm and crisp. I laid the picture down on the table with care and clasped my hands in my lap. Sassy meowed and surveyed the rest of the contents of the box. Finding little to interest her, she dropped to all fours and jumped onto the couch to attend to some much-needed grooming.

"How did I dream of a photograph I've never seen? Did I imagine the whole thing?" I raised my gaze to look out one of the two windows flanking the fireplace, which faced the direction of the cemetery, though only the shadows in the garden left by the late afternoon sun were visible from the first floor.

I forced myself to relax my aching jaw and take a deep breath. I reached for the photograph again with loving hands. I peered at it closely. Faded gray ink marked the bottom border in a delicate cursive script.

"Darius Blake Ferguson, 1880, age 28 yrs." I mouthed his name once again. "Darius Blake Ferguson."

I turned the picture over and studied his face once again—the dashing waves of hair that spread out from his forehead, the sparkle in his light-colored eyes which were blue in my dream, the soft lines of his lower lip visible below his dark mustache. A feeling of peace swept through me, warming the core of my being and spreading throughout my limbs. I pressed the photograph to my chest for a moment before compulsively staring at it once again. Whatever supernatural phenomenon led me to meet Darius in the cemetery, or whatever force had brought him into my dreams, I promised myself I would never run from him again...if only I had the chance to see him one more time, ghost or dream lover.

He existed. He had been real. He had lived...and died. I raised the photograph to my lips. And I loved him. I knew that as certainly as I knew I would return to the cemetery every day until I found him again...as certainly as I knew I would do everything in my power to see him again in my dreams.

The unmistakable sound of a car in the drive brought me to my feet. I set the photograph down on the high-gloss black coffee table and hurried to the door, anxious to ask Cynthia and Laura about Darius. Was he a relative of theirs?

"Hello, dear. Thank you," Cynthia murmured as I rushed down the steps to help her from the car.

"Did you happen to find those boxes? Boy, I hope they're here, or we're in for it with the grandkids—when they get old enough to care." Laura preceded us and threw a grin over her shoulder as she carried Cynthia's walker up the porch stairs.

"I did. They were in the attic—right where you said. I brought them downstairs."

"Thank you, Molly," Laura murmured. She took Cynthia's arm in one hand and held the walker in the other while I pushed open the door. "I could have brought them down. Were they heavy? I don't even remember; it's been so long since we saw them."

"No, that's fine. There they are." I practically danced with an overwhelming sense of anticipation. "I hope you don't mind, but I peeked in one of them."

"Not at all, dear. In fact, I wonder if we shouldn't leave a few of them here, Laura. Some of the ones of the house? I think there were some around the turn of the century, weren't there?"

I caught my breath and did my best to keep my hopeful look toward Laura just short of begging.

"Sure, we can do that. Why not? It's your house now, Molly, and all houses come with history."

I grabbed the taller woman for an exuberant hug.

"Oh, thank you, thank you," I said with a broad smile. Laura's eyebrows shot up at my enthusiasm, but she patted my arm kindly. Cynthia beamed in return.

"Well, of course, dear. We're delighted to share the history of the house with you."

"Please sit down," I said with some shortness of breath as I wondered if I dared ask for the picture of Darius. It was a portrait, not a picture of the house, and I had no idea how they would react when I asked for it.

"The refrigerator is in place and humming away," I rattled nervously, "but I still haven't been to the store—not that I know where it is, so I can't offer you anything."

I winced as I watched the sisters pause to regard my out-of-place ultramodern sofa with raised eyebrows, before Laura lowered Cynthia onto the sofa.

"That's perfectly understandable. We just finished dinner at any rate," Laura said as she took a seat beside Cynthia who ran her left hand along the fabric of the angular armrest.

"My dear, this sofa is luxurious!" Cynthia cooed. "I've seen them in magazines, but I never imagined! Sister, we have to get one of these for our place in Florida. I could stretch out on it all day long." Cynthia eyed the extensive length of the couch—one of only two pieces of seating furniture that would fit in my small Seattle apartment living room.

"Well, then I guess we'd better get two, because I have every intention of lying on a sofa myself with a pack of romance novels."

"Done!" Cynthia murmured, seemingly enthralled as she continued to run her delicate blue-veined hands along the surface.

"So, what's that you have there?" Laura turned her attention to the photograph on the coffee table. I startled, already on edge about Darius's picture.

I dropped into the small blue microfiber easy chair opposite the couch and picked the photograph up from the coffee table.

"Well, I was wondering. I didn't mean to snoop... Okay, I guess I did." I scrunched my face with a cheesy grin. "Anyway, I didn't get any further than this photograph that was near the top of the stack. It's the oddest thing—" I stopped short, unsure of how much I wanted to reveal, unsure if I really had a shred of sanity left.

"What's that?" Laura held out her hand for the photograph, and I reluctantly handed it over.

"Well, I was wondering if you know who he is. That's all. Is he a relative?" I sat on the edge of my chair.

Laura peered at the photograph and read the bottom inscription as I had.

"It says Darius Blake Ferguson, 1880, age 28 years." Laura squinted at the picture. "Hmmm...He looks familiar, but I can't—" She shook her head and turned to her sister. "Do you know who this is, Cynthia?"

Cynthia, still admiring the feel of the microfiber, brought her attention to the conversation at hand. She accepted the photograph from Laura.

"Oh, yes. I remember him," she exclaimed.

My heart pounded. She *remembered him?*

"Well, I remember hearing about him." Cynthia turned to Laura. "He's the uncle who built the house. You know...the one who died young. Well, I don't know if he died exactly. Something happened. And then his brother, our great-grand somebody or another Ferguson, came out from Virginia and took over the house." She gazed at the photograph once again. "Handsome man, wasn't he?" She handed the picture back to Laura and returned to appreciating the sofa.

"Oh, that's right!" Laura looked at the photograph once again. "I remember hearing about him, but I can't remember how he died either. Wasn't there some talk? What was it?" she asked herself.

I leaned forward to capture every word, every nuance, every change of expression—while I coveted the photo in Laura's hands.

"Yes?" I encouraged breathlessly.

Laura shook her head, set the photograph down on the table, and returned her attention to the box.

"I can't remember. I'm sure it will come to me, probably in the middle of the night. Should we go through these boxes now and see which photos of the house Molly wants to keep? I'm sure she would like to get to bed sometime tonight."

I was fairly sure I wasn't going to get any sleep that night. These women quite possibly had the key to the mystery of Darius, and they didn't understand how desperate I was. Nor did I want them to know of my peculiar obsession with him, but I couldn't resist another question.

"Do you know if he's buried in the cemetery?"

"I have no idea," Laura said as she dug further into the box.

My shoulders slumped, but I gave it one more valiant effort.

"Well, if you do happen to remember anything, I'd love to hear about it. You know. The builder of the house..." I waved an airy hand around the living room, hoping it wasn't shaking. Of course, Darius had built the house. And that is why I loved it. Had there ever been a doubt?

"Certainly, dear," Cynthia nodded. "We'll put our heads together and brainstorm."

I picked up the photograph, unwilling to leave Darius lying on the table—discarded and alone. As I had left him at the cemetery...or in my dream.

"I know this is a lot to ask—and you know where I live if you want it back, b-but could I have this picture?"

At the startled look on Laura's face, I rushed on. "It's just that I feel like... like I know him... just a little," I said with a lift of my shoulders. "You know, the house."

Cynthia chuckled.

"You have a crush on him, don't you...from his photograph? I think we all did as children. It comes back to me now. He was so handsome! Even my mother thought he was quite dashing."

Laura shook her head. "Did we? I don't remember that. But yes, you can have the photograph, Molly. We don't need it, do we, Cynthia? He didn't have any children who would want it, did he?"

"No, I don't think he did, but as I said, I don't remember the whole story. It will come to me—as Laura said—in the middle of the night or some other inconvenient time."

"Call me if it does," I urged. I set the photograph down on the glossy black coffee table with reverent care. "Thank you."

"You're welcome. I'm sure we can call upon you to provide us a copy should our grandkids or great-grandkids ever desire to pursue their family history. That seems unlikely at this time," Laura said with a shake of her head. "They're all pretty young with their lives ahead of them, and completely uninterested in old stuffy photographs...or old stuffy people, for that matter." She chuckled and poked Cynthia in the side.

"Speak for yourself," Cynthia giggled. "Florida beaches, here I come!"

We spent the next several hours going through the photographs. There were several shots of the house taken by their parents in the early 1900s with an old Brownie camera, according to the sisters. The children lined up in front of the house in their Sunday best while "Dad" took the photograph. Contrary to what Cynthia had said about poverty, the black and white photograph showed a well-tended house, the paint seamless, the garden lush and full of life. The present day garden was overgrown, but I could see the original landscaping detail in the photo. I asked for that photo, and they gave it to me willingly, having several more of the same photo session.

Laura and Cynthia reminisced while they searched through the boxes, sharing family anecdotes with me. Their stories brought the house to life, infusing it with history and warmth, and I looked up to scan it often with renewed interest and a surge of affection. I kept my ears perked for any further mention of Darius, but his name did not come up again, and I didn't want to pique their curiosity any further by interrogating them.

Their visit came to an end all too soon.

"Well, we've got to get going," Laura huffed as she bent down to grab one of the boxes.

"I'll get them." I jumped up to assist.

"Thank you, dear. That's very nice of you." Cynthia threw a last admiring glance at the couch and pulled herself up on her walker.

"Thanks, Molly." Laura picked up Cynthia's ubiquitous oversized shiny handbag, which the frail woman could hardly manage with both hands on her walker.

"Listen, Cynthia," Laura said. "I think we should introduce Molly to a few of the people in town tomorrow. You know—Bob down at the hardware store...and Sally at the grocery store." She chuckled and turned to me with an apologetic shrug. "Well, we call it a grocery store, but it's just a little shop. We still have to go into Missouri Valley to get our supplies—just like my parents used to do."

I paused, box in hand.

"Oh, sure! That sounds great!" I said. I really did need to get to a store.

"Good. We'll see you in the morning then. About ten? Do you need anything tonight? Can we loan you some food or some coffee?"

I pushed open the door with my hip while I maneuvered the box outside.

"No, I'm good, thanks. I've got a few things in the fridge already that I had in a cooler in my car."

I hoisted the box into the back seat of the town car and returned for the other box while Laura settled Cynthia in. The sun descended below the tree line, and I was about to spend my first night in a strange house in the middle of nowhere. I picked up the second box and treated myself to another quick peek at Darius's photo on the coffee table.

It seemed as if Darius gazed directly at me. And my heart swelled. Allowing myself a moment of uninhibited joy, I gave him a quick wink and hurried out with the other box.

Several hours later, exhausted from searching through boxes to find my bedding, I dropped down on the newly made bed and contemplated the task of bathing. Night had fallen, and the wind had picked up outside, blowing gently through the old window screen and filling the room with a cool breeze—just cool enough for a good night's sleep, I hoped. The absence of curtains did not bother me unduly as I suspected no one would be able to see me from any particular vantage point—unless they drove up to the cemetery and used binoculars! With that ludicrous image in mind, I grinned, wished them well if they wished to exert such effort, and pushed myself off the bed to head for the bathroom. I'd prevailed upon the inspector to have a water heater put in over the two week period that I'd been gone, and I was anxious to see if it worked. He assured me it had. There were still many, many renovations needed to the house, including replacing many of the pipes.

I grabbed a towel out of one of the unpacked boxes in the bathroom and picked out soap, shampoo and conditioner from my traveling kit. A twist of the knobs on the clawfoot tub, kindly loosened by the inspector, sent warm water flowing into the tub with some clanking and a groan or two from the old pipes. I tossed in some bubble bath to celebrate my first bath in my new/old home. As with most things in the house, the chipped and stained tub would require a facelift, and I was happy to undertake that project.

I wondered at the miracle that Darius had built this house—the house I now owned, though I felt as if I was only borrowing it. He had probably ordered the tub...and hauled it up the stairs, though I couldn't imagine how. No doubt, he had taken baths in it himself. My face reddened at the thought. I shed my clothes and stepped into the tub, slipping down beneath the bubbles.

Darius's clawfoot tub. I closed my eyes for a moment and rested my head against the back of the porcelain. Some candles would have been nice, I mused. I'd have to get some the following day at the store.

"Be careful you do not fall asleep in there, Molly, my girl."

I shrieked at the sound of the male voice behind me and jerked. Slipping further into the tub in a panicked attempt to cover myself, I banged the back of my head on the hard rim.

"Get out! Get out of here! I have a gun!" I screeched as I ignored the pain in my head and rotated onto my knees below the water line to face my attacker.

Darius leaned against the bathroom doorsill, his back to me. He glanced over his shoulder for an instant before averting his face. The adrenaline surging through my body barely allowed me to see that his cheeks were reddened. Before I could yell at him, he raised his hands above his shoulders in mock surrender.

"A gun! Good gravy, Molly! Since when did you own a gun? You hated those things."

I crouched below the water and covered whatever body parts I could. A sense of the surreal surrounded me once again. I thought I had imagined him. Was I hallucinating...again?

"How did you get in here?" I choked out. "Who *are* you?"

Darius stole a sideways glance over his shoulder—as if to see that I indeed did not have a gun aimed at him—before turning his face away.

"It is I, Molly. The same man you met two weeks ago. The same man you loved over a hundred years ago."

"You're nuts!" I spit out. "You're not here. I'm just imagining things." My knees were aching, and I shifted awkwardly in the tub to dive under the water again, keeping my neck twisted to watch him. I couldn't stay in the bathtub all night. I felt so vulnerable—even if this was a hallucination...or a fantasy.

"So, since you're not really here, you wouldn't mind keeping your face turned away, so I can get out of the tub, would you?" My heart pounded, the rhythm matching the pounding in my head from smacking it on the edge of the tub. "Please?" I couldn't keep the quiver from my voice.

"Certainly. It is not proper for me to be standing here at any rate. I simply came upstairs to see if you were here, and there you were—in my tub—a vision of bubbles and curly brown ringlets."

I pressed a hand to my damp ponytail. A sudden warmth in the pit of my stomach contradicted the cold grip in my chest.

"Go away," I pleaded. "I may want to daydream about you, but I don't know that I want to actually *see* you. It's too confusing. You can't possibly be real. If you're not a dream, then you're a gho..." I choked on the word.

"As you wish, Molly. But I can assure you...I am quite real, although you are right. I may very well be a ghost." He threw another quick glance over his shoulder, and his mouth curved into an embarrassed smile before he moved away.

I watched him disappear and panicked.

"Wait," I shrieked. "Wait!"

"Yes, dear?" He backed up to the edge of the door again, still keeping his face averted.

"Wait for me downstairs. Don't go yet. I'll be right there."

Darius inclined his head slightly to the side where I saw his profile, and I could have sighed when a single golden-brown curl fell forward in his face.

"Very well. I will be downstairs in the kitchen."

I waited until I could hear his footsteps descending the stairs and then I jumped out of the tub and grabbed my towel with shaking hands. I scrubbed myself dry with vigor before peeking down the hallway to see that all was clear. With the towel wrapped around me, I tiptoed lightly past the stairs and across the hall to my bedroom.

Easing the door shut, I scrambled onto my knees to rifle through my open suitcase on the floor for a bathrobe. I slipped it on, yanked the sash as tightly as I could and thrust my feet into my slippers. I opened the door and tiptoed out into the hallway again.

Pausing at the top of the stairs to listen for sounds below, it occurred to me that Darius was able to get into the house because I hadn't bothered to lock the door. A silly mistake for a girl from a big city like Seattle. How could I have fallen for the "innocence" of country charm?

But then again, if he was Darius Blake Ferguson, and it seemed likely he was, this really was his home, and he would know how to get into it anyway. And if he were a ghost, which also seemed likely, keys and locked doors probably weren't an issue. I swallowed hard and ignored the shiver down my back.

Calling 911 was not an option at the moment. My phone was downstairs in the living room. Should I need to call for help for some reason—though the idea seemed far-fetched at the moment as I couldn't imagine Darius ever hurting me—I would encounter Darius again long before I could get to the phone. And hadn't I dreamed him up anyway? What if *help* came? What if—after listening to my bizarre tale of cemeteries and ghosts—they took me away, ostensibly to keep me from injuring myself or some such thing?

I crept down the stairs, peering over the rail to scan the dining room—empty of furniture since I had none for the space. I looked over the other rail toward the living room. A light shone from the kitchen, and I descended the stairs. I caught sight of my purse on the coffee table and debated whether to grab my phone...just in case. The unmistakable sound of the refrigerator door opening and closing caught my attention, and, anxious to see what was going on in the kitchen, I ignored the phone and turned in the direction of the kitchen. What was the man doing? I peeked around the edge of the doorsill. I smiled to see that Darius stood in front of the refrigerator, pulling the handles on the refrigerator doors, bending down to peer up into the icemaker, poking and prodding its handle.

"It's an icemaker," I murmured. If he wasn't the most adorable thing... He looked like a little boy, albeit a tall one, playing with a machine he'd never seen before.

Darius turned to me with bright interested blue eyes. I had underestimated how gorgeous they really were.

"Indeed? This is truly remarkable. Certainly better than the small wooden icebox which once stood here. And do you still have your ice delivered from the hardware store? Nesbitt's Hardware, if I remember correctly."

I couldn't help it. I laughed outright. Darius turned a startled look on me, and I clamped a hand over my mouth to stifle another laugh. When I regained some control, I answered.

"No, we don't have ice delivered anymore, Darius." I nodded toward the refrigerator. "The machine makes it—though not at the moment. I'm waiting for the plumber."

Darius cocked his head and turned back to open the doors once again. He peered in.

"How?" As men have done through time immemorial, Darius pressed and released the button to turn the light off and on.

I watched him with amusement.

"Water is piped in through the back." I grinned and gave a slight shrug, suddenly wishing I knew more. "Some combination of magic occurs inside the refrigerator involving electricity, and the ice is formed." I chuckled. "That's all I know about the mechanics of it."

"It's wonderful," he breathed like a kid in a candy store.

He turned to survey the rest of the kitchen, running his fingers lightly along the edge of the single basin porcelain sink. "This room was meant to be filled with children and laughter, the smell of cooking and good food." His face darkened for a moment, taking on a distant look as he gazed out the kitchen window. "It did not happen as I dreamed," he said quietly.

"Darius?" The shadow of regret on his face broke my heart. If I'd had the courage, I would have wrapped my arms around his waist to comfort him. But I couldn't make myself move.

In response to my voice, he gave himself a slight shake and faced me with a tender smile.

"Please forgive me, Molly. I do not wish to cause you distress. It is foolish to dwell on a past that is gone. This is a joyful time...now that I have seen you again."

I blushed and lowered my head. I didn't know who I was supposed to be to him, but I desperately wanted to be her, to bask under the light in his bright eyes.

"And what is this?" he asked in an amused tone. I turned to see him study my apartment-sized, round, glass-topped breakfast table—completely out of place in this homey Victorian kitchen with the faded remnants of an ivy-patterned wallpaper on the walls. I seriously doubted that Darius had put the wallpaper up.

"That is certainly an interesting piece." He moved over to touch the surface. The sight of his tanned, sturdy fingers running gently along the smooth glass made my knees wobble.

"It's the furniture from my other house. It doesn't seem to fit in here, I know."

Darius turned to me with a smile that brought a charming crinkle to the corner of his eyes.

"I apologize for frightening you upstairs. I knocked on the front door, but there was no answer. The door was not locked, and I entered as you can see," he said with a self-deprecating smile. "I planned to wait in the living room for you, but your yellow-eyed spotted kitten stalked me mercilessly. And the orange cat ran inside the house when I entered. Surrounded by felines of unknown temperament, I found myself retreating up the stairs, and suddenly there you were!"

His cheeks bronzed only slightly less than mine burned. He rubbed an unsteady hand over his jaw and contemplated the top of the table once again.

"I can't believe you're real," I whispered as I tightened my robe. I rushed on in a louder voice, hoping he hadn't heard. "Can I offer you something to drink? Some hot chocolate?"

Darius inclined his head. "Yes, please, that sounds wonderful." He turned to survey the new white electric range and stove that had been delivered that afternoon. "This certainly doesn't look anything like the wood stove I put in the house." He touched the surface, again with long, masculine fingers that seemed to gently explore the texture of the smooth enameled surface.

I turned away from ogling his hands to grab some bottled water from the refrigerator, following which I ransacked one of the cardboard kitchen boxes for two mugs and two packets of instant chocolate. I filled them with water and put them into the microwave. So far, the little apartment-size microwave had coaxed the old wiring to give it just enough juice to make hot water. I hoped it would hold up for two more cups before it fried the entire electric circuitry of the house.

Darius turned to watch me. "And what is that?"

"A microwave," I murmured self-consciously. "I don't know how it works either, but it heats things up fast."

"You do not use wood?"

I shook my head.

"No, no wood. *I* don't." I jabbed a thumb toward my chest. "Maybe some other people do. I don't know what they do out here in the country."

Darius eyed me and chuckled. "And I have no idea what they do in the city...or even in this century for that matter." He crossed the room to take a seat at the breakfast table, perching carefully on the orange-cushioned, black pseudo-wrought iron chairs that went with it.

The microwave beeped, and I poured the packets of instant chocolate mix into the cups. It wasn't my favorite sort of hot chocolate, but it sufficed in a pinch. I stirred the contents and brought the mugs over to the table where I took a seat opposite Darius. I lowered my gaze, wishing we were at opposite ends of a massive wooden dining room table so I could admire him from a distance. Just not so close.

"You purchased my house," he murmured in a voice of wonder, almost under his breath.

Startled, I looked up to find him watching me steadily—a warm expression on his face.

I squirmed under his gaze, and I took a quick sip of chocolate before responding.

"I did. It's a beautiful house. You did a wonderful job." I looked around the kitchen...anything to avoid his disturbingly intimate gaze.

"It took over a year to build. I built it for you, you know. For us." He exhaled as he spoke, almost like a sigh, and I thought I might faint from the rush of bittersweet emotion his words elicited. I dropped my gaze again and struggled for control of my modern day sensibilities—fighting the sensation of being swept away in a romance that could have no happy ending.

"Perhaps for someone who looked like me, Darius. It couldn't have been me." I took another practical sip of hot chocolate. "I don't see how that could be possible." But I desperately wanted it to be.

Darius reached for my hand and covered it with his.

"It *is* possible, Molly, and I think you are not as much of a skeptic as you think. I see it in the way you try to hide your eyes from me. You are frightened, and you do not understand what has happened. Nor do I. But I know that you loved me and you were going to marry me."

I clenched my fist under his, fighting the irresistible warmth of his touch. I pulled away gently and stuffed my hand into my deep robe pocket.

"How could I be alive then and now? Are you suggesting reincarnation? And what about you? Are you alive? I thought you were just a dream."

Darius shook his head with a bemused smile.

"I do not know, Molly. But you are as I remember you. Your sweet voice, the sparkle in your eye, the soft brown of your hair."

I thrilled to his words.

"I cannot attest to whether I am alive or not," he repeated as he grinned and ran a hand down the front of his dark gray vest. "I *feel* alive. I feel pain and hunger and thirst."

Hunger and thirst? I jerked my head in his direction and stared at him.

"What? Where have you been for the past two weeks? Since I last saw you at the cemetery? Where have you been staying?"

"Here," he said.

"Here?" I sat forward. "Do you mean to tell me you've been in the house this whole time?"

"Well, yes, I am afraid so. I needed shelter." He smiled apologetically.

I gulped. "Do you mean you can't go back to...to wherever you came from?"

"It appears not. I am still here." Darius shrugged his shoulders and regarded me with a half smile.

"But...but how have you been eating?" I stammered. "Do you even need to eat?"

"Apparently, I do," Darius murmured. "I have been very hungry lately."

"How did you get food?" My eyes widened and my stomach rolled over. "You *have* been getting food, haven't you, Darius? Please tell me I didn't walk off on you and let you starve." I covered my mouth with my hands and leaned on the table. "I didn't know," I mumbled against my palms while I stared at him, horrified.

Darius chuckled, and his blue eyes twinkled.

"Do not fret, Molly. I am in good health. I have eaten from the surrounding crops and roots from the garden." He blushed. "I will admit to sniffing some of the orange cat's food that was left out for him, but the smell was quite distasteful."

"The cat's food?" I dropped my hands to my lap and began to giggle helplessly. "Oh, Darius! Surely not the cat's food!"

"Yes, well, I was not certain what the ingredients were, so I opted to let it be. I do not know how the cat eats that nonsense, but he seems to enjoy it."

I stopped my guilty laughter and studied Darius's face. On closer examination, he did look a bit leaner around the face than when I'd seen him last.

"I'm so sorry, Darius," I murmured. "Drink your hot chocolate, and I'll see if there's anything to eat."

Either he was homeless or one of us was a lunatic. I hoped it wasn't me—and I sincerely hoped it wasn't him.

Darius picked up his cup and took a sip. I was halfway to my feet to find something for him to eat when he began to sputter and cough.

"Good gravy! What is this? Did you say it was hot chocolate?" He wiped at his mouth with the back of his hand and peered into his cup.

"Yes. Instant hot chocolate." I sat down again and eyed him narrowly.

"Well, it is positively dreadful. Instant, you say? What does that mean?"

"Instant. Ready made. Just pour it into a cup of hot water." My foot began to tap. Sara would have told him that was a bad sign. Beggars really shouldn't be choosy, I fumed.

"But where is the milk?"

"I don't have any. I just moved in. I haven't been to the store. I don't have an *icebox*." I arched an eyebrow as I glared at him. "You're only supposed to mix this with water, not milk."

"Oh, dear. I think I had better show you how to make a proper cup of hot chocolate...with milk and chocolate."

"I told you." I frowned. "I don't have milk—or chocolate."

He sat back in his seat and nodded, an irritating half smile on his face.

"When you get them, of course."

"What if I don't want to get them?" I dug in my heels...figuratively—hardly willing to reveal at this point that I wasn't overly fond of instant hot chocolate either.

From the gleam in his eye, Darius seemed to be aware of my irritation, but he was not intimidated.

"Well, if you want a proper hot chocolate, you will get them."

"Why don't *you* get them?" Hah! I had him now—the arrogant man!

"I do not know that I can get down to the market."

"Oh, really? And why is that?"

"Well, because I might very well be a ghost for all we know. I am unsure of what will happen if I try to go to the store."

I pointed triumphantly. "That's right. You probably *are* a ghost! So, you probably shouldn't be telling me how to make hot chocolate, should you?"

Darius smirked. There were no other words to describe his expression.

"But why would I not tell you if you are making it wrong?"

"Because...Because..." I paused and gulped down a sip of my lukewarm, suddenly awful-tasting hot chocolate. "Because you're a guest in my house, that's why!"

Darius grinned and inclined his head. "You are right, of course. I am a guest in your house, and I have been rude."

I gave a satisfied nod.

"Except..."

I shot him a glare. Would the man not give in?

"It is also *my* house."

I sputtered and dropped my cup with a clatter on the glass top.

"Oh, no, you don't." I wagged my finger. "This is *my* house. I bought it. It's mine."

Darius tipped his head.

"It is *our* house, then. As it was always meant to be."

I bit my lip. He wasn't *exactly* wrong about that. It really was his house. I don't think he sold it willingly.

"Well..." I pursed my lips and refused to say more.

"Molly?" He leaned forward to peer into my face.

"What?" I leaned back in my chair, crossed my arms and watched him through narrowed eyes.

"I am not your father. You do not need to glare at me so crossly. Is it *our* house?"

I tapped my slippered feet.

"What would that involve...exactly?"

Chapter Six

Darius flashed white teeth and tilted his head in my direction in the most charming way.

"I am not sure. I could stay as long as I wanted?"

I gasped. *Stay here? With me?* Be careful what you wish for, I thought. Perversely, I pressed my lips together and shook my head in mute silence.

"Hmmm... I see your point. That might prove to be inconvenient for you." Darius crossed his arms and tapped a finger against his lips in mock thought. "I can stay as long as *you* want?"

I gave him a dubious look.

Darius chuckled. "That is better. We are making progress. You did not shake your head this time. What if I promise to help you restore the house? Can I stay? Surely, you do not want me wandering about that cemetery at all hours of the night, do you?" His feigned look of injury was irresistible.

I burst into laughter, unable to hold back the image of handsome Darius with his golden chestnut waves haunting the cemetery at night.

"I can just see it now," I choked out between peals of giggles. "The ladies of the town will line up to come see you and bring you cookies."

Darius joined my laughter. "And why would they do that?"

"Because you are *so handsome*," I gasped as I recovered my breath. "Who could resist you?"

A bright red flush bested the tan on Darius's face, and he dropped his gaze. He picked up his mug and took a sip of his hot chocolate.

"Stuff and nonsense." He put a hand over his mouth to cough, and my heart melted at his embarrassment. I changed the subject.

"So, what do you mean you'll help me rebuild the house?"

"Well, if you can provide the materials, I will...em...freshen it up, strengthen its weak spots, shore it up for another hundred years."

"Can you do that?" The image of this nineteenth-century man entangled in the cords of modern power tools and electrical wiring alarmed me.

"Of course, I can. I am a builder. I built the house, did I not? It is still standing, is it not? Though in sad repair, I must say." He gazed around the shabby ivy wall-papered kitchen.

"The current owners said they didn't have money to put into repairs. They haven't lived here since they left home to marry. Their parents lived here until they passed away—probably about 20 or 30 years ago, but I understand they did no modernization."

"Well, that is it then! The house just needs to be taken care of, and I will see to it."

"Can you handle modern building supplies, electrical wiring, plumbing? I'm having some people come in a few days to upgrade the wiring and plumbing, but you would still have to deal with those upgrades."

Darius waved a dismissive hand. "It should not be a problem."

I gave him a skeptical look.

"Well, I don't doubt that you can refurbish the house you built, but I wonder if you won't have some difficulties."

"I am up to the task," he said in a self-assured tone.

"And where do you plan to sleep? Umm, that is...do you sleep?" I bit my lip and dropped a nonchalant gaze to my now empty cup.

"Yes, I do seem to need sleep. I have been sleeping in a corner of the living room. Not very comfortable on the floor, I might add. I should have used softer pine flooring instead of the hard oak, but little did I know I would require it for a bed." The twinkle in his eyes matched his lop-sided grin.

I sobered up and swallowed a lump in my throat. How could I have left him so...alone? How could I have abandoned him without resources?

"You can take the couch for now. I don't have an extra mattress or I'd let you have the spare bedroom upstairs."

A thought struck me. Cynthia and Laura were coming to pick me up in the morning.

"Can other people see you?" I asked hastily.

Darius chewed on his lower lip for a moment and shrugged.

"I do not know. I thought it best to wait in the shed out back when the men came in the large conveyance to deliver your furnishings. This is a new experience for me."

"Well, the previous owners of the house—who are actually relatives of yours, by the way—are coming to pick me up in the morning. Just in case, I think you should... uh... not be seen, however you can manage that."

"Ah!" he nodded. "Certainly! I will hide in a closet if need be. And who might my relatives be?"

"Cynthia and Laura. Let's see. I think they are your—great-great-grand nieces. Something like that."

"Really! How fortunate. I still have family," he beamed. "I would love to meet them."

"No!" I barked. "Absolutely not! It's bad enough that one of us is crazy. I'd really rather not have them think that both of us are."

"Crazy..." He fingered his mustache thoughtfully. "I do not believe that *I* am crazy," he stated with a thumb pointed toward his chest.

"Well, *I'm* not either, so there!"

"Exactly!"

"Fine!" I grabbed the mugs and jumped up to put them in the sink. "The only food I have to eat right now is some fruit and oat bars that I brought along on the trip. I haven't been to the store yet. Do you want one?"

"Certainly. I'll admit to being famished."

I grabbed several out of a box on the counter and handed them to him. "I'm sorry I don't have anything else. Will that be enough?"

"Yes, this looks...delicious." Darius bent his head to study the package. He pulled it apart successfully and tasted the bar. I watched with apprehension. Would he like it? Had we been in the big city, I could have run to an all-night grocery store, but I seriously doubted Lilium had any such thing. At any rate, had I been in a big city, I probably would not have met Darius.

He smiled broadly and bit it into it. I relaxed. He seemed to like it. At least, he wouldn't starve for tonight. I had no idea what the future would hold.

"This is excellent," he pronounced with another bite.

Aware of a desperate need to separate myself from him at the moment to sort out my racing thoughts yet hating to be away from him for even a moment, I surprised myself by announcing I was going to bed.

"So, I'll leave out an extra pillow and blanket for you." I bit my lip. "Do you need those? Do you get cold?" I wrapped my arms around myself and fought off a shiver of my own. "I don't know..."

Darius rose. "A blanket and pillow would be lovely, thank you, Molly. Right now, I am feeling all of the urges I knew when I lived. Thirst, cold, hunger..." He tilted his head with a brazen smile and directed a pointed look at me. I caught my breath and turned away.

"I'm afraid you'll have to put up with Sassy wandering around. She's a night owl, and I don't usually let her in my bedroom."

Darius chuckled. "She and I will do fine. And the orange cat?"

"Oh, yes, Marmaduke. At least, that's what I call him. I don't know how he'll settle in the house at night. He might want to go outside where he's used to living. For a while anyway. He's going to be fixed next week."

"Fixed?"

"Neutered?"

"Good gravy! Why would you do that to him? He seems such a fine fellow."

"Because he doesn't need to be getting all the female cats in the neighborhood pregnant."

I watched as Darius's face colored again. He pressed his lips together and dropped his gaze to studiously examine the fruit bar in his hand.

"I see."

"Oh dear, I'm sorry." I bit my tongue—and it hurt. "That's probably not a word you all used that often back then, was it? What did you used to call it? Expecting? In the family way?"

Darius coughed behind his hand. "I am sure *I* never had occasion to use the term at all." He mumbled and turned away but swung back almost immediately. "I was wondering..."

I waited, but he seemed to be struggling for words.

"Well, that is...I was wondering if I might borrow a towel?"

"What? You want to take a bath?" I stared at him.

"Well, it has been...em...some time since I bathed. It did not seem to matter when I was alone. Rinsing my face and hands with plain cold water can only do so much. As long as I am up and about, as it were, I would like to be presentable. And since I am near you..." His eyes twinkled again.

I didn't know whether to laugh or cry—or throw myself into his arms and offer to wash his hair.

"I-I...I never thought of it." I shoved my hands deeper into my robe pockets. "Do you *feel* dirty?" I reddened at the unfortunate wording. "I mean...does it feel like you haven't bathed in...what?...a hundred and thirty years?"

Before I knew what was happening, Darius moved to stand beside me, his face only inches from mine.

"What do you think? Do I smell as if I need a bath?"

I would have jumped back except that I was pressed up against the sink with nowhere to go. I closed my eyes against his penetrating gaze, and inhaled. He smelled of the outdoors—like freshly mowed grass...with a hint of sweet chocolate on his breath.

"Ummm...no, you don't smell like you need a bath, but you're welcome to one." I pushed past him and hurried into the living room. "I'll just get the towel, blanket and pillow for you," I called over my shoulder as I tripped up the stairs, willing my erratically beating heart to slow down.

I ran into the bathroom, scooped up my discarded clothes from the floor and tidied a bit before grabbing a clean towel out of the moving box and setting it on top. Did he need a razor? Did ghosts shave? I shuddered, and dived back into the box to pull out a disposable razor and shaving lotion, placing them by the towel.

Then I headed to my bedroom, found a spare blanket and pillow in another box, and carried them downstairs.

"Your cat...Sassy, is it?...and I are getting along just fine."

And indeed the independent feline, who accepted only the occasional odd caress from me, luxuriated on Darius's lap as he sat on the incongruous modern orange sofa. A fierce whirring could be heard from Sassy's general direction as Darius stroked her ears.

I gave the innocent-eyed cat an irritated look and wondered how I could usurp her and take her place so Darius could rub the back of my ears.

"Is something wrong, Molly?"

I glanced up to catch Darius watching me with a lift of his lips. My cheeks heated and I gave my head a fervent shake.

"Oh, no. It's just she doesn't usually like to be touched, that's all."

"Well, she certainly seems to be enjoying it now." He picked Sassy up and put her aside with a gentle motion. I extended the blanket and pillow to him, keeping my distance. He rose to his feet, took the blanket and pillow from my hands and set them on the sofa.

"I have a feeling she's going to jump up and sleep with you in the night." I was so jealous of that cat.

Darius turned to look at Sassy, now testing the softness of the blanket with a tiny paw.

"I will enjoy the warmth of being near another living being."

"I'm sorry," I said. "There's no central heating or cooling yet. I think they're coming to install it next week. And I don't have any wood for the fireplace either."

Darius favored me with a pointed look.

"That is not quite what I meant, Molly." With a disarming grin, he picked up the towel, walked past me and climbed the stairs. I stared after him while my mind whirled through several different scenarios in which he enjoyed the *warmth of another living being.* Did he mean me? I fervently hoped so. Could that ever be? I remembered the feel of his lips against mine two weeks ago, the warmth of his arms as he held me tight. He seemed real enough. The sound of footsteps on the stairs brought me out of my reverie, and I looked up as Darius returned to the living room with a sheepish expression.

"Where, might I ask, did you acquire that rather pleasant-looking steamy hot water in your bath? Is there a ready source available? And a bucket to transport it?"

"From the faucet." Though it took me a few seconds to realize what he was asking, I clasped my hands behind my back and gave him an innocent gaze, prepared for a bit of fun.

"The faucet? In the bathtub?" He knotted his brow and glanced at the ceiling as if he could see the tub. He'd shed his jacket, undone his black tie and loosened the high collar of his long-sleeved cotton white shirt. His dark gray vest emphasized broad shoulders and a slender waist.

"Yes, the faucet. There's a hot water faucet and a cold water faucet. Just turn them. The water will come."

"Really? When I ordered the tub there were no such fixtures. I must go see." He pivoted and disappeared back up the stairs. I followed him to the bottom of the stairs and tilted my head upward, listening.

The old pipes groaned and gurgled once again, and I heard the sound of running water. A loud shout followed by several colorful, if old-fashioned, curses galvanized me into action, and I raced up the stairs and down the short hallway to burst into the open bathroom.

"What's the matter? What happened?"

Darius held his left hand in the air while he twisted and pulled the porcelain faucet knobs with his right hand.

"The blasted water is as hot as... as..." He glanced at me hastily and bit his lip. "How do I get the wicked thing to stop spewing forth?"

I chuckled and sauntered over to the bathtub to twist the knobs and test the water with my fingers.

"Here! I'll adjust it for you. Big baby."

"Baby? I beg your pardon! I have likely scarred my hand permanently. Do you have any salve for it?"

I turned to him with a raised brow.

"Salve? No! You don't need any *salve.* You'll be just fine. It's just a slight burn. All you need to do is get undressed and hop into the water. I've adjusted it for you, and it's quite comfy now."

"Comfy? Hmpff..." Darius reached down with his previously so-called injured left hand and dipped a finger into the bathwater.

"Well, that is better," he said slightly mollified. "Thank you. You can turn that thing off now. I take it my...em...family attempted some modernization with the addition of the scalding water." His disdainful expression showed what he thought of his family's modernization.

I watched him in amusement. He would make me laugh, this man as he struggled to find his way in a different century. My heart swelled with adoration. I wanted to grab him and hug him. At the moment, he reminded me of a precocious teenaged boy who indulged in spurts of his former childishness alternating with unexpected moments of dignity and maturity.

It occurred to me though, that he might just view me in the same way. My own behavior had been less than sensible and mature over the last few weeks.

I rolled my eyes at the thought as I bent forward to twist the knobs on the faucets. Feeling very motherly at the moment, I stood back with my arms crossed and regarded him with a raised eyebrow.

"And you think you're going to be able to handle modern power tools and wiring, eh?"

Darius straightened to his full height, an unconsciously sensual move that made my heart jump in the most unmotherly way.

"I assure you, my dear, I am quite competent," he said. "I do believe that whoever installed this 'hot water' did a poor job of it. Otherwise, I should not have burnt my hand." A twitch of his lips belied the scornful look on his face.

"And now, if you will permit me," he added. "I intend to take my first bath in a hundred years." He began to unbutton his vest with his once injured hand, which appeared to be working just fine. "Unless you would care to join me?" A daring glint in his blue eyes sent me running from the bathroom, but not before I saw the blush on his face even as he teased me. He would have died had I called his bluff.

Chased by the sound of his chuckles, I fled to my room and slammed the door shut. Sassy, apparently having followed everyone upstairs but stopping short at the hated sound of running water in the bathroom, sat on her haunches on the end of my bed, ears perked, eyes wide open and expectant.

"Oh no, you don't. You're not going to hop all over me tonight, Miss Kitty. I'm not going to get any sleep as it is." I picked her up and put her just outside the door.

Darius had apparently decided to leave the door of the bathroom open, and I could hear him humming. I would have given anything to be Sassy at the moment and tiptoe up to the bathroom door as she did, but I dared not. It was bad enough having a ghost in my bathtub. The last thing I needed to do was turn into a peeping Thomasina.

I eased my door shut, turned out the uncertain pale yellow light cast by the old porcelain light fixture on the ceiling and crossed the room to get into bed. Soft luminescent moonlight filled the room, and I relished the familiar feel of my mattress and pillow in such unfamiliar circumstances.

I lay awake, waiting to hear Darius descend the stairs. It seemed a full half hour passed before I heard the sound of footsteps going down the hall. They paused at my door, and I pulled the covers up to my chin... waiting... hoping... dreading. The footsteps moved on, and I heard Darius talking to Sassy in a low voice as he descended the stairs.

I loosened my grip on the covers and stared at the moonlight coming in through the window, hoping with all my might that Darius would still be there in the morning. We had absolutely no future together. How could we? But today was enough. Tomorrow would be even better. As he had once said to me...I could not bear to lose him.

Apparently, I must have managed to fall asleep because I awakened to the most horrible screeching sound imaginable. It sounded like someone or something was being tortured.

Darius! I jumped out of bed and stumbled to the door, stubbing my toe against the bed along the way. Fortunately, the moonlight filling the room allowed me to see the top of the stairs as I opened the door.

"Darius," I shouted. "Are you all right?" I clutched the railing and leaned against it as I followed it down in the dark. "Darius?"

"Molly! What is it, my love? Are you all right?"

I reached the bottom of the stairs, pathetically grateful to hear Darius's voice. I followed the streaks of moonlight coming through the living room window and turned in the direction of his voice. The terrible screaming erupted again, and it sounded as if it were coming from outside.

"Oh!" I gasped as I fell into Darius's arms...or rather he pulled me into them. "What's happening? What is that poor thing?" By now, I realized the sound was that of some helpless animal screaming in pain.

Darius held me against his chest, and I didn't fight him off—not for one second. At the moment, I was too terrified to think straight. For a ghost, he seemed remarkably warm. He wore no shirt. His chest was bare except for a layer of soft masculine hair, and his skin smelled clean and fresh after his bath. His heart beat loudly, although the rhythm seemed to jump a bit as I pressed my face against his chest.

"Should we go outside and see if we can help?" I whispered in dread.

I heard a deep rumble in Darius's chest, and his shoulders shook.

"I think me must not interfere. The poor creature does not have much time left."

"What?" I hissed as I pulled back to peer at his face in the moonlight.

Only the gleam of his teeth as he grinned was visible. I struggled to get out of his arms, but he did not release me, though his hold was gentle.

"I have to do something, Darius! I can't just sit here and listen to the pain. What's happening? Something is killing something out there. What if it's Marmaduke? What if he's hurt?" I cried as I twisted to face the front door.

Just then, as if he heard me, Marmaduke jumped onto the outside sill of the large picture window by the front door, and I gasped.

"Marmaduke! There you are!"

Darius released me as I headed for the front door to let the cat in. He trotted into the darkened room and ran past me up the stairs.

"Oh, no, you don't, buddy. You're not spending the night in my room. Don't even think about it!" I called as I turned to lock the front door.

"And there is your tortured creature, my dear," Darius murmured close behind me. I heard the laughter in his voice. "He looks well enough now. Quite content, I might add."

I realized then what I'd heard. I turned around to face him, a little lightheaded at his close proximity. "Oh, for goodness sake! That was Marmaduke? I take it he was—" I didn't finish. I was desperate to take a breath, but he stood so close, it seemed I would breathe the air that he did—as if that were a bad thing.

Darius braced one hand against the door above my head and rested the other on his hip. Thank goodness, he had worn his trousers to bed.

"Yes, I'm afraid he is sowing the last of his oats as it were. The poor fellow obviously realizes his days of romance are coming to an abrupt end."

I could have ducked under his arm and made a dash for it, but I couldn't make my legs move. I leaned against the door and wished I could throw myself back into his arms. However, at the moment, there seemed to be no good excuse to do so.

"Well, with a performance like that, I think it's an absolute necessity. Love should hardly be that... um... vocal or scary, I think."

I saw the flash of Darius's teeth. "Well, hopefully not frightening at any rate. It is a good thing we are more... civilized... than cats."

"Yes, well..." Feeling a flush of warmth from my head to my toes, I thought it best to make a run for it—albeit slowly. I moved away from the door, and Darius stepped back to let me pass.

"I think he probably ran into your room, smart fellow that he is," Darius teased. "I am not sure that he might not sit in the window and serenade you in the moonlight."

Almost to the foot of the stairs, I turned with a laugh.

"Oh, please, no. I couldn't take the caterwauling again. He's being evicted from the bedroom."

"Poor fellow," Darius murmured with a throaty chuckle. "Never mind. There is plenty of room on the couch."

"Good night, Darius. I'm sorry I wakened you."

"Call me anytime, dear. I am here."

I resisted the urge to call him then and there, and I felt my way back up the stairs. Darius had predicted the situation correctly, and Marmaduke sat in the window seat meowing.

"Out, Marmaduke. Next week can't come soon enough for you." I picked him up and carried him to the door, closing it behind him.

I crawled back in bed, turned on my side to face the window and imagined Darius sitting there...humming to me. His velvety voice certainly sounded like it might hum a lovely tune.

It seemed only moments later that I awakened to the sound of tapping on my door.

"Molly. It is 9:30 a.m. Did you say my nieces were coming at ten to pick you up?"

I jerked my eyes open and tried to focus on my watch. Sunlight streamed into the bedroom. What happened to the night?

"Thank you, Darius," I called out. So, my ghost was still here! My heart swelled with joy as I hurriedly jumped into a pair of jeans and threw on a T-shirt. I stuck my feet into some sneakers and skipped into the bathroom to brush my hair and teeth and rinse my face.

I dashed downstairs and rounded the corner of the living room only to run into Darius, who steadied me by my shoulders.

"Good morning, sleepyhead," he murmured. "I have prepared some of that instant hot chocolate you seem to favor. Come into the kitchen." He pulled a pocket watch from his vest and consulted it. "You have a few minutes yet." He looked relaxed without the formality of his jacket.

I caught a whiff of my shampoo as he set me from him and went into the kitchen. I followed him, wondering how my rose-scented body soap could somehow smell so utterly masculine on him.

"How did you make the hot chocolate? Did you use the microwave? I warn you...I don't know if the wiring is up to it."

"Microwave? You mean that white oven? No, no. I do not think I know how to operate that device yet. I used some of that very hot water you already have." He guided me to the small glass dining table where two mugs of chocolate awaited us.

I sat down, and he took the seat opposite me. I peered into the cup and took a test sip.

"Well, it's still pretty hot, that's for sure," I said with a smile. "I guess the water heater is working fine."

"It would seem to be," he murmured, "although I am not quite sure what that is. Another electrical device, I assume, which does exactly what it says? Heats water?"

I grinned and nodded. "I promise to get some things at the store today. Milk and what? What kind of chocolate do you want?"

Darius seemed gratified. The brightness of his smile reminded me of our close proximity the night before, and I struggled to subdue a blush—as if that were possible.

"Baker's chocolate and some sugar will be sufficient," he said.

"What else do you like to eat?" I aimed to please, certain I had much to make up for in having abandoned him.

"Well, let me think," he said as he placed his elbows on the table and rested his chin on one fist. His eyes sparkled playfully. "Ice cream and pumpkin pie and roasted corn and apples."

"Oh, sure." I rolled my eyes. "What else?"

"Truly?" Darius widened his eyes. "Will you be making the pie? Because I warn you, I am very handy with a cup of hot chocolate, but I do not bake." He put out his hands as if to ward off evil.

"Neither do I. Someone at the store does, I'm sure."

"Ah! Baked goods from the market. Yes, indeed, the oat and fruit bars. Very modern."

"Very convenient," I murmured with a chuckle. I checked my watch. Fifteen minutes.

"I'll try to head Laura and Cynthia off before they get out of their car."

"Or I could meet them?" He waggled his eyebrows.

"Not likely. They've seen your photograph. They know what you look like."

"Is that so? There is a photograph of me about?" He pretended to look around.

I colored.

"Um...yes. Somewhere. I saw it yesterday. It was in a box of family photos. Laura and Cynthia took the boxes with them." I was careful not to lie, but I didn't want him to know that I had stored the treasured photograph in the nightstand by my bed.

"I was thinking..." I changed the subject. "I'm going to need to buy you a few things—some clothing, I think. You can't run around in that suit all the time. Can you?"

He looked down at his suit. "Well, it *is* a fine suit, but a little impractical for making repairs to the house. And I will need some supplies from the hardware store to begin the renovation. I will prepare a list while you are gone."

"There's no rush about that, is there?" Suddenly agitated, I jumped up to take my cup to the sink and kept my back to him.

"If you want to be comfortable here in the house, there is." His voice came from directly behind me. He had risen when I did and stood only inches from me—so close I was certain I felt the warmth emanating from his body.

"What is wrong, Molly? Do you truly believe I am not competent enough to repair the house?"

I pivoted to face him.

"Oh, no, not that! Oh, no. I know how competent you are. Just look at this beautiful house."

I looked up at his face, only inches above mine.

"Then what is it, my dear?"

I repressed a shiver of delight at the endearment. "It's just..." I swallowed hard. "It's just... What if you disappear—when you finish the house?" I met his gaze, mesmerized by the tiny gold flecks in the blue—the same gold that highlighted his chestnut hair. "What if you're here to do just that? Fix the house, and when it's done—you vanish?"

I didn't realize that I had grabbed his shirt until I felt the warmth of his hands over mine.

"I am not going anywhere—if I can help it, Molly. I am staying with you—no matter what." He paused. A muscle worked in his jaw. "I have loved you since you were twenty-five years old, and although you may not remember our love, I do. It was sweet and lovely and full of laughter. You will love me again someday. I can be patient."

He bent his head close to my ear, and I melted against him.

"I will always love you," he whispered.

His tender words brought a sudden anguish such as I'd never known. A pain knifed through my shoulder, and I gasped and grabbed the spot.

"What is it, Molly?"

"I don't know. Pain. Here." I pulled my hand away to rub a sore spot just below my left clavicle. "Pain and a feeling of...grief." I shook my head in confusion.

Darius opened his mouth to speak, then pressed his lips together. I searched his face.

"What?"

"I feared this might happen. You might be remembering—"

A knock on the door startled us both, and I gasped and pushed him away.

"Go! Hide! Do something. Go!"

Darius stepped back and scanned the room. His gaze paused on the kitchen door.

"I will go outside into the yard and around to the shed in back—until you leave."

"Okay, go, go." I shooed him out the kitchen door at the far side of the house, and ran to the front door. My shoulder still ached for some unknown reason, but not as badly as it had. I threw a quick look over my shoulder before I pulled open the door with a broad smile plastered on my face.

"Good morning, ladies. I was going to meet you at your car so you didn't have to come all the way up the porch."

"Good morning, Molly," Laura said. Dressed in a white sweatshirt with poodles on the front and a loose pair of jeans, she looked much younger than she had the day before in her dark "I'm going to the cemetery" clothing.

I looked past her.

"It's just me," Laura continued. "I left Cynthia in the car. No sense dragging that walker of hers around more than we have to. Are you ready?" She stood back and appraised me frankly. "You look so rosy-cheeked this morning. Iowa air seems to be doing you a lot of good."

I was fairly certain my cheeks had just gotten much rosier.

"I'll just grab my purse, and we can go," I said as I dashed over to the coffee table and grabbed my bag. I noted with distress that Darius's pillow and blanket were folded neatly at the end of the couch. A quick check over my shoulder in Laura's direction revealed she had turned away to return to the car. I threw a longing glance toward the kitchen and turned with a sigh to hurry after Laura.

To my consternation, the ladies had decided to make a day of it. As grateful as I was for their help, I chafed to get back to the house—back to Darius. Please, please, let him still be there.

Our first stop was at the local post office—a tiny gray building serviced by one person—the postmistress—Martha Banks. Her rural route carrier, who just happened to be her husband, Jim Banks, was out delivering mail, she said, and she was pleased to welcome me to town. I warmed to the affable older woman immediately and waited politely while Cynthia, Laura and Martha—obviously school chums—discussed the merits of forwarding mail to Florida.

We moved on to Nesbitt's Hardware, a small store in an old two-story brick building on what might have passed for the main street a hundred years ago. In fact, the street was named Main Street. Several small businesses remained in the sadly run down turn-of-the-century brick buildings, and I wondered why the town had not thrived. The construction of what were once beautiful commercial buildings indicated high hopes for prosperity at one time in Lilium.

"So, how did this town come to be?" I asked as we descended from the car at the hardware store.

"Oh, gosh, I don't know," Cynthia murmured. "It's mostly farmers around here. Our great-grandfather was some sort of scholar back in Virginia. Then he moved out here to take the house over when his brother died...or disappeared or whatever he did. Anyway, I guess our great-grandfather took up farming. I don't think he did very well at it though." Cynthia chuckled. "At least, that's what my mom said. My dad taught at the local school—pretty much a one-room schoolhouse when we were kids."

I alerted at the mention of Darius and cringed at Cynthia's use of the word "died."

"You say your great-grandfather's brother disappeared? That's Darius, the builder of the house, right? Did he die or disappear?" I couldn't help myself. I had to ask.

Cynthia paused and turned to Laura. I held my breath.

"Laura, what was the story, do you remember? Did Mom say he died or disappeared, which was it?"

Laura, her hand on the doorknob of the faded but sturdy appearing oak door at the store's entrance, turned back with a shrug.

"Well, it seems obvious he died at some point, right? But I think there was a rumor he disappeared. Or maybe he just moved away. I can't remember much more about it."

I mumbled something innocuous, hoping they weren't making too much of my continuing obsession with Darius. I was determined to ask him the moment we returned if he'd "disappeared" or "moved away." I couldn't bear to ask him if he'd died. He seemed as confused as I about his existence in the present time. I could not wait to return to the house...to Darius...and every moment that I was apart from him seemed a terrible waste of the time we had together.

I did my best to swallow my anxiety as I followed the ladies into the store. A bell rang overhead, and the musty smell of the old building hit me in full force—something I was managing to rid the house of by keeping the windows open as much as possible.

"Molly, this is Bob Nesbitt. If you need any tools or light bulbs or anything, he's your man." Laura led me toward a stout man with who bent over a display of seed packets. Tools and implements abounded on dark-stained, albeit heavily scratched, wooden shelves that had seen better days. No modern steel shelving for this older merchant. He wiped his hands on a well-worn, faded green apron and nodded.

"Good to meet you, Molly. So, you bought the old Ferguson place."

Puffy pale blue eyes regarded me with skepticism. "Good luck. That's going to take a lot of work." He hooked his hands on the front tie of his apron as if it were a gun belt and nodded pleasantly. No single hair of his Marine-style crew cut moved with the motion.

I stiffened, instantly on the defensive.

"I've already got an electrician and plumber on the way to upgrade the wiring and water systems. And I've had a new hot water heater installed."

He raised his eyebrows. "Well, I hope they're able to make a go of it. These old places..." He shrugged with a grimace. "Sometimes, it's just easier to demolish them and start over."

"Now, now, Bob. We just sold her the house. Don't scare her off. It can be modernized." Laura's words were almost drowned out by my heated rebuff.

"I would *never* tear that house down. *Never*!"

CHAPTER SEVEN

At the unanimously startled expressions of my companions, I bit my bottom lip and lowered my head.

"Of course not, dear. It's a lovely house. Bob has been teasing us about the house for years. He's just making fun, aren't you, Bob?" Cynthia patted my arm, as one might attempt to calm a snapping dog.

"Well, not really, ladies, but I certainly wouldn't come between a homeowner and her dreams—not if I want to sell her a few things." An unrepentant Bob chuckled and winked. I relented and gave him an answering smile as I swelled with pride.

"I've already got a guy lined up to take care of the repairs, and I'll need to order some things from you shortly." As soon as the foolishly boastful words were out, I wished I'd kept my mouth shut.

Bob cocked an eyebrow, and both Laura and Cynthia swung their heads in my direction.

"Oh, really, anyone I know? What's his name? I know most of the construction guys around here," Bob asked with interest.

"You didn't tell us, dear," Cynthia said with a wide smile. "How wonderful. Is he a local boy?"

I blinked rapidly and literally sidestepped as I shuffled my feet in dismay.

"Oh, well, he's..." I focused on a small dust bunny on the wooden floor under the edge of one of the shelves. "Yes, he's local. Well, I found his name in the paper. That is...he comes recommended."

"Really? What's his name?" Bob pressed home, hopefully never suspecting how much I wanted to kick him in the shin.

"Oh, uh...I wrote it down at home."

"Is it that Stevens fellow, dear?" Cynthia asked. "Because he's just a local handyman, and I'm not sure he's up to a major renovation project."

"No, no. His name is Dar—Darren Fergland, and I think he's out of Council Bluffs. So...he's kind of local."

"Well, good for you, Molly! I'm impressed by how much you've accomplished already," Laura said with an approving nod.

I shot her a grateful glance and hoped the conversation was over.

"Can't say as I've heard of him. Well, you make sure he's got a contractor's license, and that he's bonded. I'm sure you already checked into that." Bob shot me a warning look.

"Oh, sure," I murmured. I moved over to study a shelf as if nuts and bolts were the most interesting things in the world.

Laura and Cynthia exchanged a few words with Bob and pronounced themselves ready to move on.

Bob grabbed the knob of the heavy, old oak door and hauled it open for us. The tiny bell accompanied his words.

"Don't forget to get me a list of what you need. I may not have it here in the store, but I can get it delivered in for you in two days or so."

He nodded pleasantly, and I smiled and escaped out the door, hoping the subject of renovations was closed for the day.

"Well, where to next, Sis?" Laura put the car in reverse and waited for Cynthia's instructions.

"I think we should have some lunch, don't you, Molly?"

I confessed to some hunger pains. I worried that Darius would be hungry, but could think of no way to announce to the sisters that I couldn't eat unless my ghost could eat as well. The best I'd been able to do for Darius was leave the box of oat bars out for him along with a container of crackers. Better than cat food, I thought with a wry grin. What sorts of things was he used to eating in the 1800s?

What I really needed to do was find some time alone so I could get on the Internet and figure out what to do with a ghost from the nineteenth century. Food, clothes, beverages, hot water, cold water, toiletry supplies. Entertainment? What did he need?

Laura drove a half-hour to the larger town of Missouri Valley where we had luncheon in a nice, homey café that could have used some modernization as well. The blue vinyl on the benches of the booth showed unrepaired cracks, the laminate tables were chipped with corrosion evident on the metal banding around the edges, and the creased and bent blinds had not been replaced in years. The food was delicious, however. I imagined myself ordering a sandwich to go and arriving triumphantly at the house with food in hand...like a good little provider. I looked across the table at Darius's great-grand nieces. Nope. That wasn't going to happen. As fussy as he had been the night before about the hot chocolate, I wasn't certain about his taste buds.

The server, a tiny faded blonde powerhouse who appeared to be in her late 50s, seemed friendly and outgoing. She knew Cynthia and Laura well.

"We've been coming here for years." Cynthia explained. "It's hard to live in a town without a restaurant. There used to be a nice little café next to the hardware store, but that closed down...oh, about fifty years ago, right, Laura?"

"Has it been that long? Seems like only yesterday." Laura grimaced and shook her head.

"What happened to Lilium? Has it always been so...small?" I asked.

Laura dabbed at her mouth with a napkin before she spoke.

"Well, it was a lot busier around the early 1900s...or so our mother said. Very prosperous with farming and markets and church socials and hayrides and lots of fun. But that was before they moved the county seat to Logan and redefined the boundaries of the county. I think there was some hope the railroad would come through Lilium, but it was diverted somewhere else."

Cynthia chimed in.

"No one wants to stay, of course. Most of the children tend to go away to the city as soon as they graduate from high school. Our own kids moved out. I have a daughter in Phoenix, and a son in San Antonio, and Laura's kids are in Houston. There's really nothing for us here now."

"Oh, dear. Yes, I can see how a town could shrink like that," I said.

"But look at you!" Cynthia offered with a beaming smile. "If more people like you leave the big cities and come to the small towns, they can thrive again. You said your computer work allows you to live anywhere, right?"

"Yes, look at me," I murmured in bemusement. Tempted to roll my eyes at the irony of my life at the moment—half in love with a man who was either a ghost or a very odd character—I controlled my face, smiled and turned back to my food. A sudden visual image of Darius nibbling on nothing but fruit and oat bars took the taste right out of the meal.

We returned to Lilium in the early afternoon and made the grocery store our final stop. A tiny store in an older battleship gray painted wooden building, "Sally's General Store" held most of the basics. I considered myself quite lucky to secure the Baker's chocolate Darius had "ordered." And I grinned from ear to ear when I saw freshly baked products. Apparently, "Sally" liked to bake. The owner came out from the back as we entered the store, sporting a white apron over her faded pink T-shirt and shapeless jeans.

"Well, hello, girls. And who's this?"

Introducing yet another one of their school chums, Cynthia and Laura pulled me forward to meet the short, stocky, gray-haired woman.

"Sally, this is Molly. She's bought our old house...you know, my parents' house on County Road 2."

"Really? Well, that'll be a handful to fix up. It's nice to meet you, Molly." She introduced me to her middle-aged daughter, Cathy, explaining that the equally stocky woman with the mousey brown pageboy hairdo took care of the front of the store, stocked shelves and ran the cash register. Cathy bobbed her head shyly and retreated to stocking, shuffling loaves of bread from one shelf to another.

I smelled something familiar.

"Are you baking pumpkin pies?" I asked Sally with a bright smile.

"I sure am. I've got two coming out the oven right now. Do you want one?"

"Oh, yes, please." I preened with pleasure. Darius had playfully ordered pumpkin pie, and I was actually going to be able to deliver! Not made with my own hands, but this would do in a pinch.

"I'll go throw one in a box and bring it out front." Sally bustled to the back while Cynthia, Laura and I scanned the shelves and tossed things into our respective red plastic baskets. Sally returned in short order and handed me a warm boxed pie.

"There you go. So, are you fixing the place up or are you planning on leveling it?"

I bit my tongue this time before I answered.

"No, no, I'm going to rehabilitate it. I couldn't destroy something that beautiful. It has great bones. Just needs a little bit of makeup."

"Rehabilitate it, huh? Hmmm... Who's going to do the work? My daughter's husband does some handy work." She nodded in Cathy's direction. Cathy's hand stilled, and I knew she was listening, but she didn't turn around to look at us.

"Hey, Laura, did you tell her about Cathy's husband, Rick, you know, for the house? He could do the work," Sally called out toward the back of the store.

Cynthia and Laura, examining a carton of eggs in the cooler, turned. I watched them exchange a glance. Laura strode toward us while Cynthia shuffled along.

"Well, I guess Molly already has a contractor lined up—a fellow out of Council Bluffs. I think she contracted with him right after she bought the house a few weeks ago."

"Council Bluffs? Well, we like to use local help around here—to support the economy and all, but since you already made arrangements with this guy..." Sally pursed her lips as she looked at me with narrowed eyes.

I threw Laura a grateful glance, and dug myself in deeper.

"Yes, he's a specialist in Victorian homes." I beamed at my heretofore unsuspected creative imagination. Out of the corner of my eye, I saw Laura turn a sharp glance in my direction.

"Oh, well. Rick's pretty good with his tools, but he's no specialist," Sally huffed. Cathy resumed shelving.

"Well, there ya go," Cynthia murmured in a smooth voice. She favored everyone with an innocent grin when all eyes turned on her—especially Sally.

"Okay, I've got everything I need," Laura said hastily. "Are you ready?"

"Yes!" I stepped up quickly to the single register at the counter and laid out my groceries. Cathy made her way over to the register, gave me a small smile, but remained silent as she rang everything up. We were out of the door in no time at all with a farewell to Sally.

"That was close," Cynthia murmured behind a giggle. "Rick would be the handyman we told you about who probably isn't skilled enough to work on the house."

"I didn't know you'd hired a 'specialist' in Victorian homes. You didn't mention that before." Laura met my eyes in the rearview mirror with a dubious look. I had known this subject would come up again at the exact moment I elaborated unnecessarily in the store, and I tossed off a few airy words.

"Oh, yes, I found him on the Internet. That's why he's from Council Bluffs. I would have preferred someone more local, of course." I took a breath. "Yes, apparently restoring Victorian homes is a real big thing right now. That's what I've read. Uh huh..." I brought my babbling to a halt.

"Hmmm..." was Laura's reply. It seemed likely she wasn't buying my story.

"Well, that sounds very interesting," sweet Cynthia said. "I can't wait to meet him, dear. Will he be starting soon?"

"Oh...uh...Yes, soon. Yes," I repeated, trying to sound more definite.

"Before we leave for Florida?"

"When is that?" I stalled.

"I thought we mentioned that at lunch. We're going to hit the road—as they say—in about three weeks."

"Three weeks! Really! Well, I'm not exactly sure when he's starting. He has another project he's working on. I'm not sure."

"I hope we get to meet him," Cynthia murmured.

I smiled faintly and grew silent. I hated lying to the kind women.

Unable to sort through my lies, I found it easier to remain mute on the way back to the house.

I waved goodbye to them moments later, and waited on the porch with my two bags of groceries to ensure they pulled out of the driveway and disappeared down the road.

Then I turned and called.

"Darius!" The name that repeated itself over and over again in my mind like a broken record, albeit a beloved broken record. I picked up the bags, wrestled the knob and pushed open the door with my shoulders.

"Darius!" I called again, expecting to hear his footsteps. Silence filled the house. With a growing sense of unease that was never too far away, I dropped the groceries on the coffee table and dashed into the kitchen. It was empty. I pulled myself up the stairs, taking them two at a time, calling his name.

"Darius!" No answer.

Outside! He must be outside, I thought as I began to hyperventilate.

I tripped back down the stairs and ran through the living room back to the kitchen, noting with a panicked eye that the mugs had been washed and left on the counter. So, he had come back into the house.

Wrenching open the kitchen door which led to the side of the house , I pushed open the screen with a responding creak, poised on the top wooden step and called his name, heedless of any nearby listeners.

"Darius!"

Still nothing. Nothing but the sound of the wind in the oak trees that shaded the side yard.

I ran around to the back, stumbling several times on the vast expanse of overgrown grass. Several ramshackle and weathered wooden buildings—an old barn and some sort of shack—butted up against a seemingly endless field of green corn stalks which marked the edge of the property line. I cupped my hands and shouted with all my might.

"Darius! Darius!

I paused to listen for a response, my knees shaking as I tried to catch my breath. Panic robbed me of oxygen. There was no sound except the wind rustling the corn stalks.

I ran across the back yard and dived into the open door of the barn, shouting Darius's name. He wasn't in there. I ran next door to the shack and pulled at the door which hung precariously on one rusty old hinge. The hinge screeched ominously as I half supported the door and peered inside. The shack was, in fact, some sort of cabin, and consisted of one dusty empty room. I could barely see inside, so dirty were the windows at either end of the cabin. An old stovepipe stood in a corner.

"Darius," I whispered hoarsely. No answer. It seemed clear he wasn't in there.

He was gone. Gone.

I turned away, at a loss for what to do or where to look. Despair overwhelmed me, and I dragged myself back to the porch at the side of the house to sink down onto the steps. I buried my face in my hands to fight back my sobs. *I shouldn't have left the house. I shouldn't have left. He'd still be here if I hadn't left.*

"Please don't let him disappear," I whispered. "Oh, please don't leave me, Darius!" Surely if I repeated the words enough times, he would come back to me. "Please stay with me, Darius. Please," I begged in a ragged breath.

"Molly, my love, what is wrong? What has happened?"

I jerked my head up to see Darius striding toward me from across the yard near the tree line. I gasped and rose on shaking legs to reach for him through blurry eyes.

Darius reached me as I almost fell off the step, and in one fluid motion, scooped me into his arms. He lowered himself to the bottom step, holding me in his lap like a child while I sobbed against his jacket. He pressed his face against the top of my head.

"What has happened, my love? Tell me what is wrong," he murmured in a husky voice.

"I thought you were gone," I clutched his coat and wailed, nowhere near calming down.

"No, no, my sweet." Darius's embrace tightened, and I pressed against him. "I am sorry. I just went for a walk...to the cemetery actually. I did not mean to alarm you."

I stiffened and lifted my chin to look at him, simultaneously giving his lapel a fierce tug.

"The cemetery!" I choked out tearfully. "Haven't you been there long enough? Don't do that to me again! At least, leave me a note next time. I can't tell you what I thought..." I wiped at my face and hiccupped.

"Forgive me, Molly. I did not think..." He paused and leaned in to kiss my forehead. "You love me, Molly. You still love me."

I pulled myself upright in his lap, unwilling to leave the place I wanted to be most in the world—encircled in his arms, and equally unwilling to allow myself to become any more enamored of him than I already was. The events of the previous few minutes had proved a point. He could disappear at any time, and I didn't think I could bear to live with the pain.

With every ounce of willpower I had, I pulled myself from his arms and struggled to stand upright on the steps. My wobbly legs misbehaved and failed to give me support. I gave up and plopped back down on the step beside him.

I sighed heavily.

"I don't know how I feel about you, Darius. I really don't. And even if I did, I don't think I'd admit it. I don't want to lose myself...anymore than I already have." I bit my lower lip, knowing I'd already given away too much. "All I know is that when I came back, and couldn't find you..." I muttered and refused to look at him, instead choosing to stare at the oak trees lining the side of the property.

"Forgive me, Molly. Truly. I did not know I would be missed."

"Well, you were," I responded gruffly. "I worry about it." That's it. That's all I was giving him.

"I am grateful to hear it," Darius replied. "I worry about you as well. It cannot be easy living with a ghost." I heard the hint of laughter in his voice, but I refused to join the frivolity. The near loss—as my wayward heart understood it—was still too raw. My throat was too tight, my chest still constricted.

"It's not funny."

Darius acquiesced and dutifully sobered. "I am sorry I frightened you, my love. How was your day?"

"Good, thanks." I smacked a hand to my forehead and jumped up. "Oh, shoot! I have to put the groceries in the refrigerator."

"Shall I help?" Darius stood. He bent down to brush the dust from the wooden step off his pant leg, and I shook my head as I watched him.

"We need to get you some clothes. No chance you can just conjure up something to wear, is there?" I pulled open the screen door and stepped inside the kitchen.

Darius laughed as he followed me in. "I do not think so. I have never tried. How should I proceed?"

I retrieved the bags from the living room and shrugged with a half smile, though I was still unwilling to meet his gaze. The intensity of my desperation to see him once again shocked me, and I wasn't sure I trusted myself at the moment—or any time he was around.

"I don't know. Sit down and imagine a new set of clothing, something comfortable. Some tennis shoes?"

"Tennis shoes?" Darius peeked into the sacks of groceries and began to pull things out and examine them with interest.

"Rubber shoes. Surely, they had tennis even in your day."

"Well, certainly they do. But I have not heard of these rubber shoes."

I allowed myself a short laugh. Relief made me giddy.

"Well, let's go into Council Bluffs tomorrow morning and get you something to wear. Did you have something to eat while I was gone?"

Darius's blue eyes widened. "Council Bluffs? That's quite the journey. Will we be staying the night?" He checked his pocket watch. I wondered how the watch could still work after all these years.

"It will take several hours to get to Missouri Valley, supposing that we can get a conveyance," Darius continued as he studied his watch, "and then another hour and a half to the city from there which will, of course, depend on your modern train schedule."

I laughed to myself as I put things away in the refrigerator. Before I turned around, I pressed my lips together to compose my face.

"I've got a car, Darius. You'd be surprised how fast we can get to Council Bluffs from here. I'd say not more than an hour one way."

"An hour?" He shook his head slowly and regarded me with amazement. "That seems difficult to believe. Very well, then. Tomorrow it is!"

"First thing," I promised. "The electrician is coming in the afternoon, and we'll have to figure out where to stash you while he's here."

"By stash, I suppose you mean hide." Darius grinned. "I could always wander up to the cemetery once again," he teased. "I feel very comfortable up there."

I huffed and turned a shoulder to him.

"Very funny," I muttered.

Darius laughed and changed the subject.

"I examined the house while you were gone, and I have decided on a course of action for the necessary repairs. Shall we review my proposals?"

For the next few hours, Darius walked me around the house, inside and out, showing me what he thought needed to be done. I trusted his judgment implicitly. Though he'd built the house over a hundred years ago, it seemed likely that the fundamentals of carpentry hadn't really changed.

I looked forward to the sight of him with a tool belt strapped around his waist, hammer in hand with a hardhat perched atop his chestnut waves. Something like a calendar pinup. The macho image, though, soon evolved into another vision of Darius tangled up in the cord of a power saw. I couldn't repress a grin, and I refused to answer Darius's questions regarding the source of my amusement.

Darkness descended, and I made my way into the kitchen to eye the microwave and contemplate whether it could hold up under the strains of heating dinner. I ogled the new electric stove and wished the hours would roll by so the electrician could do what he needed to do and get it hooked up—along with my washer and dryer in the alcove off the kitchen.

Darius could be heard knocking on walls on the second floor, presumably looking for studs. I had rounded up some paper and pencil for him to start writing notes and listing supplies.

My cell phone rang and I ran into the living room to retrieve it from the depths of my purse.

"So, how's it going?" Sara asked when I answered. I plopped down onto the sofa, forcing Sassy to open one eye from her roost on the top of the couch. Though Sara couldn't see me, I know I blushed foolishly.

"Good!" I said in an unnaturally high voice. I tried to tone it down. "I went out with Laura and Cynthia today and met some of the local folks, got some groceries, hired a guy to renovate the house, and—"

"What!"

I was hoping to breeze through that portion, but Sara was quick—or maybe she was used to listening for anything out of the ordinary when it came to me.

"I hired a guy. I haven't seen him yet or anything, so I don't know if he's going to work out..." I rapidly ran out of lies.

"Good gravy, you're moving fast. Well, just make sure he's licensed and bonded." I swore she must have been related to Hardware Bob in another life.

"Yes, Mother. Speaking of which, how is she? How's the cruise going? Have you heard?"

"Not a peep. They're too 'frugal' to call from somewhere in the Pacific Ocean, you know."

Sara laughed, and I smiled at the true words. I heard Darius's continued tapping, and I covered the phone with my hand.

"At any rate, I'm sure they're having a good time," Sara said.

"Well, maybe Mom. Somehow, I don't see this as Dad's cup of tea."

"So, how was your first night in the house?" Sara asked.

I thought of my eventful first night and opted for at least one truth. I hated lying to my sister.

"Well, the orange cat, Marmaduke, certainly made a commotion last night. I guess he's out sowing his wild oats while he can because I'm having him neutered next week."

"Poor kitty," Sara murmured. "Still," she sighed, "if he wants to be an indoor cat, it's the best thing for him...and you."

"Well, I can't be responsible for little orange kitties over running the neighborhood," I said dryly.

I heard Darius's footsteps on the stairs, and I covered the phone again. He appeared on the stairs, streaks of dust on his white shirt and a smudge on his face. I held my finger to my lips. He stilled at the bottom of the steps and tilted his head with curiosity.

"So, what are you doing?" I asked Sara, hoping Darius wouldn't speak. I was out of luck.

"I am just getting ready to wash up," he said, and I jumped to my feet and pointed to the phone while making exaggerated faces and shushing gestures in what must have seemed like a bizarre mime performance.

"Did you say something? Wait, let me turn my music down," Sara said.

"I asked you what you were doing," I repeated with relief that she hadn't heard Darius's voice. He, in turn, shook his head in confusion but finally seemed to understand that I wanted him to be silent. He approached me tentatively, and I took a step backwards, trying to remember what I had asked Sara.

"Oh, I'm just reading a book. Brad is out of town at an engineering conference, so I'm having a single girl's night out with a romance novel." She laughed.

I froze as I could back up no further with the couch behind me, and Darius continued to approach. He came to stand beside me and bent his head near the phone. It occurred to me that I was having my own girl's night out with a romance novel—only mine was standing right next to me

"Molly? Are you there?"

"Yes, I'm here," I said as I smiled up at Darius who looked at me and back to the phone again. "What did you say you were reading?"

"Well, it's a time travel romance. Do you ever read those?"

"Once, a long time ago," I mumbled, distracted by the feel of Darius's breath near my cheek. "I can't remember the author, but I loved the story."

Darius raised his head, startled and voiced a silent apology, having realized he was listening in on someone's conversation. He turned to leave, but I caught his arm. Not only did I enjoy watching him see and experience new things—like the phone—I thought it was a fine excuse to keep him close.

"So, what's this one about?" I asked as I inhaled Darius's scent.

"Oh, this gal travels back in time to the Victorian era. Something about boarding a train which has some magic power to transport her in time. Then she meets a handsome man and falls in love."

I grinned, reluctantly letting go of Darius's arm as he bent his head near me again.

"And then what? Does she stay with him or go back to her time?" I murmured.

"I don't know. I haven't gotten that far," Sara said.

"I wish we could travel through time. Wouldn't that be great?" I heard myself sigh. Out of the corner of my eye, I saw Darius turn a curious look on me.

"I don't know. Why? Don't tell me you think you have to travel in time to meet Mr. Right?" Sara chuckled. "Are you looking for a Victorian man? Is that what you've been holding out for all these years?"

I blushed, and decided Darius had heard enough. I moved away from him, and he understood. He nodded and retreated to the stairs.

"No, I don't think so. Maybe," I said, barely paying attention to the conversation as I watched Darius climb the stairs. As if he knew my gaze followed him, he glanced over his shoulder and threw me a brash grin before he disappeared from sight. I sighed. And said the first thing on my mind.

"Do you believe in ghosts?"

CHAPTER EIGHT

"What?" Sara asked as if she thought she'd misunderstood.

I sank down on the sofa once again.

"Do you believe in ghosts? You know, people that come back from the dead." I shivered. I wasn't explaining it well. "Not like white and pale and spooky, but people who...well, like your book...travel through time. Maybe for love?"

Sara coughed. "Well, let me put it this way. I'd be more inclined to believe in time travel than I would in ghosts. Does all this ruminating come from living so close to a cemetery? *You* picked the house, sis."

I forced a chuckle, albeit a high-pitched one.

"I love that cemetery."

Sara grunted in response. "Well, listen, I'm going to get back to my time travel to see what happens. I'll keep you posted on the outcome. You're welcome to your ghosts."

"I have to admit," I chuckled again. "I'd rather meet a man who traveled in time myself. Even if I do live near a cemetery." I said goodbye and hung up.

I heard the moaning and groaning of the pipes upstairs, though it sounded more like the sink than the bathtub. At least, I hoped so. I was going to try to make dinner soon.

I pulled my knees up under me on the couch and rested my chin on them. The conversation with my sister had given me food for thought.

Time travel, I repeated silently. If only time travel were possible. Then Darius would be...alive, wouldn't he? He wouldn't be a...a ghost.

I felt a corner of my mouth lift. If ghosts were possible, then why wasn't time travel? Who said Darius had to be a ghost? That he was out of the ordinary, there was no doubt. That something supernatural was at play also seemed a certainty. But there really was no evidence that he was a ghost. Was there?

My heart thumped against my chest.

Wait, now, Molly. Don't start imagining things. Either way, it's all too bizarre. Why couldn't you just fall for some nice lawyer or doctor who was born in this century?

I shook my head and jumped up to head for the kitchen, muttering silently.

Time...Time...Time was all I had. Time would tell. Time heals all wounds. All it takes is time. Time in a bottle.

A peek into the still near-empty refrigerator settled the menu for dinner as soup and salad. I hoped Darius liked tomato soup. I would have to do some major grocery shopping in Council Bluffs. The local store simply didn't have the room to stock a large variety of food.

I heated up the soup, standing guard over the microwave and begging it to hold out for a few more minutes. It managed to do so, and I threw a salad together and set it on the table along with some sliced bread from the store. I loved French bread but had a daunting feeling that my favorite foods would not necessarily be available in this small town. I couldn't imagine special ordering through Sally.

"Darius," I called. "Dinner is ready."

As if he'd been waiting for me to call, Darius clattered down the stairs and appeared at the kitchen door, smelling of soap. His hair was neatly combed and his coat, slacks and shoes were clean and free of dust. I studied him thoughtfully, Sara's words playing in my mind. His clothing looked brand new, though he'd been living in the same things for the last few weeks. Surely, a ghost's clothing would have a musty smell at the very least? Wouldn't the garments look old, cobwebby, tattered? I lowered my head with a wry smile, cursing Sara for putting even more confusing ideas into my head.

"What was that contraption you spoke into, may I ask?" Darius asked as he pulled a chair out for me. I blushed—feeling quite the lady of the manor—and took a seat with a murmur of thanks.

"It's called a phone. It used to be called a telephone, but now we just call it a cell phone."

"Ah! I heard rumors of such an invention, but have not seen one. And you talk to people who are not here with it? How exactly does that occur?"

I grinned when I saw Darius searching for a napkin. No doubt, he was looking for something in linen. I pushed one of the squares of paper towels that I'd brought to the table for just that purpose.

"Here! Your serviette," I chuckled.

He glanced up at me, raised one eyebrow and laid the paper towel across his lap with aplomb as if it were made of the finest Brussels linen edged with lace.

"Yes, of course," he murmured.

"I don't know how the phone works, exactly. Cell phone towers communicate with satellites in space which send signals all over the world to other cell phone towers?"

"I beg your pardon?" Darius, who'd been in the act of picking up his spoon, paused to stare at me with a knit between his brows. "I am quite certain, Molly, that every single word you used was English and yet...I have no earthly idea what you just said."

I shook my head and gave him a rueful smile.

"I wish I could explain how things work to you, Darius, but the truth is—I don't know how everything works. I hope you don't think I'm..." I shrugged, feeling wholly inadequate. "Well, I mean, how does one educate someone who wasn't born in the last hundred years? But then again, who plans to meet someone from another century?"

Darius's hand covered mine as it rested on the table.

"Molly. I know how intelligent you are. That is one of the things I loved about you—one of the things I love about you. Only tell me what you can. It is enough." His smile grew broad and the twinkle appeared in his eye. "And did I hear you finally admit that I was not born in your millennium?"

I delighted in the feel of his hand over mine—the warmth, the strength, the sense of safety I felt when he touched me.

"I'm pretty sure I said century—not millennium," I smirked, completely bowled over by his touch.

"I stand corrected," Darius said with a solemn face, although the corners of his lips twitched. He squeezed my hand before releasing it to pick up his spoon.

"Darius?" Now was as good a time as any, I thought.

"Yes?" He stilled his hand and lifted his blue eyes to mine. Under his gaze, I almost lost my train of thought.

He gave me an encouraging nod as I struggled to organize my thoughts.

"That was my sister, Sara, on the phone," I stalled.

"Yes, I gathered," he responded. "You have mentioned her before." He smiled gently. "Is she well?"

"Yes, she's fine, thank you for asking." Why was this conversation so difficult, I wondered? I looked at him for a moment—handsome, alive, vibrant, even normal—except that he wasn't.

"Do you believe in time travel?" I asked, seemingly out of the blue.

At least, to see his startled face, it was unexpected.

Darius burst out laughing—a deep-throated, warm and hearty sound that would have thrilled me had I not been so intent on discovering his origins.

"Well, If I didn't believe in time travel by now, that would be quite naïve of me, don't you think? After all, have I not traveled through time. For you?"

His face sobered on his last two words, and he reached for my hand again, but I slid my hands into my lap so I could focus. I simply could not think straight under the spell of his touch. And I really could not think when he said such ridiculously romantic things to me. I knew that if this man could not stay with me, I would do my utmost to go with him—no matter where he came from. No other future presented itself to me any longer.

"I'm serious, Darius! I know you think that you're a...spirit...ghost or whatever." I scrunched my face as I searched for an acceptable term—acceptable to me, that is. "But what if—" I stumbled over my words, my thoughts as incoherent as my words. "Well, it's just that Sara was talking about time travel, and I wondered..." I raised my hand when it looked as if he would interrupt. "Don't get me wrong. We don't actually believe people can travel through time—even in this *millennium*." I avoided his gaze as the entire conversation sounded foolish—even to me. "But a lot of people don't believe in ghosts either. So, isn't it just as likely that you've actually traveled through time? Rather than..." I gulped, "...died?" I lifted my gaze from my cooling cup of soup and checked his reaction.

He sat back in his chair regarding me with an indecipherable expression. I swallowed harder under his scrutiny. The *discussion* hadn't gone as well as I'd hoped. Perhaps my delivery needed finessing.

"Darius? You think I'm a kook, don't you?"

A twitch of his lips reassured me only slightly.

"I am not sure. What is a kook?"

"You know, eccentric...odd." I found it hard to meet his direct gaze. All of a sudden, he seemed quite normal, and I felt like the oddity.

He smiled broadly. "Well, you certainly are different from anyone I've every known. Even the Molly I once knew."

"That sounds bad." I grimaced.

He shook his head. "Not at all. It is a compliment. You are like Molly—yet different somehow." He leaned forward and placed his elbows on the table, the soup forgotten. "So, if you believe that I have traveled through time—how does that explain your presence here?"

I blinked.

"Me?"

"Yes, you, my dear. I may have been speaking of Molly as if she was some other woman, but she is not. She is you, and you are most definitely she."

I shook my head.

"That's just not possible, Darius."

"Stop hiding your hands and give them to me," he commanded in a tone that brooked no argument. I complied, and was not at all unhappy about it. He held my hands in his warm grasp and rubbed his thumbs along the tops of my fingers. "It seems I cannot think very well unless I touch you," he murmured with a wry smile.

I realized I was holding my breath and released it.

"Why do you think it is possible for me to have traveled through time and not you?" he repeated.

My initial reaction was to pull my hands back so that I *could* think, but Darius held them firmly.

"And *I* can't think straight while you touch me," I mumbled, avoiding his direct gaze. I closed my eyes for a moment, trying to ignore the blissful feel of his thumbs as they traced delicate patterns along the back of my hands. It was impossible.

"I don't know what I believe, Darius." I opened my eyes and did my best to meet his beautiful blue gaze. The soft expression in them nearly undid me, and it was all I could do not to leap across the table and throw myself in his arms. "I don't have any memory of a past beyond this life," I shook my head slowly. "And apparently you do. So, that suggests that you *have* lived in another time." I shrugged helplessly. "Why wouldn't *I* remember something like that? Why wouldn't I remember *you*?" A small smile tugged at my lips. "I would not be likely to forget *you*."

I watched Darius's face bronze, and my heart fluttered in response. Who didn't love a man who could blush? He gave my hands a light squeeze before settling back in his seat. He crossed his arms and stared unseeingly at the uneaten food on the table, seemingly lost in thought. A frown between his eyes worried me. Though the evening was warm, I felt suddenly cold, and my shoulder began to ache again. Darius glanced at me with a troubled look on his face, but his eyes flickered and he returned to staring at the table.

"Darius? Did I say something wrong?" Whatever I had said took the light out of his eyes, and I felt absolutely awful. I wanted to run, but my legs seemed frozen. I put a hand to my left collarbone and rubbed it.

Darius saw my movement, and he grimaced.

"I have seen you do that several times today. Does your shoulder pain you, Molly?"

"What?" I looked down at my shoulder and dropped my hand hastily.

"Yes... No..." I shook my head in confusion. What had I said? "Yes, it does, but that's not important. Is something wrong? You—you pulled away...I don't know what I—"

Darius leaned forward and captured my right hand in his hands. "You said nothing wrong, Molly. I apologize. Forgive me." He gave me a slight smile. "I am not usually given to moods, but I find myself in strange circumstances."

"Is it..." I struggled for the right words, but they failed me. "Is it the other Molly? Are you still in love with her? What happened to her? Where is she?" I asked in a low voice.

Somehow, I knew. Whoever she was, he was still in love with her. And though I might look like her—or remind him of her in some way—I wasn't her, and he was never going to love me that way.

He blinked for a moment before freeing his right hand to run gentle fingers along the edge of my jaw as if exploring my face. Unexpected tears sprang to my eyes, and I closed them for a moment.

"You are one and the same, my love. I know you don't believe it, but you are the same Molly I have loved for years."

I swallowed hard and fought for control as I opened my eyes to see him watching me intently, as if he tried to decipher my thoughts.

"I just don't see how that's possible." I shook my head.

"Neither do I, sweeting, but I am not mistaken about you...about us. You remembered me. You knew my name. You cannot deny that some unexplained force is at work here."

I rubbed my face against his hand for a moment.

"What happened to your other Molly? Is she still there? Did you leave her behind?" The thought of what she must be going through—losing him. I couldn't bear to think of her pain.

Darius stiffened for a moment, and his gaze flickered away from mine.

"What?" I pulled back, and he let my hands go. "What aren't you telling me, Darius?"

"I cannot speak of it, my love," he said in a husky voice. "Not now. We will talk of it another time, I promise. It is enough that I have found you again and all is well with the world." He gave me a lopsided smile. "Come, we must eat. The food grows cold."

I looked down at the soup in some confusion. All was well with the world, he said. Then why had his face shown such grief?

He rose to his feet, the smile remaining on his handsome face, though it didn't meet his eyes. I sank back into my chair. Deflated, confused. There was a mystery surrounding the "other Molly," and I needed to know what it was. Darius was unwilling to discuss it with me at the moment, and short of demanding to know what was essentially his private business, I had no choice but to wait for a better time.

He paused for a moment to look at me with a softness in his eyes that warmed my heart. He bent and lowered his face to mine. He cupped my chin gently and stared into my eyes.

"I love you, Molly. I love *you.* The woman you have become... Do not doubt that for a moment."

He lowered his gaze to my mouth and rubbed his thumb along my lower lip. My head swam under his touch, and I held my breath. Would he kiss me...as he had two weeks ago? Would I lose myself in him, emerging only to scream in agony when he disappeared from my life?

I begged him with my eyes to kiss me as I held my breath. He bent his head toward me, and I closed my eyes in anticipation. Warm lips caressed my cheek.

"I will wait for you, Molly," he whispered in my ear. "Until you are certain that I am here to stay. I will wait for you."

My mouth dropped as I opened my eyes to see him straighten. He cleared his throat and flashed me one of his boyish grins.

"Let's see now," he said huskily. "Where were we?" He looked down at the table in some confusion. "Ah, yes, I believe we were speaking of dinner. I shall take our soup to that little contraption you have to see if we can make it hot once again." He picked up our cups with a slight tremor in his hands and headed for the microwave. I snapped out of my trance and jumped up to intercede, never doubting that he was fully prepared to attempt to operate it himself.

"I think I'd better show you how to use this. I have a feeling you're going to use it anyway." I struggled to focus on more practical matters, certain that Darius kissed me, dinner would have had to wait...until the morning.

"Just remember that we're operating on very old wiring, and the microwave may not hold up much longer—at least until the electrician comes," I heard myself saying.

"Yes, dear," Darius murmured.

How many women had heard that domestic line before? I would never tire of hearing it from him. The warm look in his eyes and intimacy in his tone gave the trite acknowledgement a sweet validation of our strange, yet wonderful, relationship.

With the soup re-heated and Darius semi-trained on the basics of the microwave, we sat down to dinner again, leaving questions and mysteries until another time.

We ate as if we'd been doing so together for years, with Darius expressing delight in the salty flavor of the soup, the freshness of the salad and surprise at my acquisition of the requested pumpkin pie.

Though I demurred and informed him I had made nothing from scratch, I nevertheless beamed at his praise and considered my first attempt at domesticity with a nineteenth century ghost...time traveler—no, make that enigma, I thought as I eyed him speculatively—to be a resounding success.

"A fine repast," he said as he wiped his mouth with my best paper towel napkin when we finished eating. "Thank you, Molly. I believe I shall enjoy the food in this time." He grinned approvingly, and I beamed, delighting in the sparkle of his playful eyes.

"I think I must return to inspecting the house so that you can order supplies soon." He picked up the dishes and carried them to the sink while I watched in surprise.

"Darius... You don't normally clear your dinner table, do you? I thought men in your time..." I faltered.

He turned to me with a rueful expression and shook his head.

"No, not really. I have staff who help with those tasks."

I blinked.

"Staff?" I cleared off the rest of the table. "What kind of staff?"

"Well, just a few people, that is all."

"How many few people?" I closed the refrigerator and turned to stare at him.

He seemed embarrassed.

"A housekeeper who also cooks, her daughter who helps out, a man who takes care of the farming and gardening—who also happens to be her husband—and her son—who takes care of the animals, horses and carriage."

I raised my eyebrows at just about the same time as I dropped my jaw.

"A carriage?"

He cleared his throat.

"Well, perhaps buggy would be a more apt description. A carriage is simply not sturdy enough for these country roads. I used to have a carriage though when I lived back East. It was lovely! Black and gleaming." He sighed rapturously.

"Darius! Were you... I mean... Are you..." I shook my head. "No, I guess the word would be...were. Were you wealthy?"

His face reddened.

"Well, I was not without means, although I must say that I am as poor as a church mouse at the moment." He grinned, and the twinkle in his eyes showed no hint of regret.

I closed my mouth, hoping I didn't look as astonished as I felt. A thought popped into my head, and I surveyed the kitchen.

"This house isn't really that big, Darius. Did everyone live here...like live-in staff?"

He shook his head.

"No, they live...lived in town. Mrs. White rules the roost over her husband, daughter and son," he grinned. "I am...was very fortunate." He shook his head and rubbed his chin in that endearingly confused way I had come to love. "I find it hard to speak in past tense—as if my life is in the past."

My face must have drooped at his words because he instantly crossed the kitchen and took me into his arms. I stood quietly still, my arms at my sides, though I longed to wrap my arms around him. I hesitated to let him know how completely love-struck I was, as if exposing my love somehow would hasten its end. I seemed to be made of mush lately, without backbone or will or rational reactions.

"Ahhhh, Molly, that is not what I meant at all. I am very pleased to be here—to be here with you. You have no idea how much I have missed you." He pressed my face against his chest and laid his chin on the top of my head. I listened to the rumbling in his chest as he spoke and wished we could stay that way forever.

I had no idea what he was talking about when he said he missed me, but I didn't want to see the grief on his face as he spoke of the "other" Molly, so I didn't question him again. If I was serving as some substitute for a woman he once loved, so be it. That was good enough for me. But the fear that he might disappear lingered ever present in the forefront of my mind, and I continued to try to hold back one last piece of my heart from the strange mystery that was Darius Ferguson.

He pulled back and peered down into my face with a gentle smile.

"This will take time, I think, won't it, my love? I cannot rush you."

I kept my eyes downcast, unable to meet his gaze—especially after his intimate term of endearment.

"You certainly know how to turn on the charm, Mr. Ferguson. You're awfully hard to resist," I quipped as I maneuvered my way out of his arms and crossed the kitchen to run water into the sink to wash dishes.

I tried to keep my back to him, but there was no response, so I gave in to curiosity and threw a glance over my shoulder. Darius leaned against the refrigerator where I'd left him, in a relaxed pose, with his arms crossed over his chest.

"Perhaps you should quit trying," he said quietly. "To resist, that is."

My face heated, and I'm certain my heart stopped for a moment as I looked at him—tall, devastatingly handsome, full of life, and seemingly in love with me.

"I will wait, Molly, as long as it takes. I am not going anywhere," he said in a husky voice. He gave me a final lopsided grin before he turned to leave the kitchen. "I will take this time to check a few more things in the house," he threw over his shoulder as he walked down the hallway.

I must have smiled the entire time I washed the dishes. When I'd finished cleaning up, I went upstairs to take a bath, this time ensuring that the door was firmly shut just in case Darius planned on another bathroom raid.

I lay in the bathtub listening to him continue to tap about the house, and I wondered he'd managed to find the one occupation that would bring to reality his possible ghostly status—tapping and rattling on doors, walls, ceilings and floors. He was a walking cliché. I grinned.

Personally, I was opting for the time traveler persona versus the ghost, and I wondered if I would ever know the truth. It seemed likely that we could not go on exactly as we were—I just didn't see how—and I would know sooner or later which he was. Whatever brought him to my time—to me—might very well take him from me. I swallowed against the painful lump that formed in my throat and dunked my head under the water as if I could wash the unwanted thoughts away.

A short while later, feeling clean and refreshed—if a little waterlogged—I climbed out and dried off, wrapping myself in my robe.

"It's all yours," I called out on my way to the bedroom. From the noise, it seemed Darius was above me in the attic.

He opened the attic door and peered down at me.

"What's that?"

"The bath... It's all yours. I'm done."

"Bath? I just bathed last night."

I paused in the middle of towel rubbing my hair and stared up at him. His startled look brought a quiver to my lips, and I pressed the towel against my face as I bent over to laugh.

"What do you find so amusing?" He ran a hand through his hair. "Is my hair askew? Do I have dirt on my face?"

I peered up at him and inched the towel to just below mouth. It hadn't succeeded in stifling my giggles at any rate.

"You're killing me, Darius, killing me!" I squealed. "Here in the United States, in the twenty-first century, unless we're camping in the wilderness, we try to bathe or shower every day. I'm afraid you're not in the nineteenth century anymore, Dorothy!"

To my surprise, Darius grinned broadly as he hopped down the stairs, taking them two at once.

"Wonderful! I am so pleased to hear of it. I confess that I am very ready for another bath after crawling about in the dust up there. But I did not want to waste your water." He nodded toward the ceiling. "And I'll have you know that some people in the nineteenth century bathe every day...or so I heard." He turned into the bathroom but paused at the doorway to look at me. "Who is Dorothy?"

I went off on another peal of giggles, stuffed the towel to my face again, shook my head and ran into the bedroom, wondering if I were close to hysterics given the bizarre events of the past few days.

As I readied for bed, I berated myself for mocking him and promised to do better in the future—if I could help it. The sincere curiosity on his face when he asked about Dorothy promised to set me off into another round of giggles.

I hopped onto the end of my bed and brought my knees to my chest, resting my chin on them. I felt like a teenager. His presence had brought a ray of golden light into my life. I wanted to smile and laugh under the gaze of his turquoise eyes. When I wasn't terrified he might disappear, that is.

I slipped off the bed and opened the door to call out a goodnight. Darius had left the bathroom door open, and I exerted every ounce of control to keep myself from tiptoeing down the hallway to peek inside. Sassy had no such qualms as she sat by the bathroom door and stared at the object of her affection, who hummed quietly as he bathed. I noted Marmaduke sprawled across the head of the stairs, effectively making sure neither Sassy nor Darius made a move without his permission. I decided to keep him inside so there was no repeat of last night's noisy festivities.

"Good night, Darius. I'll see you in the morning."

"Good night, Molly. Sleep well."

I shut the door and crawled into bed, wondering what the following day would bring. Electricity, a shopping expedition and the sight of Darius in a pair of blue jeans. What more could a girl ask?

I fell asleep, although I never thought it would happen—not with Darius so near. I dreamed of a woman who looked like me. The other Molly, I guessed. She stood with me on the windy hill of the cemetery, long skirt flapping around her legs, arms outstretched, her fingers touching mine as we laughed and pretended to soar over the valley below. Her brown eyes sparkled, and her dark curls flew around her face. Darius relaxed on the bench beneath the oak tree—an expression of satisfaction and love on his face as he watched us.

****

I awoke in the morning to a lovely fresh breeze drifting in through the open window of my bedroom. I rolled over onto my side to face the gentle light filtering in, and I bemusedly contemplated the image of a pair of delicate white lace curtains framing the window. The wind would lift the curtains softly, gracefully, while I lay in bed and admired the pattern of light streaming through them. Darius's arms would be around me, and we would face the beauty of the morning together...in each other's arms.

I inhaled deeply as if I could smell him near me. Was he thinking of me as I thought of him? I wrapped my arms around my chest and hugged myself tightly.

Today, we would be together. We were going to Council Bluffs. I would buy frivolous white lace curtains, and Darius would hang them while I sat on the bed and admired him. He would turn to look at me, and his face would light up with love and affection. He would pull me into his arms and kiss me.

I hugged myself tighter and took deep breaths as I closed my eyes and indulged in my daydream for a few more moments. Darius was just downstairs. Why dream about him when I could just get up and be with him?

I jumped out of bed and threw on a knee-length blue denim skirt and a white cotton blouse. I slipped into some flip-flops, and opened my door to listen for sounds of Darius. The house seemed quiet. Was he still sleeping? Did he sleep? I still didn't know.

I tiptoed down the stairs to find the couch unoccupied, the blanket and pillow neatly folded once again at the end of the couch.

"Good morning, my dear." Darius emerged from the kitchen, beaming and holding a mug, which he held out to me. I felt my face redden as I reached for the cup. Hopefully, Darius couldn't tell from my face that I'd been fantasizing about him.

His hand stilled in midair, and I watched his eyes drop to my skirt and widen. He blinked for a moment and dragged his gaze back to my face with effort. I could have sworn a blush that matched my own bronzed his cheeks.

I looked down at my skirt for an instant before raising my gaze to his face. I took the cup from him with uncertain hands.

Darius cleared his throat.

"You slept in this morning. It is half past nine," he murmured as he studiously consulted his watch. "We have a journey ahead of us today."

I nodded, suddenly mute, and brought the warm cup to my lips, wishing I'd put on some jeans instead of the skirt.

"I must say you look very lovely in that skirt, Molly, though you look equally delightful in those...em...blue trousers you often wear."

I blushed and preened...just a little.

"Thank you."

Darius cleared his throat again. I looked up.

"I see that the length of women's skirts has changed over the years...er...centuries." He hesitated, and his eyes flickered to my skirt—or my legs. "Quit a bit, I think." He averted his eyes and directed his gaze to my face.

I surveyed my skirt again.

"Yes, they have. Is it bothering you?" I said with a coy look at his embarrassed face. "I know women didn't run around exposing their legs in your time, but we do in my time, Darius." I didn't know if I was teasing him or flirting with him. I suspect it was a little of both. But what was the fun of having a nineteenth century man around the house if one couldn't embarrass him occasionally?

"A bit," he murmured with an even smile, "but I shall learn to adapt." His eyes twinkled appreciatively. He seemed to have recovered his equilibrium very quickly, I thought.

I took a hasty sip of my drink to hide the flush on my cheeks. A slightly sweet, dark chocolate flavor assailed my taste buds, and I peered into the cup.

"Darius! This is delicious! Is this your special recipe?"

Darius clasped his hands behind his back and beamed, the bronze color of his face emphasizing the whiteness of his teeth.

"It is not such a special recipe, but I am glad you are pleased. It is very common in my time." He turned toward the kitchen. "Come, we will have breakfast before we go."

I followed him in to the kitchen to discover the glass-topped table set with bowls and spoons. The box of raisin bran cereal and the gallon of milk sat in the center.

"I am afraid I could not find a pitcher for the milk," he said as he pulled out a chair for me.

"I don't have one," I mumbled in bemused fascination. "I just pour it from the jug."

"Well, this looks delicious. Shall we?" he asked.

Darius picked up the cereal box and turned it several different ways before finding the opening at the top. Molly watched with a swelling heart as he studiously read the instructions on the top of the box.

"I suspect you didn't always build Victorian houses for a living, Darius. What did you do?"

He had mastered opening the box of cereal, and I put my hand out to stop him from filling my bowl to the brim.

"You are correct. This is the first large house that I built on my own, though I had some experience assisting with the building of other homes as a youth working with my grandfather. I certainly learned a great deal from the experience." He grinned and looked around the kitchen. "When I first came here, I built the cabin out back and lived in that. And prior to that, I practiced law for several years in Virginia, but I felt too confined in offices, so I left that behind." He studied the picture of a bowl of cereal on the cover of the box and picked up the milk jug.

"A lawyer! So, you went to college then? Did your family have money?" There was just something about the way he carried himself that didn't quite fit with "farmer".

"Yes and yes. I wanted to come out here to try my hand at farming. My parents and brother stayed in Jefferson County."

I took over the pouring of the milk since Darius seemed only too happy to fill the bowl all the way to the top.

"You owned all of this land? Even up to the cemetery?" I paused with my spoon in midair and gazed out the breakfast nook window toward the open expanse of cornfields.

"It wasn't a cemetery then, but yes, this was my land." He gave me a wry smile.

"I can't imagine farming all of this without machinery. You just don't look like a farmer." I grinned, hoping to soften my observation in case he was dead set on presenting the image of a farmer.

I needn't have worried. He grinned and took a bite of cereal.

"Yes, well, I would venture to say that Sam White and his son, George, probably did most of the farming. I seemed to be somewhat inept at it in the beginning. But I learned"—he grinned again—"just as I learned to build the house. It is hard work, I must admit. But I enjoy being out of doors."

I watched him savor the sweetened cereal.

"And then I met you."

"Me?"

"Yes, you, my dear one, and I knew that my bachelor cabin simply would not do, so I set about building this house for us." His gaze bored into mine, with a sparkle in the golden specks of his eyes. It was as if he tried to draw me out, to compel me to remember.

I dropped my gaze to my food.

"Don't stare at me like that," I mumbled. "I can't remember anything. And batting your eyes at me isn't going to make me remember."

Darius's unexpected snort of laughter broke the intensity of the moment. I looked up.

"Batting my eyes?" he sputtered. "I beg your pardon. Batting my eyes, indeed!"

He grinned and resumed eating. I returned his smile. I still had more questions for him, but I didn't want to spoil the moment, and I feared a return of the pain I saw in his face when he spoke of the "other" Molly.

We finished eating over a general discussion of house repairs.

"Are you ready to go?" I asked as I took the dishes to the sink.

"To ride in a car for the first time? I am!" Darius grinned as he shrugged on his dark jacket. The jacket seemed molded to his broad shoulders and slim waist, and I watched him with a sigh.

"I can't wait to see you in blue jeans," I thought out loud. Darius's face reddened, and I clapped a hand over my mouth.

"I trust they will not fit as...em...much like a glove as your trousers do you." He cleared his throat. "I could not possibly get any work done that way."

I blushed. "You'd be surprised. They're very comfortable."

Darius coughed behind his hand and lowered his gaze to my skirt.

"Comfortable... Yes, of course. Shall we go?"

I grinned, loving his old-fashioned embarrassment. I grabbed my purse from the coffee table and led the way to the car, pulling open the passenger door for Darius. I beamed as he expressed wonder, both verbally and by action, in the materials and feel of the car. I laughed outright as I showed him how to hook the seatbelt, and argued with him that he simply had to wear the belt—no matter how uncomfortable it felt to be tied in.

Marmaduke, who had followed us out of the house—with permission—given his last few days of freedom, jumped onto the hood of the car as if he, too, were going for a ride. I shooed him off. He continued to dash from one side of the car to the other, and I worried that he intended to jump inside the car, but he finally came to a halt and stalked over to the side of the drive to watch the activities.

Having bested Darius's recalcitrant objections over the seatbelt as a mother might, I went around to the driver's side and climbed in, feeling self-conscious as he watched my every move. He asked a myriad of questions, some regarding the mechanics of the car, which I could not answer, of course.

Unsure of Marmaduke's exact location, I backed slowly down the driveway. With relief, I noted he continued to stare at us from his position near the house. It amazed me that the cat never wandered far from the grounds—if at all. Darius turned around to watch the movement of the car with fascination.

I backed onto the road.

"Molly, stop!"

I slammed my foot down on the brakes at the urgency in Darius's voice. The car came to a jarring halt, and I swung my head around to look for an oncoming vehicle. I could see nothing.

"What!" I cried out as I turned to look at him.

"Something is wrong."

Before my horrified eyes, Darius's normally tanned face paled to an almost translucent white. He raised his hands in front of his face to look at them...or the transparent haze that they'd become. I could see right through his hands...to the car door beyond.

CHAPTER NINE

I began to shake.

"Take me back to the house. Take me back now, Molly," Darius whispered.

"I can't, Darius!" I cried. "I can't move. I'm too scared. What if I do something wrong? What's happening to you?" My hands shook as I gripped the steering wheel and my legs seemed frozen, incapable of action—the action I so desperately needed.

"Molly, listen to me," Darius's voice seemed to come from a long way off. "I do not think I can leave this place. And I do not think I can walk. I feel so weak. If I do not get back..." His voice trailed off.

"Darius! Darius!" I couldn't make out the features of his face and could barely see the outline of his body. Everything was a blur. Some force finally galvanized me into action, and I hoped against hope that I could get the car back into the drive without losing him. I slammed the car into drive, yanked the wheel and gunned the car. The car jerked forward and roared back into the driveway. Marmaduke jumped out of the way as I slammed the car to a halt next to the house. I shut off the engine and turned to stare at the faint white silhouette that was Darius, desperately willing him to come back to me.

"Darius," I shrieked. "Darius!" I reached for him but my hand passed through his shape, and I jerked back, terrified and helpless to stop what was happening.

"Darius, please don't leave me!" I sobbed helplessly. I scrambled out of the car and ran to the passenger's side door. I yanked it open and stopped short. Darius sat in the seat—in the flesh—staring at his hands.

"Darius! What happened?" I grabbed the lapels of his jacket to hang onto him. "What happened?" I repeated, but he seemed not to hear me.

"Darius?" I choked out. Blinded by tears, I let go with one hand to rub my eyes.

He turned to look at me, his eyes unfocused, a vacant look on his face.

I reached for him again, terrified that I wouldn't touch solid flesh. But the skin of his face was warm to my fingers.

"Darius?" I whispered.

He seemed to see me at last and grabbed my hand to bring it to his lips. As if exhausted, he closed his eyes and rested his forehead against my open palm.

"I don't think I can leave this place," he muttered. "Perhaps I am just what I seem. A ghost. And tied to this land I once loved so much." His voice held such despair that I ached for him—and for me. I swallowed hard, refusing to dwell on the future implications, and I reached to unlock his seatbelt.

"Come on. Let's go back to the house. I can go to the store later. I'll get what we need."

I tugged at Darius's arm, unwilling to let him go, and he climbed out of the car—albeit on unsteady legs. He put his arm around my shoulders, and we walked toward the house. He resisted going inside though, preferring instead to take a seat on the loveseat on the porch.

I sank down beside him, staving off logistical concerns or the terror that threatened to send my body into another spasm of terror.

"Look, Darius. Everything is going to be all right. I'll get what we need. Just please don't disappear like that again."

He looked at me for a brief moment, his face grim, and then he leaned forward over his knees to stare at his clasped hands.

"What future can I offer you like this, Molly? Never able to leave this property? I was afraid this would happen. I tried to walk out of the cemetery that day—to follow you. I could not bear to see you go."

I felt a hot tear slipped down my face.

"But something happened when I stepped into the road. I felt weak. Strange images and sensations came to me—colors, confusion, weakness. I made my way back into the cemetery, and it passed." He grimaced. "Unable to understand what was happening and unwilling to attempt it one more time that night lest I die, I slept on the bench. In the morning, I tried to leave once again, but I decided to attempt the path between the cemetery and the house," he nodded his head in the direction of the trees beyond the pond. "As you see, I am still here."

"I don't understand, Darius."

He shook his head, and his shoulders sagged.

"Nor do I, my love."

"So, you can go back and forth between the cemetery and the house? But you don't think you can go anywhere else?"

His wry smile said it all.

"Well, the cemetery is where I first 'appeared,' don't you remember? It seems likely that I cannot leave the land that was once mine. The land that I loved." He raised dejected eyes to survey the property. "The land that now holds me prisoner."

I jumped up. "Don't say that! You're not a prisoner here. I'm here." I pointed toward my chest.

Darius grabbed my hand and pulled me back down to sit beside him. He wrapped me in a fierce embrace and whispered in my ear.

"That is not what I meant, Molly. I would willingly be your prisoner for the rest of our lives—whatever that may be. But I cannot be the man I want to be for you. I cannot take care of you, provide for you, protect you."

I squirmed restlessly in his arms, preparing to argue my case—our case. I pulled away to look at him.

"I can take care of myself, Darius. I've done it all my life. *I'll* take care of us."

Darius stared at me for a moment, his eyes hardening. He rose abruptly and went to stand by the railing, staring down the driveway to the road beyond.

"I am unmanned by the thought, Molly. How will we go on then? Will I cook and clean for you while you take care of me and buy my clothing, my toiletries, my food?"

The bitterness in his voice frightened me, and I fell silent—unsure what words might make the situation worse.

He turned to face me, bracing his palms on the railing behind him, a harsh set to his jaw.

"I could wish that I had never 'appeared' here—in your time—but I cannot bear the thought of losing you again. I love you, Molly. I think I must set about proving my worth to you. I will rebuild this house such that it will protect you from all harm. I will take care of you so that you have the strength to provide for us." The break in his voice tore at my heart. "I will tend to your every need as best I can given my limited means. And if you should find me a burden, you have only to say the word, and I will be gone. If nothing else, I now know how to leave." On that bitter note, Darius turned and strode down the length of the porch and around to the side of the house and out of sight.

I sat in stunned silence for a moment, staring at the emptiness where he had stood only a moment ago. Then I gave myself a quick shake, jumped up and ran after him. I stopped short, though, when I saw him on the other side of the pond. He was down on one knee with his head bent.

I had to let him grieve.

Tears flowed down my face as I backed away. I returned to the front of the house and sank back down onto the loveseat. With my hands lying limply in my lap, I let the tears fall silent and unchecked.

I had no idea what the future would hold for me, but any time I could spend with Darius was precious. I would work at home as I always did, go to the store if needed, order things online and over the telephone. And we would manage.

The tears froze on my face as I remembered that Sara was coming for a visit in two weeks. What were we going to do? How would I explain Darius to Sara? Would I tell her he lived at the house? Sara would never understand. I bit my lip. It didn't matter because I didn't understand either. I rubbed the tears from my face and jumped up restlessly. We had a few weeks. I would deal with it another time.

For the rest of the morning, I wandered around on the pretext of unpacking boxes while I watched Darius from various windows in the house. He paced back and forth from the front yard to the back yard, pausing occasionally in the garden to stare skyward at the oak trees, then back down to the ground as he jammed his hands in his pockets and scuffed some imaginary leaf. He reminded me of a caged animal. I followed his progress toward the back of the yard, and from the kitchen window, I watched him explore the old cabin and shed out back. My heart jumped to my throat when I saw him take a tentative step into the corn field. I froze as I watched him stretch a hand out in front. He was too far away for me to see if there was any reaction, but to my relief, he dropped his hand and strode back to the side of the house next to the garden.

I ran to the living room window and then around to the large picture window next to the front door to follow him as he walked down the driveway to the end of the road. He paused at the edge of the drive and put his hands out in front as a blind man without a cane might do.

I couldn't see what happened, but whatever transpired, he swung around and stalked back up the drive with one hand on his forehead. I couldn't take it any more. I wrenched open the front door and burst out onto the porch.

"Okay, so what happened?"

"I beg your pardon?" He climbed the porch steps.

"So? Did you disappear again? Your hands?"

He pressed his lips together and nodded.

"Yes, it is the same. Strange images and sensations come to me. Colors, weakness."

"Okay, so we'll deal with it. You can 'provide for me' by rebuilding the house. You can take care of me by protecting me here. It's actually terrifying to sleep alone in an isolated house." I hoped he didn't read too much into that statement, though perhaps he wouldn't be misreading. "You can take walks with me to the cemetery. I love it up there, and I would welcome your company. You can be a man, if that's what you feel compelled to call it, by accepting your fate—our fate—and learning to live with it."

Darius narrowed his eyes and stared at me for a moment with an indecipherable expression. Then he moved toward me and swept me into his arms.

"Our fate," he whispered as he pressed his lips against mine, ignoring my half-hearted and disingenuous efforts to push him away. I gave up the pretense and clung to him, winding my hands through the soft chestnut curls that I adored.

"I love you, Molly. I will always love you."

"And I love you too, Darius. I still don't know how or why, but I'm pretty sure I have loved you forever."

I pulled away and cupped his face with my palms.

"We're going to be all right, Darius. Just please don't leave me. I don't know how I've managed without you all these years."

Darius smiled and wrapped an arm around my shoulders. He raised his head to survey the house.

"Well, if I am to be your carpenter, then I had better find some suitable work clothing. Any ideas?"

I chuckled with relief and dragged him into the living room where I pulled my laptop from its case, tethered my cell phone to it, and connected to the internet.

We spent the next few hours cruising the internet, while I watched Darius with loving tenderness as he ogled the screen, pushed buttons at random and occasionally lifted the computer to look under and behind it.

Life with him would likely never fail to surprise me. His interest in new things reminded me of the curiosity of a small boy, but one look at the set of his jaw or the strength of his muscular forearms left no doubt as to his maturity and masculinity. I sighed as if I had a schoolgirl crush.

We ordered some clothing on line based on calculations of his size. I tried very, very hard to keep a straight face when we got to the underwear. Darius preferred boxers, which appeared similar to the undergarments of his time—so he said—versus briefs, which shocked him with their skimpiness. He accidentally clicked on a page showing women's undergarments, and the sight of the colorful and dainty lace lingerie brought a dull flush to his face. He looked away toward the garden window while I hurried to find the men's clothing once again.

"You're such a prude," I murmured with a laugh.

"Am I?" he said in a bemused tone. "I did not know. I do not think I have been...tested...as much as I have in these last few days."

Darius allowed his gaze to travel back to the computer and visibly relaxed when men's shoes appeared on the screen.

"Now, these are interesting!"

We poured over the different sorts of shoes available while I recommend a pair of sneakers, some work boots and something casual like sandals. Darius couldn't fathom the idea of wearing open-toed shoes but professed himself willing to try when I demonstrated my own flip flops by wriggling my toes and expressing my pleasure in their comfort.

I alerted to the sound of a vehicle coming up the drive. I jumped up and ran to the front window. A white van pulled up to the porch area.

"The electrician is here. You've got to hide."

Darius slumped. "Again? All right! I'll either be in the cabin or the shed out back, or perhaps I will take a walk to the cemetery. If you have any regard for me at all, bring me something cool to drink while I linger outside. One would even do that for livestock on such a warm day as today."

I laughed and pushed at him.

"You'll be all right. I'll bring you something later. I'm sorry it has to be like this, but until we figure out a way to make you look like you belong in the twenty-first century—or at least some less historical clothing—you need to stay hidden."

I backed him up to the kitchen door.

"My clothing?" He glanced down at his suit. "What's wrong with my clothing? It is in good repair—in fact, quite new."

I opened the kitchen door and pushed him out.

"It's a hundred and thirty years out of date. Now, go!" I ran back to the front of the house and let the electrician in.

The electrician, a burly middle-aged man of few words, set to work immediately. I knew he'd worked on old Victorian houses before, so he knew what he was getting into. Once he'd done a cursory examination of the house, he gave me the news.

"This is a big house, Miss Hamilton. The wiring isn't really half bad. It's knob and tube wiring. Needs some upgrading, for sure, to get it up to 200 amps. That's what you need to run modern appliances. It's gonna take me a couple of days though. I can get started on it now, but I'm gonna need to finish up tomorrow."

"Oh! Well, that sounds great, Mr. Cooney. The plumber is coming tomorrow. Will he get in your way?"

"Nah," Mr. Cooney answered as he headed for the door. "Water and electricity don't mix too well—so we won't get in each other's way." He paused and rubbed his nearly bald head. "Except maybe when I set up the outlets for the washer and dryer."

"Okay," I murmured. What was I going to tell Darius? I couldn't possibly keep him standing outside in the heat for the rest of the day and all day tomorrow. "Well, I'll be around if you need me," I called out to his back as he went out the front door.

I turned and headed back through the kitchen and out the side door. I stalked through the unkempt grass until I reached the small shed at the back of the property. A rattling of metal caught my attention, and I peeked inside the dim interior.

"Hello there!" I called out. "What are you doing?"

Darius had thrown his jacket on a hook, folded up his sleeves and loosened his collar. He bent over a rusted push lawn mower.

"I am testing the blade. It is time to start earning my keep." He threw a grin over his shoulder. "Has the electrician come and gone already?"

"No, he's just gone to get what he needs out of his van. He says it's going to take two days to upgrade the wiring."

Darius straightened and wiped his hands. I eyed him speculatively.

"You know, you could pass for...um...modern day—if you leave the jacket off, remove the vest and take off your tie."

Darius looked down at his clothing.

"Remove my vest? Whatever for? I would feel half dressed. This suit requires a vest."

"Because then you won't have to spend half of today and most of tomorrow out here." I had a quick thought. "That is...if anyone can see you anyway."

Darius tilted his head and gave me a sly grin. "Shall we go find out?" He ripped off his tie, unbuttoned his vest and hung it up with his jacket. He gestured toward the house with a gallant bow.

"Shall we?"

I already had second thoughts.

"Okay, but I warn you. Don't mess with the electrician, and for goodness sake, don't tell him you built the house."

"Molly, I am not an imbecile!" He pretended to look insulted, but the sparkle in his eyes told me otherwise. "And what do you mean...*don't mess* with the electrician?"

"I mean...don't get in his way. I have a feeling you're going to be all over him—just don't get in his way. I don't think they like that."

"*All over him?* I cannot imagine such a sight. I think I know what you mean, but I find some of your expressions...visually revolting."

"As long as you know what I mean, my friend!" I quirked an eyebrow and gave him a warning eye.

"Yes, my love," Darius murmured docilely. I turned and walked out of the shed, hiding the broad grin that felt like it stretched from ear to ear.

I pulled open the screen door a moment later and tiptoed inside.

"What are you doing?" Darius asked behind me.

"Shhh." I put a finger to my lips and whispered. "I'm not sure what to expect. Will he see you or won't he? This is huge, Darius!"

The electrician rattled about in his vehicle, no doubt pulling out tools and other equipment.

"Why?" Darius joined me in whisper.

I turned to face him.

"Because...think of what this means. If he can see you, then everyone will be able to see you—the plumber, the mailman, Cynthia and Laura, who know what you look like from your photograph, my sister..."

"Your sister?"

"I forgot to tell you. She's coming to visit the week after next."

"Ah! A guest! I look forward to meeting her. I wonder if she is the same sister—"

"Shhh... He's coming inside."

I glided out to the living room to greet Mr. Cooney once again, refusing to turn around to see if Darius followed. I suspected I would soon find out.

"Mr. Cooney."

"I prefer Bill," he stated flatly with a nod as he looked beyond me.

I glanced over my shoulder to see Darius jump into action. He extended his hand, and Bill adjusted his tools to one hand while he grasped Darius's hand with the other.

"Oh, this is my...friend, Darren Fergland, Bill."

"Darren," Bill repeated curtly.

"The pleasure is mine, Bill."

"Well, if y'all will excuse me, I'd better get going. I'm gonna start in the basement." His face seemed etched in a permanent scowl, but that could have been from years of staring at tiny wires in dark spaces. He lumbered off as if his back hurt, dragging coils of wire, clanking tools on his waist belt and hoisting another bag of tools over his shoulder.

Darius turned to me with raised brows. "Darren? Fergland? Egads, woman. I am Irish, not German!"

"Well, I had to give you a name that no one would recognize, so there you are." I grinned without mercy.

A nearby clunking and clattering indicated Bill had found the basement stairs leading off from the kitchen and was descending the narrow opening.

"I think I should just accompany him to see what he is about." Darius turned to follow.

"Darius," I warned, giving him my sternest look. He paused for a moment and gave me one of his endearing lopsided smiles.

"Molly, my dear, I need to know what changes he is making so that I can make repairs in the future, would you not agree?"

The word "future" sounded wonderful to me. I hoped there would be a future for us.

"Please don't mention anything about building the house." That would be all we would need, I thought. Gossip about the strange man in the Victorian house in the small town, although Bill really didn't look like he talked very much at any rate.

"A foolish notion, indeed." Darius beamed and turned away. Within seconds, I heard him clattering down the stairs behind Bill.

Hours later, following a dull day of emptying boxes throughout the house, interspersed with curious visits to the kitchen where I listed to the frequent loud pop of a staple gun mingled with masculine voices, I heard footsteps coming up the basement stairs. I dashed into the kitchen to study their faces.

Bill emerged first, an unexpected toothy grin on his rounded face, followed by Darius who put a companionable arm around Bill's shoulder as they passed me with my mouth no doubt hanging open.

"Your man here knows quite a bit about Victorian houses, Miss Hamilton," Bill nodded approvingly. "Good thing he was here. Saved me a lot of time, tracing the wiring."

Darius threw me a quick discreet wink, and they walked to the front door where Bill said his farewells, promising to the return bright and early in the morning to finish the work.

Darius waved him off and turned to face me. He leaned against the doorsill and put up his hands in mock defense.

"I did not tell him that I built the house."

"I can see that," I murmured. A smile tugged at the corners of my mouth, and I shook my head. What an irresistible man he was. It seemed he had even charmed the scowl right off the taciturn electrician.

"You goof!" I punched him playfully in the arm—if only to break the spell he had over me—before I turned in the direction of the kitchen.

"Ouch!" He pretended to nurse his arm as he followed me. "I am sure the term...em...'goof' is not a compliment, but your eyes tell me it is not necessarily an insult either."

I gave him a sly smile but held my tongue, as I handed him a glass of lemonade and set a bowl of chips and dip on the table.

"This is just a snack to tide you over till dinner—whatever that will be. You missed lunch."

Darius sat down at the table and picked up a chip.

"What are these? Fried potatoes?"

I joined him.

"Yes, potato chips. You dip them in here...and eat them." I popped one in my mouth and crunched.

Darius tasted it, and then took a bite. Crumbs fell onto his shirt, and he tried to capture them as best he could.

I laughed outright.

"It's better if you put the whole thing in your mouth at once. They're messy."

"And very greasy," he noted as he reached for a napkin on the table. The next chip went into the dip, and I could see from the glaze in his eyes he was hooked.

"These are wonderful. Just wonderful," he praised.

"They are, aren't they? And they're not good for you, either."

Darius loaded another chip with an excessive amount of dip.

"Why not?" The chip went in, and he wiped at his mustache once again.

"Because they're oily and salty, and none of that is good for us." I hurried to get some dip before it disappeared.

"You have crumbs on your mustache," I noted, my gaze never far from him.

"Do I?" He wiped his mouth again.

"So, how long have you had a mustache?" I asked. "Does everyone wear mustaches...I mean, did everyone? Does..." I gave my head a quick shake and snagged another chip. "You know what I mean."

"No, not everyone. I have always had a mustache, ever since I was a young man. Why? Is it displeasing to you?" He stopped chewing and fingered the thick band of silky dark brown hair above his lip.

"I'm just not used to it," I conceded. I would have loved to see the entirety of his mouth, certain that it was as beautiful as I suspected.

"I will shave it off immediately." He rose from the table, strode from the room and could be heard clattering up the stairs.

"Wait! Darius! Wait! I didn't mean you should shave it off." I rushed after him and pounded up the stairs. He was already facing the mirror in the bathroom, my shaving cream in his hand, the disposable razor at the ready.

"Darius. Please wait!"

"No, I think I will do this. Bill looked quite comfortable without a mustache or beard." He bent down to wash his face.

"Bill didn't have much hair, Darius...anywhere."

He straightened and grabbed a towel from the rack, and shot me a grin.

"Will you be watching then? I welcome your company, of course."

I sighed, wishing I'd kept my mouth shut. It seemed as if there was nothing he wouldn't do to please me—and I needed to honor that wonderful trait of his. I had to make certain that my needs were few, to keep him from going to extreme lengths to meet them.

"Are you sure about this?" I asked.

Darius nodded firmly and lathered his face, pausing once to regard the shaving cream in his hand.

"I love this can—how the cream simply squirts out without the necessity of mixing it up. Wonderful invention."

I took a seat on the edge of the tub. "Well, yes, I'll watch then—if you don't mind."

"Not at all. You can come to my aid should I slice myself with this silly pink razor." The brightness of his grin outshone the white shaving cream on his face.

Darius stretched his upper lip over his teeth and began to scrape the top edge of his mustache with the razor. I winced.

"Don't cut yourself," I warned, suddenly anxious. What if shaving the mustache took all the character from his face? What if he suddenly became a stranger to me?

Darius glanced at me in the mirror and winked, and I sighed at the gesture. No, there was no chance that he wouldn't be as handsome—if not more so—without the mustache.

The process took a good deal longer than I imagined, and involved repeated applications of shaving cream and rinsing. At one point, Darius mumbled for another razor as the one in his hands seemed suddenly dull. I jumped up and fished another one out of the box, suspecting the pink disposable razors were never intended to shave off a mustache as thick as his.

At long last, Darius took one last swipe with the razor and bent down to rinse his face. I lowered my head to stare at my shoes, afraid to look at him. Would I recognize him?

"Well, what do you think, Molly?"

I looked up with some reluctance. Darius patted his face with the towel and lowered it to his waist. Without the mustache, he seemed suddenly vulnerable, the expressions of his mouth now fully exposed. I stared at him as my heart pulsed in my throat. His face reddened under my continued ogle, and he dropped his gaze for a moment.

As if it were even possible, he was, in fact, more handsome without the mustache than with it. His face took on a more angular look than I'd previously observed, his cheekbones suddenly pronounced. His mouth was symmetrical, wide and generous, with full firm lips, the top just a bit smaller than the bottom lip. At the moment, they were slightly curved into a tentative smile as he waited for my opinion.

I swallowed hard and plastered a playful grin on my face.

"You look very handsome, Darius. Good job!" I jumped up and passed him to exit the bathroom, suddenly in a hurry to put space between us.

He grabbed my arm. "Is that my only reward?"

I could do nothing but tilt my head back and meet his bright blue gaze. My gaze traveled to his lips—his beautiful smile.

He pulled me to him and bent to kiss me. His kiss was the same, yet different—warm, insistent, smelling of the aloe-enhanced shaving cream. I rose on my toes and wrapped my arms around his neck to bring him closer, matching the curves of his body with my own.

I thrilled when his arms tightened around my waist. I felt at home in his embrace—loved and secure in a safe world where nothing could harm me.

Where nothing could harm me? What did that mean?

I broke off the kiss and slid my hands over Darius's now smooth cheeks. He pressed his face into my palms as a purring cat might. I traced the line of his lips with my fingertips.

"Darius?"

"Yes, my love." He kept his eyes closed while I caressed his face, but he continued to hold me against him.

"I just had the strangest sensation that I felt safe in your arms—that nothing could harm me."

He opened his eyes and smiled gently. I knew I would never stop craving the sight of the movement of his lips.

"And nothing *will* harm you, love—not while I am here."

I thrilled at his words and I believed them, but I could not dismiss the strange thought.

"It was such an eerie feeling," I murmured. "I've never known danger in my life. Well, not really. Nothing more than a walk to my car at night from the grocery store. I didn't know I was feeling unsafe."

Darius's eyes darkened slightly.

"What?" I prompted.

"Nothing, love." His arms tightened around me. "I am happy that you feel safe with me. I only wish I could protect you when you leave this house." He jerked his head in the vague direction of the door.

I knew how powerless he felt at the moment, and I tried to put the odd sensation behind me to keep from worrying him. My shoulder ached again.

"Well, I don't go *out there*"—I jerked my head in the same direction with a forced grin—"that much, since I work at home. And you're here."

"That I am, my love, that I am." He bent to kiss me again. "Now go." He gave me a gentle shove. "I really must bathe. I have a lot of dust on me."

I grinned, left the bathroom and wandered down to the kitchen to find something for dinner. A pizza delivery would come in handy right about now, I thought.

Was there a pizza place in town? I realized I didn't even have a phone book yet. Aha! But I did have the internet...

Fifteen minutes later, I sat down on the couch in a state of bemusement—a large pizza on the way, to be delivered by someone at the local bar/lounge, which advertised itself on the internet as making the "best homemade pizza in Harrison County."

Darius came downstairs with a rueful smile, with Marmaduke at his heels.

"I really must wash these clothes out, but I am not quite sure what I would wear in the interim."

Relaxing on the couch and marveling at the modern world of online dining, I tilted my head and regarded him with amusement as he surveyed his clothing with mild distaste.

"Well, I could loan you my bathrobe!" I pumped my eyebrows and smirked.

Darius put his hands up in mock dismay. "No, thank you. I will just have to wash these things out tonight and hope they are dry by morning."

"I wish the washing machine and dryer were working, but they're not hooked up yet."

Darius came to sit beside me, and Marmaduke sauntered over to the window and jumped on the sill to survey his domain.

Sassy, resting on the back of the couch, immediately jumped on Darius's lap. He ran a hand along her black and orange marbled coat.

"Sometimes, Molly, I have *no* idea what you are talking about. I wonder if it would help if you spoke slower." He shook his head with a playful grin. "What is a *dryer?*"

I chuckled.

"We wash our clothes in machines now. None of this scrub board stuff anymore."

Darius nodded.

"Ah, I understand. But the wiring and plumbing are not adequate for these machines, is that correct?"

Sassy's purring grew loud. I fought the strongest urge to relocate the cat to the floor and jump onto Darius's lap myself. I knew I could purr louder than Sassy. But I controlled myself...again, and focused on the subject at hand.

"Yes, that's it. You catch on fast, Darius."

"Thank you. I have always been known as a quick study." He gave his head a mock conceited shake and pretended to preen.

The sound of a car in the drive caught my attention, and I jumped up.

"The pizza is here. That was fast!"

I scanned the living room for my purse. Where had I left it?

"*Peetsah*," Darius rose to his feet. "What is that?"

"Pizza, pizza. Food. Italian food—kind of."

I ran to the kitchen and found my bag on the counter. Grabbing my wallet, I headed back to the front door, and pulled it open.

"Surprise!" my sister squealed.

Chapter Ten

I froze, wallet in hand, staring at the apparition.

"I wanted to surprise you," Sara crowed. "I knew you'd be feeling kind of lonely in this big old house by yourself. Not to mention I thought you could use some moral support with the electrician and plumber."

I watched in horror as Sara slipped her black soft-sided bag off her shoulder and dropped it onto the porch.

"Can I come in? Are you all right?" Sara scanned my face.

I shot a desperate look over my shoulder, expecting to see Darius standing in the living room behind me where I'd last seen him, and wondering what on earth I was going to tell my sister, but Darius was not in view. Sassy had disappeared as well. Marmaduke had come to stand by my feet.

"No! Yes! I'm fine. Yes, of course, you can come in. I-I..."

Stuttering, I pulled the door open and let Sara in. Another scan of the living room and entry to the kitchen showed no sign of Darius.

"I'm stunned," I muttered. A thousand thoughts ran through my mind at the moment—none of them coherent or productive.

Sara laughed and pushed the loose curls escaping her ponytail back off her face.

"You look it. I guess I did surprise you." I saw Sara's gaze stray to the blanket and pillow on the couch, and I babbled the first thing that came to mind.

"I slept on the couch last night. You know... New house, strange sounds."

Sara dropped her bag on the floor.

"Yeah, I know. Well, might as well leave them here. I'll take the couch. You still don't have a spare bed, do you?" She rubbed her hands and looked around the room.

I shook my head in dumb silence. The complications of Sara's surprise visit seemed insurmountable...and all of them involved Darius in some way.

"No, you couldn't fit a lot of furniture in your apartment, could you?"

Another mute nod. Where was Darius going to sleep? Eat? Where was he now?

Sara brought her attention back to me. "What's up? You're quiet. It's all right that I came early, isn't it?"

Straining to listen for any sound from Darius to tell me where he was, I nodded.

"Oh, sure. Sure. Yeah, that's great." I forced myself to focus on Sara and stepped forward to give her a belated hug. "It's good to see you."

"Well, it hasn't been that long," Sara shrugged with a smile. "Like I said, I was worried about you all alone out here."

I tilted my head. *Alone? When?*

"I've been so busy I haven't noticed. Laura and Cynthia came by and took me 'out on the town' to meet the local folks, and the movers were here and the electrician and—" I pulled herself up short.

"And?" Sara moved away toward the kitchen with the air of someone inspecting a house, and I chased after her, willing myself to show a little restraint and avoid blurting out the truth—at least the truth as I understood it.

Darius. Where are you? Please don't jump out and scare her...us.

"Wow! The new appliances look great." Sara threw me a look over her shoulder. "You said the electrician had already been here today?"

I noted the door to the basement was closed. Had Darius gone down there? Was he in the back yard again? I froze for a moment. He hadn't disappeared, had he?

"Ummm...what?" I tore my gaze from the basement door. "The electrician? Oh, yes, he was here today. Still has to come back tomorrow, so most of the appliances aren't hooked up yet. But the refrigerator is running." I waved a distracted hand in the direction of the tall, two-door appliance in "bisque"—the first refrigerator I'd ever bought.

Sara opened it and peered inside.

"It's huge! What's this?" She pulled out the large square of semisweet chocolate I had bought according to Darius's instructions. "Are you binging on chocolate? This looks pretty hard core." Sara broke off a piece and popped it in her mouth before returning it to the refrigerator. "Well, Sis, it looks like I came just in the nick of time to save you from blowing up like a balloon."

Despite my anxiety, I couldn't hold back a grin. "Oh, please. I've been experimenting with making old-fashioned hot chocolate. Everything about this house makes me want to do things the old way."

Sara tossed her head in the direction of the microwave.

"Well, almost everything."

A knock on the door made me jump.

Sara narrowed her eyes. "Good gravy, Molly, you're acting like that silly cat of yours. Go see who it is."

"I ordered pizza... Maybe it's the pizza." I moved toward the door in slow motion, grabbing my wallet again off the coffee table along the way. Where was Darius? He wouldn't... He wouldn't knock at the door and pretend to be someone, would he?

I pulled open the door, with much more reluctance this time, and found a tall man in his mid-40s, standing on my porch, a pizza warmer in his hand. I blinked. He looked a bit older than the usual teenage pizza delivery boys I'd seen.

"You ordered a pizza?" he said in a flat tone.

"Yes, yes, I did. Thank you. How much?"

He gave me an amount, and I fumbled in my wallet for the money, uncomfortably aware he was peering around me to see into the house. I felt rather than heard Sara come up behind me.

"I heard you bought this place. I'm Rick, Cathy's husband. I think you met my mother-in-law, Sally, at the store yesterday."

"Oh!" My hand shook as I handed him the money. Lilium was getting smaller by the minute. "Yes. It's nice to meet you." I accepted the pizza and the hand he proffered to shake.

"So, this guy you hired to remodel, this 'Victorian specialist'—does he need any extra help?" Rick continued to peer over my shoulder toward the inside of the house. "What's his name again?"

I froze for an instant, before pulling my hand from his to balance the pizza, now burning my left hand. Out of the corner of my eye, I saw Sara's head jerk in my direction. How was I going to get out of this?

"Oh, I don't know. I could ask him. Ummm...Dari-Darren Ferland. His name is Darren Ferland. No, Fergland. Fergland."

Rick, a man of nondescript features and a two-day growth of beard, pocketed the money. "Well, let me know. I'm pretty handy with a hammer. And I live locally." He attempted to give me a pointed look, which fell short of impressing me with its message. Poor Cathy, I thought.

"Sure. Like I said, I'll check with him. Thanks for the pizza. Good night." I pushed the door shut in his face and held the pizza out to Sara. "Here, take this. It's burning my hands."

Sara grabbed the pizza while I rubbed my so-called burnt hands together and tried to think of something quick.

"I didn't know you'd hired a contractor. What's this about a 'Victorian specialist'?"

"Let's go eat first. I'm starved." I led the way to the kitchen, and we settled at the small kitchen table. I dug into my first slice with what I hoped looked like hungry enthusiasm, but the food tasted like cardboard. I turned to look out into the back yard, now shadowed as the sun began to set. Was Darius out there somewhere? I had to do something. I couldn't just let him wander around outside alone...hungry...in the dark—ghost or time traveler.

I dropped my food and lifted a napkin to my mouth.

"As a matter of fact, I did hire a contractor...and he's actually staying here." I avoided Sara's gaze and looked out the window. "I'm not sure where he is right now. Probably out back checking out the siding or something."

"What?"

I kept my gaze firmly fixed outside.

"You have some guy staying here? A stranger? Are you nuts? Where is he?"

I grabbed my slice of pizza and stuffed it in my mouth. In a brief moment of hysteria, I wondered how it tasted, because I certainly had no idea. With appalling manners, I mumbled through my food...maybe hoping to distract Sara from my jumbled words.

"Well, yeah, I know it sounds weird, but he's from Council Bluffs, and I thought it was best if he stay here...you know...so he doesn't have to drive back and forth every day."

I slid my gaze toward Sara who stared at me with a gaping mouth.

"That just doesn't make sense, Molly. I mean if you had a husband or a man around to make sure you were safe...I could understand, but a stranger? How long is he going to be here? And where is he?"

"Until the remodel is done?" I offered with a tentative smile. "I really don't know where he is right now. He doesn't exactly report to me, you know."

"So, is he the one who's been sleeping on the couch?" Sara eyed me sternly. "Why did you tell me it was you?"

I jumped up to grab a couple of glasses and a carton of prepared lemonade from the refrigerator.

"Because I knew you would say something about it," I murmured over my shoulder.

"Well, yeah! I would say something about it. I think it's pretty odd," Sara said as she took the glass from me. I sat down again, albeit on the edge of my seat.

"So, when is he going to start?" she asked with a frown on her face.

"When I get the supplies in. I have to go down to the hardware store and order them."

"He doesn't even do that?" Sara dropped her pizza. "Look, I don't know much about contracting or renovating, but don't they bring the supplies with them at least?"

I grabbed another slice of pizza from the box and shoved it in my mouth as I thought fast.

"Yes, I guess, normally, but his work van broke down. It's in the shop, and I offered to pick up what he needs."

"What?" Sara peered at me. "I can't understand you. Since when did you talk with your mouth full? Mom would have a heart attack. They're sailing around Hawaii now, by the way."

"Oh, good, I'm glad to hear they're having a good time. I've just been so busy."

"So, I've heard," Sara said dryly. "Let me get this straight. You hired a 'Victorian specialist' from Council Bluffs to renovate the house. He has no car, no supplies, no crew, and he's staying at the house with you...alone."

I chewed slowly and beamed. It sounded odd, improbable, and downright dangerous, but frankly most of it was the truth.

"That about sums it up, yes."

"Well, I want to meet this guy." Sara rose from the table. "Let's go find him."

"What? But I'm not done eating," I wailed, trying to stall. Where could he be? "For all I know, he's taken a walk somewhere...maybe up to the cemetery."

"The cemetery? Why would he do that?"

"Well, *I* don't know. *I'm* not his keeper, am I? I just hired the guy."

"Oh, come on!" Sara headed for the kitchen door, and I galvanized into action. I reached the door first and opened it, pushing the screen door open.

"Oh, Darren," I called out through cupped hands. "Darren! Are you out here?" His "new" name came awkwardly to me.

"Can I go outside?" Sara asked with a quirk of a dark eyebrow as I seemed to be blocking her exist.

"Oh, sure." I moved down the wooden steps to the grass.

"Darren! Helloooo!" I yodeled. I listened carefully but heard only the wind blowing through the corn. Maybe he really had gone up to the cemetery. My heart ached. I wanted him to come home—no matter what. This is where he belonged.

"Listen to that wind," Sara said in awed tones.

"Isn't it great?" I sighed. "It's one reason I bought the house. I love it." I turned around. "Well, I guess he's not out here." *Where was he?* A growing sense of urgency was nagging at me. *Oh, please, Darius...*

I pulled open the screen door and bumped into Darius's broad chest as I attempted to enter the kitchen.

"Hello, ladies. You were calling?" He held the kitchen door open and gave us a friendly smile.

With Sara close on my heels, I stepped past him into the kitchen—unable to warn him of anything I had told Sara.

"There you are, Darren. Look, my sister has come to visit," was the only hint I could offer him.

"Wonderful news," he murmured with composure.

"Hello, Darren. I'm Sara, Molly's sister."

I turned to see Sara reaching for Darius's hand.

"So, I understand you're staying here while you remodel the house, is that right?"

Darius slid a quick glance toward me and kept his warm smile. I thought I even detected a twinkle in the golden flecks of his blue eyes.

"Yes, that is correct," he replied without embellishment.

Sara crossed her arms.

"She says your van is in the shop. Any idea when that's going to be fixed?"

Darius sent another glance in my direction. I sank down at the kitchen table, my shaking legs unwilling to support me adequately any longer. Darius cleared his throat.

"No, it could be some time. Is this dinner? I am famished. May I?"

He pulled out a seat for Sara, who took it with a look of surprise on her face, and then he sat next to me.

He peered at the remaining pizza in the box and seemed to search the table. I knew him well enough by now to know he was probably looking for a plate. I grabbed yet one more piece of pizza, though I thought I would choke if I really had to swallow another bite, and I tapped his foot under the table.

"This *pizza* is really good. Have some more, Sara."

"Pizza..." Darius repeated the word as he followed my example and picked up a slice. He took his first bite and chewed it deliberately, as if exploring a new food, which seemed likely.

I searched Sara's face. She was definitely skeptical.

"No more for me. I'm full, thanks," Sara said as she kept her gaze on Darius who smiled pleasantly in her direction before dropping his gaze to study his slice with interest.

"Lovely. This tastes lovely. Very spicy," he murmured.

"I think it's the basil," I offered, aware of a surreal atmosphere in the room. Darius explored new foods, I primed him with hints to act normal, and Sara eyed us both with suspicion.

"Basil," he repeated. "I do not believe I have tasted basil before."

I kicked him under the table again.

"Of, course, I have heard of basil," he said airily. "I think perhaps my mother did not like basil and so did not use it." He bit into his slice of pizza again and smiled beatifically as he chewed.

"Are you from Council Bluffs originally, Darius?"

I tensed as he swallowed, took a napkin and patted his mouth.

"Yes, Council Bluffs, indeed."

"When did you get into restoring Victorian homes?"

I held my breath for the answer.

"Restoring Victorian homes?" Darius coughed behind his napkin. "Well, many, many years ago." He grinned again and took another bite of food.

I finished off my last piece of pizza and patted my bloated stomach with a groan.

"Ohhhh, I ate too much," I mumbled, hoping to add some domestic normalcy into an impossibly bizarre situation.

"I'll say," Sara said flatly. "You almost ate the whole thing by yourself."

To my dismay, she continued to watch Darius closely, though, to his credit, he managed to act as if he didn't notice. I watched Sara study his clothing, his hair, even nonchalantly looking down to his shoes. Luckily, Darius had shed his jacket, bow tie and vest somewhere.

At one point, Sara opened her mouth to speak and then closed it again, much to my relief. But she couldn't hold back. Never could.

"Are you licensed and bonded or whatever it is contractors have to be?"

"Sara!" I jumped up. "I already checked all that out. Don't worry about it. He's fully qualified to restore the house. Shall we go get your things and take them upstairs? It looks like you'll be sleeping in my bed with me—just like when we were kids." I grabbed her arm and pulled her up. "Let's leave Dari—Darren to his dinner in peace, shall we?" I threw him a quick searching look over my shoulder as I dragged my skeptical sister away. Darius relaxed back in his chair, stretching his long legs before him, and winked. I fought back a responding grin. This was going to be a long week.

I helped Sara grab her bag and took her upstairs, showing her the bathroom and the bedroom. Sara, still throwing occasional suspicious glances down the stairs, said she needed a bath, and I showed her how to work the faucets. Both Sassy and Marmaduke cruised the halls checking out the new guest.

"The plumber is coming tomorrow, so hopefully, things will be better. Here's a spare towel. Just hang it on the rod over there—" I eyed the rack with two towels already draped on it. I blushed at the intimate implications and hoped Sara didn't look at my face. She knew me very well.

"Oh!" I gulped. "Well, just hang it on the doorknob. I have to get some laundry done." I left her to bathe, shut the door, and tiptoed back down the stairs. When I reached the bottom landing, I raced into the kitchen.

Darius was cleaning off the table. I rushed into his arms and mumbled against his chest.

"I can't believe she came two weeks early. I mean, we were going to have to deal with this anyway, but I was so surprised."

Darius wrapped his arms around me. I heard a rumbling in his chest, and alarmed, I looked up. His face was contorted into a mask of laughter, and his shoulders shook.

"Well, things have certainly turned exciting, have they not?"

"This isn't funny! She's my sister! Do you think I like lying to her like this?"

He sobered. "No, my love. I do not imagine you do. Do you want me to leave? Would that make it easier?"

I reached up to curl my hands around his neck, holding on to him tightly.

"Don't you dare! Don't you even think about it. I bought this house because of you. I bought it for us—even though I didn't know if I would ever see you again. If you leave—I leave."

Darius cupped my face in his broad hands. His blue eyes sparkled.

"Shhh... There, there now. I love you, Molly. I will not ever leave you—not while you still want me here."

I pulled him to me with ferocity.

"I'll always want you here, Darius. Always!" I rose on my toes to kiss him—the man I knew I could not live without.

"Molly!" Sara called from upstairs.

We pulled apart. Darius brought my hand to his lips before he released it reluctantly.

"Yes!" I sang out as I ran my fingers lightly over his chest. "Coming!"

I moved away from Darius and climbed the stairs to find a bottle of cream rinse for Sara who was already immersed in the tub. She asked me to stay and chat.

A short while later, Sara and I descended the stairs to the smell of something sweet in the air. I followed my nose to the kitchen where Darius had laid out three cups of steaming hot chocolate on the kitchen table. He jumped up as we entered and gallantly pulled out chairs. Sara shook her wet hair, pulled back the sleeves of my borrowed robe and settled in with a wary eye in Darius's direction. I knew the treat that was in store for Sara, and I longed to show Darius my appreciation but forced myself to hold back.

"This looks delicious, Dari...Darren! Thank you!"

"You are welcome, Molly."

"Try it, Sara. Darren really knows how to make hot chocolate...from scratch."

"Really?" Sara murmured as she lifted her cup in both hands for a sip. "I thought that was you experimenting with hot chocolate."

I winced.

Darius and I watched as Sara drank. The knit lines between her eyes eased, and she settled back into her chair. A smile lightened her face.

"This *is* delicious, Darren. So, how did you make it?"

"An old family recipe. If I shared it, what need would you have of me anymore?" He pretended to mourn.

"Oh, please," Sara rolled her eyes, but a smile played on her lips nonetheless.

I chuckled inwardly as I hid my face behind my mug. Sara was falling for Darius's charm. It was inevitable. Who wouldn't? Now, if only I could keep his name straight.

"I think I'll go into town and order some of the supplies for the renovation tomorrow, Dari...Darren." I coughed to cover up the slip. "Don't forget to put a list together."

"Ah, I have it here!" Darius produced a sheet of lined paper and laid it on the table. I took one look at it and snatched it off the table and onto my lap.

"Let me see," Sara said as she craned her neck.

"It's just a list of stuff," I demurred.

"Well, let me see anyway." Sara held out her hand, and I had no excuse for not letting her see the list. I shot Darius a pointed look, but the confusion in his eyes told me he didn't know what was wrong.

Sara looked at the list and blinked.

"Wow! Where did you learn to write, Darren? Your handwriting is beautiful, almost like calligraphy. In fact, it looks like all the writing we've seen on the old census information when we were tracking down our ancestors, doesn't it, Molly? Look!" She showed me the paper, but I'd already seen it. Darius's handwriting was beautiful—a style I recognized as copperplate—straight out of the nineteenth century.

"Oh, look at that," I murmured as if completely surprised. I dared not look at Darius for fear I would either start crying or burst out laughing. At the moment, I had the inclination to do both...at exactly the same time.

"My handwriting!" Darius was nothing if not quick to understand. "Yes, I have indeed been studying calligraphy, as you say, and I am just practicing." He smiled pleasantly at everyone in general and took a sip of his hot chocolate.

"But it's not calligraphy, is it? What is this style called? We read about it somewhere, Molly."

"Copperplate," I intoned. I suspected I might as well just scream nineteenth century and tell Sara everything.

"That's it! Copperplate. The way he makes an 'f' out of his first 's'. That is so neat!"

"Thank you," Darius murmured. "I have been practicing for many years."

Sara handed the list back to me; I took it with a shaking hand.

"Why?" Sara asked as she lifted her mug.

I thought it was high time we all went to bed.

"I fancy myself a student of the nineteenth century."

"Really? Well, you picked the right job for it."

I relaxed at the conversational tone in Sara's voice. Was my smart sister really falling for all these lies? I swallowed a pang of guilt. What other choice was there? The truth? Would Sara even believe the truth, or would she try to drag me into the nearest mental health lockdown facility? And what was the truth anyway? That Darius came from another time, and we had no idea how or why?

I stretched my arms over my head.

"Well, I think I'm ready for bed. Are you about ready, Sara?" I had no intention of leaving her alone with Darius to hammer him with questions.

"Oh, sure," she said.

We rose from the table and picked up our cups to carry them over to the sink.

"Good night, ladies." Darius stood, shoved his hands in his pockets and gave us a nod. His gaze lingered on me, and I blushed, wishing I could stay with him.

"Good night, Darren. See you tomorrow," I murmured.

Sara said goodnight and led the way out of the kitchen. I followed after turning to throw Darius a look filled with all the longing I felt. He nodded, smiled gently and blew me a kiss. My knees wobbled, and I turned away to follow Sara up the stairs in a trance.

An hour later, the lights were out and I lay awake as a night breeze from the open window swirled around the room. Moonlight filtered in through the window, and I watched it as Sara slept by my side, wishing I could be with Darius more than anything in the world. I thought of him downstairs, lying on the couch, Sassy curled up at his feet, and I wondered how I was ever going to get any sleep. I wanted to be near him, to feel his warm hands covering mine, his soft lips on my face, his strong arms around me.

I listened for Sara's breathing, now steady and deep, and I gingerly pulled back the covers and slipped out of bed. I grabbed my bathrobe, shrugged it on and stepped into my bedroom slippers before pulling open the door and easing it shut behind me. I tiptoed down the hallway but a creak in the old floor made me pause. I held my breath and waited. Sara didn't throw open the door and demand to know just what I was up to.

I slipped down the stairs and headed into the living room. Moonlight filled the non-curtained room as well, and I stared at the empty couch. The blanket and pillow were neatly folded. Sassy slept on the back of the couch, but Darius was nowhere to be seen.

An edge of panic took hold of me, the same panic that seemed to squeeze the breath out of my lungs every time I couldn't find Darius—more so since I'd seem him literally disappear before my eyes in the car. I rubbed an ache in my shoulder.

"Darius," I whispered as I crept through the living room and into the kitchen. "Darius."

There was no answer.

CHAPTER ELEVEN

I moved to the kitchen door, peering into the back yard—the high grass and corn fields now a pale silver hue under the moonlight. I opened the door, holding my breath at the creaking of the screen. Hopefully, Sara hadn't heard. She slept pretty soundly.

"Darius!" I hissed from the top step of the porch. I waited. Nothing moved, except the steady wind rustling through the trees. Darius did not answer.

My teeth started chattering though I wasn't cold, and I gritted my teeth. Where could he have gone? I re-entered the house and returned to the living room, slumping down onto the couch. I didn't think I could go through this turmoil and anxiety every time I couldn't find him. But it seemed likely that I would. Whatever force or spell or act of nature that brought him to me remained a mystery. And I would never know when he might disappear again as he had.

The cemetery! Where else could he be?

The thought of creeping back upstairs to find shoes seemed risky at best. I had no idea what to say if Sara awoke. I wriggled my toes in my slippers, jumped up, tightened my bathrobe and headed for the front door. I lived in the last house on a long county road. No one was going to see me wandering around in my jammies.

I opened the door, and Marmaduke ran past me to get outside. He accompanied me down the driveway to the road.

"No, you stay here," I told him. "I don't want any of my men disappearing by coming out to this road." I hurried up the road—thanking my lucky stars the moon was almost full, providing me with adequate light to see the way. Ten minutes later, I reached the entrance to the cemetery.

The wind gusted up on the hill, even more so at night, and my hair flew around my face.

I hesitated to shout for Darius. The idea of standing about a cemetery screaming for someone—and I didn't know that he wasn't a ghost yet—was even too much for me to contemplate as "normal."

"Darius," I whispered. I moved up the path toward the oak tree.

"Darius?" I dared to raise my voice just a little. But the rustling of leaves in the oak trees drowned my voice.

"Molly! What are you doing here, love?"

I shrieked as Darius came up behind me and enfolded me in his arms. I twisted and grabbed the lapels of his jacket, giving him a shake.

"Why do you keep disappearing on me? I can't handle it. I'm terrified I'll never see you again."

"I am sorry, Molly. I did not mean to worry you. And here I am thinking that you are safe and sound tucked up in your bed without a care in the world."

I tilted my head back to gape at him.

"Without a care in the world? You must be joking. Since I met you, I've had nothing but worries."

Darius *tisked* with a half smile. His white teeth gleamed in the moonlight. He pulled me closer, and I wrapped my arms around his waist as he rested his chin on top of my head.

"I know, love. I hate adding to your concerns. I fancied myself your protector, the man who would ease your burdens."

The wind encircled us, and I smiled.

"You are all that, Darius. Though I seem to worry a lot more daily, I think that's probably the price of love. I wouldn't have it any other way."

Darius bent to peer into my eyes. The moonlight allowed me to see the hope on his face.

"So, you *do* love me," he said with something that sounded like wonder.

"Yes, Darius, I love you. I love you with all my heart. I don't think I've ever loved anyone else," I said simply.

He brought his mouth down on mine and kissed me with a passion that drew the strength right out of my body. I clung to him, reveling in the feel of his lips on mine, the strength of his arms around my waist.

He lifted his head and smiled tenderly.

"We had better get you back home. It is not seemly for you to be traipsing about a cemetery in your nightclothes." He grabbed my hand and led me down the path whitened by moonlight.

"Why did you come here tonight, Darius?"

"I could not sleep. I could not sleep last night either."

"What's wrong? Why can't you sleep? Do you sleep?"

Darius chuckled.

"Yes, I sleep, dearest. Not as much as I was once did though. I must admit to laying awake these past few nights since I 'arrived,' thinking of you, missing you, wishing I were with you, holding you in my arms, laughing with you, kissing your lips."

I melted, and my heart swelled with love. "You certainly do know how to flatter a girl, sir."

Darius squeezed my hand. He led me away from the road.

"Where are we going?"

"By the path that runs down the hill through the woods. It has always been there. You and I used to walk it as we came up here to the hill to enjoy the wind. Apparently, it is still safe for me to travel, as I have used it to go back and forth between the cemetery and the house."

We entered a line of trees at the end of the cemetery, and followed a small footpath down the hill. The wind continued to shake the leaves overhead, but the slope blocked any breeze.

"I still don't understand how you think you've known me in the past."

He squeezed my hand. "Not just 'known' you, Molly. Loved you."

I could almost believe him.

"I wish I could remember," I murmured. My shoulder ached for just an instant.

"Perhaps you will someday."

We reached the house in less than ten minutes and came out into the side yard near the pond. Marmaduke met us at the edge of the trees and followed us as Darius led the way toward the front door. I pulled back.

"Wait! I don't want to go inside yet. I want to stay with you."

"You read my mind," Darius murmured. "Come, sit with me here."

He lowered himself to the love seat and pulled me down beside him to rest in his arms in a half reclining position. I nestled into his embrace and listened to the beat of his heart against the side of my face. We sat together in companionable silence while Marmaduke settled himself into one of the chairs and watched us with interest.

"Molly." I heard the rumble of Darius's voice against my ear.

"Yes?"

Darius's embrace tightened. I felt a tremor run through his hands.

"I want to marry you. I want to have children."

I stiffened at the unexpected words and held my breath, a million images racing through my mind—not all of them pleasant. I pulled out of his arms and straightened, trying to read his expression in the dark.

"How?" The simple word hung in the air between us, summing up everything that was wrong.

Darius sighed and reached for my trembling hand. I couldn't steady it, and I couldn't stop the horrible rush of images in my mind. I pulled my hand from his and jammed it into my robe pocket. He stared at me for a moment, tightened his lips and rose slowly from the love seat, moving to stand by the railing with his back to me. I felt the loss of him almost immediately and ached to slip into his arms once again, but I held back.

Children? How?

"So, we come to the crux of the matter, I see." Darius's voice held a hoarse note that seemed distant.

I remained mute, unable to tell him what I feared.

"Molly?"

"Yes." I watched his stiff back. My shoulder ached.

"Am I so repulsive to you?" A break in his voice caught at my heart and twisted it painfully.

"No, Darius! No. I love you." I jumped up to stand at his side, but his body emanated an aloof rigidity that kept me from touching him.

"Then how shall we proceed?" He grasped the railing. "Do I just live here, always a ghost or—if you had your way—a time traveler?" Skepticism filled his voice. "Am I to go away when the house is finished? How will you explain my continuing presence to your sister, your family, your friends—without the benefit of marriage, without a future?"

I rubbed an exhausted hand across my eyes. If only it were still five minutes ago—when I was in his arms.

"I don't know, Darius. I haven't thought that far ahead. I'm willing to marry you. That's not the problem."

"Ah!" he said on a bitter note. "Children."

"Yes," he dragged out of me. "Children. How can we have—" I bit my tongue, unwilling to say more. Any words now would only hurt us both and could never be retracted.

"How can we...?" He prompted as he inclined his head to look at me. I pretended to stare straight ahead into the moonlit front yard though I watched him from the corner of my eye. "Shall I finish for you? How can we have children when I am...as I am?" He sighed the last words. His shoulders slumped.

"As you are," I repeated in a gentle voice. "What are you exactly, Darius? We don't even know." I shrugged helplessly.

Darius dropped his head to stare at his hands on the railing.

"I do not know. A ghost?"

I wiped away a tear that ran down my face.

"Sometimes, when I look at you," I breathed, "all I see is the man I love, and I want to be in your arms...forever. But every now and then, I remember where you came from, and I wonder if I'm losing my mind." I grabbed the railing as if to hold onto something tangible.

"And so you fear some monstrosity from our union." The words were out, and I couldn't bear to hear them. I nodded mutely in the darkness.

Darius turned to me, but I resisted looking at him. One glance from his eyes, and I would be lost forever.

"I understand, my love. I truly do." He remained silent for a moment. His voice, when he spoke, held a finality that broke my heart. "There will be no children. We will not marry."

"But—" I broke in with desperation.

Darius held up a hand. "I will not come between you and a normal life among the living. When the house is finished, I will leave." He stared into the darkness. "You have made me see that my dreams have been selfish, that I have been thinking only of what I wanted, and not what is best for you."

"Please, Darius—" I tried to break through the unyielding words. This wasn't what I wanted at all.

"No, Molly. This is as it should be. I love you, and I believe you love me. But we have no future together. I would not keep you from living a full life, with a husband and children."

"I'll marry you, Darius!" I whispered, but I spoke into the wind because Darius had swung on his heels and walked away toward the side of the house. Marmaduke jumped up to follow. I wanted to run after him as well, but I held back.

Children. I had always wanted children. But the images in my mind haunted me. I shuddered. I didn't know if Darius was a ghost or a time traveler, and I wasn't sure it mattered. But children...

I pulled open the door and went inside. Darius had not come in through the back door. I wrapped my arms around my stomach to think of him wandering around outside—alone, rejected. I stared at the couch, longing to lay there and keep vigil until his return, but Sara would be awake in a few hours, and I suspected that I had better be up there when she did.

****

When I opened my swollen eyes in the morning, Sara was already awake and dressed. I dressed quickly, anxious to see if Darius had returned. We came downstairs to find him sipping a cup of hot chocolate in the kitchen. My relief to see him still there was palpable, and I offered him a tentative smile.

"Good morning, Darren," Sara said. "Do you have any of that

chocolate left?"

"Certainly. Let me pour you both a cup." With a return smile that did not reach his eyes, he rose and prepared two more cups. My stomach rolled over to see him so distant, and I found breathing difficult.

Eager to please him in every way but one, I made plans to run down to the hardware store and get the order ready.

"Darren, Mr. Cooney, the electrician, will be here soon. Are you going to be working with him again today?" I met Darius's flat gaze. The gold-flecked sparkle in his blue eyes was gone, and I bit my lips together against a cry of anguish.

"Certainly. I would be happy to work with him again today." His voice lacked that subtle laughter that I loved.

"We should be getting a package today as well. You'll remember we ordered a few things?" I did my best to talk around the subject of the clothing we had ordered for next day delivery.

Sara, eating a bowl of cereal, gave me a curious look but said nothing.

"Yes, of course." He turned to look out the kitchen window, and I wished I could find a rock to crawl under somewhere. While Sara ate, I sat there silently watching Darius's rigid back, feeling guilty and wrong and very unhappy. I could only take the misery for so long before anger set in to help me stave off the pain.

"Well, that's that then," I pushed my chair back with a clatter. "Are you ready, Sara?"

Sara looked in no way ready, having managed to eat only half her cereal, but she jumped up and carried her bowl to the kitchen sink.

"Sure, let's go," she said.

I turned my back on Darius and marched out the door, completely unconcerned with whether Sara followed or not. Luckily, Sara had parked her small blue rental car on the side of mine, so I didn't have to stand around while she maneuvered her car out of the way. I had every intention of pulling out in a cloud of dust—for Darius's benefit!

We got into the car, and I searched my handbag for my keys with an occasional glare toward the house. I certainly didn't want Darius to think I was reluctant to go. I was more than happy to leave the house! Happy!

"So, is something going on? A lover's quarrel?" Sara buckled her seatbelt and grinned.

"What? No! What a silly thing to say!" Having finally found the blasted keys, I accidentally dropped them on the floorboard and glared at my sister.

Sara threw up her hands. "Whoa! I'm just kidding." She glanced at the house and sighed. "He *is* a handsome man, though. Do you think he's married?"

I ignored her comment for a moment while I bent double to find the keys. Managing to retrieve them, I jammed them into the ignition, and kicked the car into reverse.

"Well, I'm sure I don't know, but I do know that *you're* engaged...last I heard."

I would have loved to peel out of the driveway with tires screeching, but the best I could manage was the cloud of dust.

"Oh, yes, dear Brad." She smiled angelically. "But I'm getting married, not dying. Isn't that what men say?"

"Something like that," I muttered under my breath. I drove down the road with a white-knuckled grip.

"Hey, I know! As long as Darren is already staying at the house and likes Victorian homes, why don't you just marry him? That way he can keep up the house. And I'll bet he makes beautiful babies..." Sara sighed with a backward glance.

I jerked my head toward my sister and lost control of the wheel. Luckily, I'd already been driving slowly on the dusty country road. I slammed on the brake before the passenger front tire went into a drainage ditch.

"Molly! What is the matter with you?" Sara shrieked as she braced herself on the dashboard. "You just about ran us off the road."

I gripped the wheel and froze. "I'm sorry. I'm sorry. I don't know what I was thinking. I turned to look at you and then...zoom...there went the car. I must have jammed on the accelerator."

"Well, good gravy, calm down." Sara tightened her seat belt and eyed me with a frown. "It's a good thing there's no other traffic on this road. Do you want me to drive?"

I shook my head. "No, no. I've got it."

"Okay, well, let's go. Turn your wheel to the left so you don't run us into that ditch."

"Stop being so bossy!" I barked as I pulled back onto the road.

"Well, learn to drive better."

"Fine!"

"Fine!"

We looked at each other, though I only took my gaze from the road for a split second, and started to giggle. That exchange had always signaled the end of an argument for us, and I was glad. I hated fighting with Sara.

We pulled up to Nesbitt's store. Sara ogled the old brick building.

"Well, this sure isn't what I had in mind when you said hardware store. No chance they have fabulous carpets and great lamps for me to gawk over while I wait for you to do your business?"

I wrapped an arm around Sara's shoulder, still feeling the sting of snapping at her...and still in shock over the irony of her innocent teasing comments.

"No, I don't think he's got any room for all the good stuff. Pretty much just tools, nails, nuts and bolts. I don't even know if he has to order the lumber from somewhere else. Probably."

Sara paused. "Why are we buying this stuff again? Isn't Darren supposed to be doing all of this as the contractor?"

I couldn't quite remember myself. My lies had become so convoluted.

"Oh!" I remembered with relief. "It's because his van is in the shop."

"But why didn't he just come with us to place the order? Isn't it easier for a contractor to do that than you?"

Sweat broke out on my forehead.

"Ummm...because he needed to stay at the house and work with Mr. Cooney."

"Oh, that's right." Sara grinned and followed me into the store.

"So, what can I do for you today, Molly? Are you ready to order those supplies?" Bob stood behind a small dented and nicked wooden counter that looked as if it were original to the building.

"Hi, Bob. Yes, I am. This is my sister, Sara." Sara gave him a brief wave before she wandered off to inspect the small store.

"I have a list here. Are you ready?"

"Well, why don't you just leave it with me, and I'll get to work on it right away? I might have to order some stuff. Could get it delivered by tomorrow maybe." Bob reached for the list, but I had anticipated that.

"You know I would, but the contractor's handwriting is really hard to read." I squinted at the paper. "I'll just read it off to you, if you don't mind."

"I'm sure I can read it," he said with a faintly condescending smile as he reached for the paper.

I snatched it out of reach and parried his thrust. At least, I suddenly felt as if I was fencing.

"Probably not," I said firmly. "I had to ask him to read everything for me again. Let me just read it off to you."

Bob sighed, and picked up a notepad lying near the old-fashioned cash register.

"Okay. Shoot," he intoned as one showing a great deal of patience.

I read off the supplies while Bob wrote them down. I noted his occasional sighs and the odd shuffle from foot to foot—no doubt indicating I was putting him out by requiring his undivided attention, but I didn't care. There were no other customers in the store, and I still hadn't forgiven him for suggesting the house be torn down. I smirked and continued reading the list.

Sara cruised by a few times, her hands clasped behind her back, looking as bored as possible.

"Okay, that's it—for now."

Bob dropped his pencil and stretched his fingers.

"Well, that's enough to get a real nice head start on a remodel. I'm going to have to call down to Council Bluffs and see if they have a few of these things. I'm not even sure they use some of these tools anymore. This contractor of yours... Not a fan of power tools?"

I grinned. "Oh, I'm sure he is. We'll be ordering some of those soon."

Sara glided up to the front.

"Ready?" she asked with a nod in Bob's direction.

"Sure," I said. "Thanks, Bob. Call me about delivery."

"Sure thing, Molly. Nice to meet you, Miss."

Sara led the way out the door.

"What's this about power tools? Don't tell me Darren doesn't even have tools?" She lifted her brows.

"Oh, well, yes. Well, no." I thought fast. "You're not going to believe this, but his tools were stolen from his van. Can you believe it?" I hurried toward the car. "That poor guy. So much bad luck."

"You're right," Sara muttered when she climbed in the passenger side. "I don't believe it."

"Let's drive down to Council Bluffs and pick up a few things for the house at the store. You know... Some new sheets and stuff. I need curtains," I rattled on as I backed up onto the quiet street.

"Sounds good! We'll have lunch there."

"Great!"

"I still think there's something very fishy about your contractor, Molly. He may be a dreamboat and charming as he can be, but no car, no tools, and strange clothes worry me."

"He comes recommended," I said with finality. "So, I was thinking long, lace curtains for the upstairs bedrooms. White. What do you think? Oh, and I guess I should get a second bed. For guests..." I beamed at Sara and turned onto the local highway toward the interstate.

We spent an enjoyable afternoon picking out linens and accessories for the house, sisterly jibes and giggles abounding. I fretted several times that I hadn't had a chance to let Darius know we would be gone all day, but then I remembered that Darius and I were at an impasse...estranged for the moment. My shoulders slumped at the lonely thought. I did my best to shove it to the back of my mind in Sara's lively presence, and I picked out things I hoped Darius would like.

After a stimulating day in the city, we pronounced ourselves ready to return to the house and rest our weary feet.

I turned to pull into the driveway, and hit the brakes, throwing Sara slightly forward for the second time that day.

"What is it now?" Sara glared at me.

I stared at the driveway. The electrician's van was not there. In its place was a long, dark town car. And on the porch, seated comfortably on the pillowed wicker furniture, were Laura and Cynthia, along with a smiling Darius.

"Oh, you've got visitors. Those are the two ladies you bought the house from, right?" Sara's calm voice normalized everything.

"Yes," I said shortly. "What are they doing here?"

I caught Sara's curious look out of the corner of my eye.

"Well, I'm sure they just stopped by to say hello and see how you're doing. Just being nice, you old hermit. You'd better drive up there, or they'll think they're not welcome."

I gave Sara a startled look.

"Oh, dear, I am being rude, aren't I? And they're so sweet."

I pulled the car forward slowly, catching an odd flash of a pale blue from the porch.

"Besides, it looks like Darren has been entertaining them."

I gritted my teeth. Would the older women recognize him? Even without his mustache?

"I'll get the bags later," I murmured as I parked alongside the town car.

"Well, I see he finally found a change of clothes," Sara snorted.

Chapter Twelve

With my gaze riveted on Darius, I tripped on the first porch step. A change of clothes, indeed! My jaw gaped. He relaxed in one of the easy chairs, ensconced in a fairly snug-fitting pair of blue jeans. Light brown work boots and a faded light blue denim long sleeve shirt completed his look—that of a modern day man. Apparently, the clothing we'd ordered had been delivered.

I grabbed the handrail to steady my steps. He looked magnificent in modern day clothing, and I dreaded the day he would disappear from my life.

"I'm afraid we stopped by without calling," Cynthia called out. "I know that's rude. But we met Darren here, and he's been very hospitable." She beamed. "We've just been hearing his plans for renovation of the house."

I opened and closed my mouth. Cynthia, Laura and Darren each savored a glass of lemonade and looked to be on the best of terms. The blue of Darius's shirt enhanced the color of his eyes. I dragged in a steadying breath. Darius smiled pleasantly, but his eyes failed to sparkle when his gaze met mine.

"No, no, I'm glad you stopped by." I turned to Sara. "Here's my sister, Sara. You met when I bought the house. She's staying with me for a while."

"May I get you a cold lemonade?" Darius offered as he rose. I ran my eyes up and down his tall, handsome frame, and I dropped into the nearest chair, due mostly to my weakened knees.

"Sure, that sounds good," Sara said as she took a white wicker chair.

Darius didn't wait for my answer before he went inside.

"Darren said you've been shopping. I think he was expecting you back earlier." Laura, who'd been watching Darius enter the house, turned back to us. I cringed. Did she recognize him?

"We went down to Council Bluffs and bought some things for the house. I didn't tell Darren how long we'd be."

Cynthia glanced over her shoulder toward the front door and leaned forward to whisper.

"He certainly is a handsome fellow, Molly. Where did you find him?" She waggled her eyebrows.

My cheeks flamed. "He's just here to remodel the house. It seemed easier if he stayed here while he was doing it because he lives in Council Bluffs—I think."

I ignored Sara's sharp look. Swimming in a confusing sea of lies, I didn't know which end was up.

"Well, you need to find out if he's married, Molly," Cynthia twittered. "You don't want that one to get away."

"He's not married," Sara affirmed. She drew her brows together and turned to me. "Is he?"

"Cynthia, leave the girl alone. Maybe she's not in the market for a romance right now." Laura shook her head and eyed me with sympathy.

I pressed my lips together, wondering if heads really could explode. It certainly felt like mine would at the moment.

"Who doesn't love romance?" Cynthia mused with a dreamy look in her faded sky blue eyes.

The screen door opened, and Darius returned, setting two lemonades on the small glass-topped white wicker table in the center of the group.

"Thank you, Darren," Sara said. I mumbled something similar.

"You are welcome." He reclaimed his seat.

"Well, Molly ordered the supplies for the renovation this morning," Sara said after a sharp look in my direction.

"Oh, wonderful! Maybe we'll get to see some of the restoration before we leave next week."

"I am sure you will, ladies. I hope to begin as soon as the materials arrive."

"Some of them should be delivered tomorrow. Did the plumber come?" I swung a quick look in Darius's direction.

"Yes," Darius nodded. "He came. The task was more than he anticipated, and he will have to return tomorrow with more supplies."

"Oh." I couldn't hide my disappointment. I was ready to do some laundry. "And Mr. Cooney? Did he finish?"

"He's a good guy. Done lots of work for us over the years," Laura interjected.

Darius nodded. "Mr. Cooney came and went. The electrical wiring has been updated. I can show you later, if you like."

I nodded and looked away, devastated by the polite but blank look in his eyes when he spoke to me. I would have done anything to bring back the love that made his eyes sparkle. Anything, except...

"I was just saying to Darren before you arrived that he looks a bit familiar, doesn't he, Laura?" Cynthia chimed in. "Maybe like an actor?"

I froze. Sara cocked her head with interest. "Really?"

A dull red flush crept up Darius's face. He dropped his gaze for an instant and raised a self-deprecating hand.

"Please, ladies. I have never aspired to the stage in my life. I am a simple carpenter."

"No, I think someone in the movies," said Laura as she cocked her head and studied him.

"Moovees?" Darius repeated the word slowly. I shot him a warning look, but his attention was on Laura.

"What about that one actor? The one in that one movie set in... Where? It was a western. A romance." Laura turned to her sister. "You should know, Cynthia. You love romances."

"I don't know which one you're talking about, Laura dear, but I can see Darren as the lead of a romantic western." She beamed again while he fidgeted in his seat.

"Would you like to see what we got for the house today?" I piped in with an overly bright smile. "Why don't I just go get our bags and then you can tell me what you think of our rugs and curtains and stuff? Could you help me, Darren?"

I jumped up with an urgent look in Darius's direction. He rose without hesitation and strode down the porch to the stairs.

"Well, this is getting awkward," I mumbled under my breath as I opened the trunk.

"I admit to feeling somewhat...inspected. It is as if my...nieces...seem to know what I look like?" He ducked under the trunk hood to reach for bags.

"Of course, they know what you look like, Darius. I told you there was a photograph of you in their box of family photos. You still had the mustache, of course, so I think they haven't recognized you...yet." An imp urged me on. "And Cynthia practically swooned over it...if that's still a word today."

Darius lifted his head and hit it on the hood.

"Ow!" he muttered, rubbing a spot on his head with his free hand. "Swoon, indeed," he fumed.

I crossed my arms. "Oh, yes. Cynthia has had a crush on you for years. As did her mother."

A dull red stain colored his cheeks. "Good gravy!"

"I'll say," I muttered.

Darius straightened with all of the bags, and I grabbed several from him.

"I was thought to be quite homely in my youth," he murmured.

I turned to eye him, modern in clothing but still Victorian in speech. "I find that hard to believe." I stalled. "Are you all right with all these questions from the women? Is there anything I can do to help?"

Darius met my gaze. The flat expression in his eyes almost brought me to my knees.

"I am holding up reasonably well. I can manage. It is not for too long at any rate."

He turned and moved away.

"Darius, please," I whispered almost to myself.

He paused. His back stiffened, and then he stepped forward without a backward glance.

I looked skyward for a moment, my hands too full to attempt to wipe my eyes. As soon as the quick tears receded, I plastered a smile on my face and hurried back to the porch.

An hour later, the ladies left, and I announced I was going to make supper on the new stove that was now functional—according to Darius.

"What do you think about grilled cheese sandwiches? I may not be much of a cook, but I can whip a few of those up!"

Sara looked up from the kitchen table where she read a magazine and sipped a cup of fresh coffee from the newly purchased coffee pot.

"Sounds good."

"Dariu-Darren?" I called. He had gone into the basement, and the door stood open.

I heard his footsteps on the stairs. When his head emerged, I marveled again at how charming he looked in modern day denim.

"Would you like a grilled cheese sandwich for dinner?"

Darius wiped his hands on a rag.

"Grilled cheese?"

Sara's head lifted. I winced.

"Do you mean melted cheese?"

"Haven't you ever had a grilled cheese sandwich?" Sara asked.

"Yes, yes, of course. We called them melted cheese in our house." Darius wiped his hands more vigorously. "Yes, that sounds lovely. I will be downstairs. Call me when supper is ready."

He made a hasty escape, and Sara turned to me.

"Is it just me, or is there something distinctly odd about that man?"

"Hmmm?" I turned away and bustled about in the kitchen, pretending not to hear. I relished the increased brightness of the lighting with the new wiring, but at the moment, I could have used a little more shadow on my face.

"Nothing," Sara muttered. I stole a glance at her from under my lashes. She continued to stare at the empty door leading to the basement with a frown marring her usually happy face.

To his credit, Darius bit into the sandwich as if he'd been eating them all his life. He didn't scrunch his nose or bat an eyelash when he tasted the processed American cheese—a product I was certain did not exist in the late nineteenth century. He happily snacked on the potato chips which accompanied his sandwich, pausing often to wipe his fingers on a paper napkin.

I watched Sara watch Darius but relaxed when I saw that Darius had the situation under control. He'd become quite the expert at subterfuge—as had I. I kept my attention on my food, unwilling to see Darius go through the pretense of smiling at me without really smiling.

Hours later, I still lay in bed wide awake, thinking about Darius and wishing I could creep downstairs to see him. I imagined marriage to him and all the complications that process might involve such as birth certificates and identification. I continued to shy away from any thoughts of children though, still unable to cope with the unknown.

Sara slept soundly beside me, and I envied Sara her fairly uncomplicated life of career as a teacher, engagement to a successful attorney, and mutual plans to have three children, one within the first year. No human life was without its difficulties, but Sara's life came very close to near perfection. She worked hard at stability, much like our father, a retired college professor of economics. I took after my mother—a dreamer, an artist who taught art history at the local community college when she felt like it.

I rolled on my side into the fetal position and sighed. I missed my mother and wished I could talk to her. But they were out of reach on the cruise.

I shrugged mentally. I couldn't discuss Darius with my mother at any rate, but it would have been nice to hear her voice.

Sara turned over and mumbled something unintelligible. I closed my eyes and hoped for sleep.

****

It seemed as if only moments had passed when I smacked my alarm clock to stop its incessant beeping and rolled out of bed, certain that I had not slept at all.

"Why is that thing going off?" Sara mumbled from under the covers.

"The plumber is coming this morning," I answered as I fumbled in my dresser for a T-shirt and shorts and dragged them on. The breeze coming into the now sunny room felt wonderfully warm, and I welcomed the chance to wear shorts instead of the usual jeans suitable for cooler Pacific Northwest summers.

"You can sleep in if you want," I murmured. "There's no hurry to get up." I left the room and paused in the hallway to listen for Darius. Dishes clattered in the kitchen, and I ran into the bathroom to rinse my face and brush my teeth before tripping down the stairs.

"Good morning," I said breathlessly as I stepped into the kitchen. I caught my breath. Darius, in his light blue denim shirt with the sleeves rolled up to his elbows, continued to make my heart flutter.

"Good morn—" Darius turned from the stove and stopped short, his gaze riveted on my legs. "What in the world are you wearing?"

I looked down at my knobby knees.

"What? Shorts." I looked back at him and saw a dull red stain on his cheeks. He looked away quickly and returned to stirring something in a saucepan on the stove. His back was rigid as he spoke to me.

"I would say they are very short, indeed. Do you sleep in those?"

I dropped my gaze to my shorts again.

"Sleep in these? No. They're just shorts."

"Do you mean to say you wear those in public?" Darius's hand stilled, but he didn't turn around.

"Well, yes, of course. This is the twenty-first century, Darius. We get to do a lot of things that women couldn't do in the nineteenth century. Thank goodness," I mumbled the last words.

"So it would seem," he muttered.

"I heard that," I retorted. Feeling somehow semi-naked, I stepped behind him to open the refrigerator in search of something to drink.

"Good," he threw back. "I am preparing hot chocolate. Would you like a cup?"

I stiffened. I should say no, I thought.

"Sure." I turned a shoulder on him and went to stand at the back door looking out onto the fields beyond, doing everything in my power to prevent myself from running upstairs and switching the shorts for jeans.

"The plumber should be here soon," I muttered.

"Yes."

I refused to look at him. Fine! If that's how he was going to be...

"Some of the supplies should be delivered today. I'm not sure which," I tried again.

"Good."

I took a deep breath to loosen my jaw.

"You have lovely limbs. I always wondered..."

Startled, I swung my head to look at him, but he continued to stir the saucepan. The lobes of his ears beneath his chestnut hair glowed red. The corner of his mouth twitched. He raised his head and looked at me, the twinkle back in his blue eyes—at least for the moment.

"Thank you, Darius," I choked, holding back a laugh. "So do you."

"Nonsense." He turned away to pour the hot chocolate into two cups. A third cup stood by. "Does your sister still sleep?" He kept his back to me for a moment. I sighed. It seemed as if I'd seen more of his back than his face over the last few days.

"Yes. She always liked to sleep in—ever since she was a little girl."

I gazed at the curve in the small of his back, emphasized by the cut of his jeans. We'd forgotten to order a belt, I realized. Against my will—or maybe propelled by my will—I moved toward him and wrapped my arms around his waist, pressing my face against his back.

"I love you, Darius," I murmured against his back.

Darius stiffened. I closed my eyes and savored the moment, fully expecting rejection. Warm hands covered mine.

"I love you, too, Molly. That will never change." He raised the palm of my right hand to his lips before pulling out of my arms and striding past me out of the kitchen.

With an agonizing ache in my chest, I stared at the empty doorway. I heard the front door open and close—the sound so final—a wall between us.

"Oh, no, you're not, mister," I whispered as I roused myself out of self-pity. "I'm not letting you go."

I ran through the living room and wrenched open the front door. Darius leaned against the railing on the porch. He didn't turn around to face me.

I came to stand at his side but did not touch him.

"Darius. Please don't walk away from me. I hate that. Don't run from what is wrong with us. Stay and fight. Fight for me, fight with me. I don't care which. Just stay."

Darius dropped his head for a moment. His shoulders sagged as if my words took the fight out of him instead of challenging him.

"I cannot change what I am, Molly."

"I don't want you to change." I quirked an eyebrow. "Well, I'll admit to wishing you were...not as complicated as you appear to be, but I love you just the way you are."

He turned to me then, the blue in his eyes darker than I'd seen. He took my hands in his and pulled me to face him.

"I would fight for you for the rest of my life if I thought I was the right man for you, my love—if I were not as I am." A tremor ran through his hands. "But even I repulse myself. I shudder at the thought of what I must be."

I moved against him, pressing myself into his arms. He held me against his chest in a tight embrace.

"How do we know you're a ghost, Darius? Where is your tombstone? Are you buried in the cemetery?" I leaned back to watch his face.

"I do not know," he said quietly.

"Do you remember dying?" My voice squeaked. What a stupid thing to ask. How did one remember dying?

"Molly." He gave me a slight shake as if to snap me out of my fantasy. "Of course I do not remember dying. How could one know that? One moment, I was in the cemetery, standing over a grave, and the next moment, I was here...in your time."

I grabbed the front of his shirt. "I know it's crazy, but what if there is a chance that you traveled through time? A chance that you're actually alive. Not..."

He covered my hands with his. His smile, though patient, seemed dubious.

"How would we know?" he asked with despair.

In unison, we both turned our heads toward the road at the end of the drive.

My heart began to race.

"No!" I said with an anxious look in his direction. "Absolutely not."

"We must find out some day, Molly." He squeezed my hands. "*I* will find out some day, Molly. Why not today?"

"Oh, no. That's not what I meant. I don't know what I meant, but no, no, please don't go out there." I gave his shirt a tug.

Darius cocked his head and bent to kiss my lips.

"If something feels wrong, then I will step back onto the property. I do not know what happens beyond the colors and the weakness. What if I wait it out? If I can make it to the road without...disappearing, that will prove that indeed I am no ghost. Perhaps you are right. Perhaps I am not...undead after all. Perhaps there is hope for us."

He pulled my hands from his shirt and moved past me. I grabbed his hand.

"Oh, no, you don't," I almost growled.

No match for his strength, I felt myself in tow as Darius stepped down from the porch and onto the dirt and grass drive. Marmaduke, having watched us with curiosity from the love seat, jumped down to follow.

"Darius, please don't do this." I tried digging my heels in, but Darius continued moving forward. I clung to his hand with all my might.

"Come, Molly. Watch over me. I may need you if I go too far."

"No, I don't want you to do this. What if you can't come back? Stay with me, Darius. Please don't leave me."

We reached the end of the drive, and I pulled against him.

Darius turned to me and took my other hand.

"Molly, my love, I would not knowingly leave you. I cannot bear the thought either, no matter how much I threaten to do so." He turned to look at the road. "But if there is some other recourse for us, I must discover it." He raised my hand to his lips. "Watch for me, my love. If I begin to fade, come for me and bring me back." He disengaged his hands from mine and turned resolutely toward the road.

Fighting back the terror that threatened to freeze me into place, I followed, trying to direct my focus on the task at hand. I had no doubt he would begin to disappear once again. Could I bring him back before it was too late?

I primed myself to jump.

Darius took several hesitant steps onto the dirt road. The rigidity of his body revealed the extent of his concern, and that frightened me even more.

"You don't have to do this, Darius," I whispered.

Darius looked down at his feet and turned to me with a hopeful half smile.

"I am still here," he murmured. He raised his arms and gazed at his palms.

And then it began.

CHAPTER THIRTEEN

Darius's hands took on a transparency that began to spread to his arms. His smile faded, and he turned to stare at me, alarm in his eyes.

"Molly!" he said urgently. His knees buckled as if he were about to faint.

"Darius!" I screamed as I lunged for him. I wrapped my arms around his chest as he sagged against me. I faltered. His weight was too great. I couldn't pull him from the road. I fell under him, hitting the dirt with a thud, and Darius fell against me...at least what was left of him.

Sobbing with terror, I threw a frenzied glance over my shoulder. Only four feet to the drive. I could do this, I swore! Marmaduke ran back and forth across the entrance, meowing, tail twitching, the fur on his back standing on end.

Out of the corner of my eye, I saw Sara running down the path toward me, shouting something, but I could not hear her words.

"Help me, Sara," I tried to scream, but I couldn't hear my own words.

A dizzying kaleidoscope of images flashed across my consciousness. Darius stood over a grave in the cemetery, blood dripped from my shoulder, long skirts hampered escape, a man shouted at me. I clutched at Darius, but I could not feel him. Our surroundings whirled around us like a vortex. The wind picked up and blew my hair around my face. Blackness descended, and I felt myself slump.

****

"Molly? Molly? Can you hear me?"

I lifted heavy lids to see Darius's face close to mine. We still sat on the dirt road, but Darius now held me in his lap as he had that day at the cemetery. Had I fainted again?

"Darius?"

"Thank goodness you are awake, Molly."

I jerked upright. Everything came back to me. Darius stepping into the road. His smile. The transparency of his hands. I stared at him with wonder and grabbed his shirt.

"Darius? Are you still here?" I looked past him and saw something that seemed completely out of place. I distinctly remembered a crop of corn growing across the road—tall, green, luscious stalks that swayed in the breeze. But now the corn was gone, replaced by a much shorter field of something resembling green hay.

"I am, my love, but I am not certain that we are where we were." He followed my gaze. "Something is not quite as it was only moments ago."

I pulled out of his arms and struggled to my feet. A wave of dizziness caught me by surprise. I put out a hand to steady myself and Darius caught it as he stood.

"Do you feel well, Molly?" he asked.

"I think so," I murmured with a hand to my head. I looked over at the field of hay once again.

"Wasn't a field of corn over there this morning? I could have sworn..."

Darius glanced over his shoulder and returned his gaze to my face.

"I think you should turn around, my dear. It seems you were right."

I turned slowly, avoiding another wave of dizziness, and followed Darius's gaze toward the house.

I gasped and squeezed his hand.

There, before me, stood the house—no longer sporting faded pastel paints and a dingy white porch. The house shone with fresh gray paint and bright white trim.

I took an involuntary step back. Darius grabbed me into his arms and steadied me.

"Where are we?" I mumbled, straining to focus on the house, though I had a feeling I knew. The small bushes separating the yard from the road in no way resembled the massive hedges I'd grown accustomed to. The tall oak trees to the right of the garden seemed little more than saplings.

"Well, my dear, it appears that we are at the house, but it seems we are now in my time. The house is as I left it. This must be 1880."

I thought I might faint again, but the strength of Darius's embrace kept me on my feet.

A rumbling sound from the left caught my ear, accompanied by snorting and wooden creaking. I looked down the road, and saw a wagon pulled by two horses.

"Is that a wagon, Darius?" I asked incredulously.

"Come, Molly, we must get you into the house. I may be able to explain your presence, but I cannot explain away your bare limbs." While I gawked at the unusual sight, Darius grabbed my hand and whisked me down the dirt path toward the house. I threw a last look over my shoulder at the approaching wagon. A bent figure hunched over the reins, a dark wide-brimmed hat shading his face. He was still too far away to see distinctly. The jingling sound of the livery sounded as if it came straight from a Western movie.

I followed Darius toward the house in a daze past a fairly well-manicured lawn, the smell of freshly cut grass in the air. He pulled me onto the porch and strode toward the door. The white paint of the porch gleamed, accentuating the graceful dark black wrought iron furniture. Darius pushed open the door and pulled me inside with a quick glance over my shoulder. I followed his gaze, amazed that I could see the length of the road without the tall hedges. Two dark horses continued to mosey along the road as if the driver had all day.

Darius shut the door behind us, and I caught quick impressions of the house before I turned to Darius. The living room looked familiar yet different as Darius had furnished it with blue and rose upholstered couches and chairs. Delicate lace curtains fluttered in the breeze of the open windows.

"What's happening?" I leaned into him, disoriented, confused, wondering if I was caught up in a dream.

Darius wrapped his arms around me.

"Mr. Ferguson, is that you? Where have you been?" The warbling female voice was soon followed by a plump matronly woman in a brown ankle-length dress with a white apron tied around her waist. She stopped short when she saw us.

Darius put me behind him—as if he could hide me.

"Ah! Mrs. White. It is so good to see you again. Have I been missing for a while?"

I peeked around Darius's back to see that she stood stock still with her jaw gaping open. I don't know who she was more shocked to see—Darius or myself. She seemed astonished to see us both.

"Oh, my goodness, Mr. Ferguson. We had no idea where you'd gone. You simply disappeared without a word." I heard a note of reproach in her voice, but I also heard genuine affection and concern. I knew exactly how the woman felt. Loving Darius was not always an easy task.

"Yes, I am so sorry, Mrs. White. Circumstances beyond my control..." Darius kept me at his back and gave me a quick reassuring squeeze. At least, I hoped it was meant to be reassuring. If it were a warning to run, I didn't act on it.

"And you said I've been gone how long?"

"Several days, Mr. Ferguson." She wiped her hands on her apron and attempted to peer around him. "Bring the young woman out, Mr. Ferguson. No one is going to hurt her."

"Yes, well, the problem is, Mrs. White...em...she has had a mishap and is not quite...properly dressed." I almost burst out laughing to hear Darius struggling with this explanation. His first attempt wasn't going very well.

"Yes, Mr. Ferguson. I can see from her bare legs that she wants for some proper clothing. Perhaps I could provide an old bed sheet or something until..."

"That would be lovely, Mrs. White. Yes, if you would be so kind."

"I'll take her upstairs with me, shall I, and help her with it?"

I gave Darius's arm a strong tug, willing him not to leave my sight.

"Ahh...Mrs. White. Perhaps if you would just direct me to where you keep the spare bed clothing, I could assist her."

Her expression of astonishment accelerated into a look of shock.

"Oh, Mr. Ferguson, I am sure that it would be more proper if I—"

I could feel Darius's tension in his grip on me.

"You are right, Mrs. White, it would be more proper if you were to assist her, but I will maintain as much propriety as I can—given the unusual circumstances. Do you keep the old bed linen in the hall closet upstairs?"

"Yes, Mr. Ferguson," she acquiesced. "Can I make you some tea?"

"That would be wonderful, Mrs. White. And then you may leave. Miss Hamilton and I will manage by ourselves for the rest of the day."

Mrs. White had been about to turn away when she stopped abruptly. She turned back to stare at Darius.

"Miss Hamilton?"

"Yes, Mrs. White, Miss Hamilton." Darius's subdued voice frightened me, holding that note of grief I'd heard before.

"Miss Molly? Is that you?"

"Not the same person, Mrs. White," Darius said sharply. "Please leave us." He softened his tone. "I will see you tomorrow. I may need your assistance then."

I had the distinct impression that something was happening which I didn't understand.

Mrs. White paused and nodded her head. "I am so pleased, Mr. Ferguson, so very happy for you. Whatever I can do, Mr. Ferguson, please let me know."

"Thank you, madam. If I could ask for your discretion... Please do not speak of this to Mr. White or your children just yet. I need...I need time."

"As quiet as a church mouse, Mr. Ferguson. You can depend on me."

"Thank you. Good day, Mrs. White."

"Good day, Mr. Ferguson. Good day, Miss Hamilton."

"It was nice meeting you," I chimed from behind Darius's back.

Mrs. White, in the act of turning away, paused and looked back at us—confusion obvious on her face. She shook her head and turned away again to head for the kitchen.

Darius released me and put his fingers to his lips for a moment. The side door opened, and Mrs. White stepped outside with a bonnet on her head. She walked around to the front of the house and headed down the driveway. We watched her from the living room picture window. She turned back once at the end of the drive to stare at the house for an instant and then turned right and disappeared from view.

"Darius! What was that all about?" I looked down at my legs. "I mean I know I'm not dressed very well...for 1880"—I gave him a pointed look—"but there was something else going on there."

Darius pulled me into his arms, his smile bright, his blue eyes twinkling like stars. He seemed more joyous than I had ever seen him. He picked me up and swung me around.

"Nothing for you to worry about, Molly, my love. Nothing at all."

I couldn't help but relish his moment of joy, though I suspected it was because he had returned to his time. I was thrilled to see him so happy.

He put me down but held onto my hand.

"Would you like to see the house, my love?"

"Yes, I would. Show me your house, Darius!" I laughed. Because it was his house now, long before I came along and bought it, before Cynthia and Laura were born, before Sara and I were born.

"Come," he said, and he pulled me up the stairs—the wood highly varnished and free of scratches, the stairs without creaks—to the second floor. He threw open the main bedroom door, and I peered in to see the walls gleaming with white paint. Landscape paintings adorned several of the walls. The highly polished wood floor sported a luxurious oriental carpet of blue and gold. A massive four-poster bed topped by a very thick, comfortable looking blue quilt crowned the room. A cherry wood highboy and matching dresser completed the furniture. My window seat had a blue velvet cushion on it, and I crossed the room and looked out the window.

The pond sparkled under the direct midday sun. The small saplings that would soon grow to be massive trees fluttered in the breeze. I squinted toward the hill in the distance. I could see no tombstones from this vantage point.

"The cemetery is still very small, only a few stones or so. You will remember I donated it to the town, but that was just last year."

I held onto his hand and nodded. My shoulder ached a bit, and I absently rubbed at it as I stared out the window. Darius placed a warm hand on my collarbone, and I turned to him with a smile.

"Your shoulder continues to hurt," he stated quietly.

I looked down at his hand and covered it with my own.

"Yes, I guess it does. I don't know why." I shrugged. "Let's see the rest of the house," I urged.

We left the master room and peeked into the second bedroom. It was fully furnished with another four-poster bed, dresser, wall cupboard and an armchair of gold velvet. There was no seat beneath the window in this room.

I turned to him. "This is a lovely room. Do you live with someone or is this room for guests?"

He shrugged. "No, I live alone. I have a guest now, though, so perhaps we should negotiate who should have which room?" He grinned. "Do I take the master bedroom because it has always been mine? Or do you take the master bedroom because it is now yours—or at least it is in your time?"

I chuckled with him. "But we're not staying that long, are we, Darius? I have to get back home. Sara will have called the police by now. She must be beside herself. She saw us disappear."

Darius took a deep breath and stared at me. I tried to read his expression, but he wasn't giving anything away. An awful thought occurred to me. Surely, he didn't want to stay in his time, did he?

I dropped my gaze. But, of course, why wouldn't he?

"Darius," I tugged at his fingers, "I can't stay here. In fact, I'm half tempted to run out to the road now. I need to find out what happened after we left."

Darius stiffened, and he gripped my arms.

"No."

I jerked and stared at him. His face took on a mulish look. I'd seen it before—narrowed eyes, his chin prominent, a muscle working in his jaw.

"Darius! You don't get to tell me no, no matter what year you think we're in." I wriggled and he loosened his grip.

Darius stared down at me.

"Please don't go out there, Molly. Don't force this decision on us. We are together now. I am not dead, I am not a ghost. That is what you wanted, is it not? What we both wanted? Don't tempt fate."

I backed up a step.

"Darius! I don't want to leave you either, but I have to know if I can get back...when I need to."

Darius reached for my hands.

"Please don't go yet, my love. I do not understand what is happening, but I do not want to lose you right now. What if I cannot return with you? What if I am destined to stay here...in my own time?"

I watched in stunned silence as he took both of my hands and put them against his lips.

"You came once," I mumbled half-heartedly.

"Do you want to risk it again?"

I shook my head.

"No, I don't want to take the chance, but I can't stay here, Darius."

"Stay for a while. Now that I am back, I have some matters that I have to attend to. Then we will try to travel together. I will return with you...forever. Marriage and children?" He bent to peer into my face.

I blushed and threw myself into his arms, all fears resolved in that respect.

"Marriage and children," I breathed against his ear.

He captured my lips with his for a long, languorous kiss before raising his head to gaze into my eyes.

"I love you, Molly Hamilton."

"I love you, too, Darius. I'm so glad you're not a ghost."

"As am I, my love. As am I." He gave me a hard embrace before setting me from him. "We must find something for you to wear, and I fear I must change out of these very comfortable garments."

I sighed and walked over to the window in the spare room. The view was similar to the master bedroom.

"Why can't I just wear my clothes—if I can't leave the property? I suppose I can't step out into the road like you couldn't, right?"

Darius came to stand behind me at the window and wrapped his arms around me.

"I assume if you step into the road, you will disappear...return to your time. But there is still a chance that someone might come to the house and see you, perhaps in the garden?" He chuckled. "It certainly happened enough to me while I was in the twenty-first century. You seemed to have many visitors. And Mrs. White will return in the morning."

I raised my face to look at him.

"I have to be honest with you, Darius. I'm very worried about Sara. She'll probably send an emergency message to my parents—after she calls the police and reports my disappearance...our disappearance. And the cats. Who's going to take care of the cats if she leaves the house and goes back to Seattle? I can't stay, Darius. I have to get home."

His grip on me tightened.

"Wait! Wait a day or two. I cannot go with you until I have set my affairs in order, and I am afraid that if you leave without me—I will never be able to reach you again."

I swallowed hard. I could not bear to lose Darius. I turned to him and pressed my face against his chest, listening to the rapid rhythm of his heart.

"What affairs do you have to set in order? Can you tell me?"

His chest rose and fell with a deep breath. He set me from him, keeping his hands on my shoulders and peered down into my face.

"I have to prepare a will. If I leave without designating heirs, it is possible the land and house will pass out of the family. Then it will not be yours."

"Oh," I whispered. I couldn't contemplate such a horrible thought. What if someone bulldozed it? Someone like Bob Nesbitt?

"I need to go into town and see the attorney."

"Yes, you do," I urged. "What if we returned and the house wasn't even there..."

His face looked grim as he nodded.

"Just so," he said. "And the land is turned over to farming."

I shuddered.

"Oh, Darius. I can't imagine. I don't even want to think about it."

"So, you will wait for me?"

I nodded quickly.

"I will wait for you," I whispered.

He pulled me into his arms and buried his face in my hair.

Just then, a thudding sound near the front of the house caught our attention. Darius ran out of the room and down the stairs, with me in his wake. The jingle of livery tinkled, and I could have sworn it sounded like someone pulled up in front of the house on a horse—just like out of a Western movie.

Darius ran to the picture window in front and pulled the curtain aside just an inch to peer out. I peeked around him. I could hear a horse snorting, but I couldn't see anything from this angle.

"Go," Darius whispered urgently. His grim expression and set jaw frightened me. I froze, not knowing what he wanted me to do. My shoulder burned, but I ignored it. "Go now. Run upstairs and lock yourself in the bedroom. Go now!"

I gaped at him for a moment, but obeyed without question. The sounds of heavy steps on the porch galvanized me to dash for the stairs. I ran up them as silently as I could, throwing terrified glances over my shoulder. I couldn't leave Darius down there alone! I just couldn't.

I paused at the top of the stairs, where Darius could not see me from the living room or the front door. A pounding on the door below raised the hair on the back of my neck.

"Ferguson. Open the door. Where is she? Where's Molly Hamilton?"

I gasped. Me? Who was looking for me? In 1880? What was going on? My heart pounded in my throat and my mouth tasted like dust. I flattened myself against a wall, unable to see what was happening.

I heard the front door open quietly, and Darius's controlled voice.

"Calm down, James. She is dead. You should know that. Your brother killed her."

"Then why did Old Man Briggs say he saw her—not half an hour ago—out there on the road?" the voice shrieked. "If my brother hung for something he didn't do, I'll find her and kill her myself," he raged.

"She's dead, James. I don't know what Mr. Briggs said, but he didn't see Molly. And if they hadn't hung your brother, I would have killed him myself." Darius's voice was unlike how I'd ever heard it—deadly, filled with venom and hate. I couldn't begin to understand all the references to Molly's death. Had she died violently? My shoulder burned.

"You da—" I heard a scuffle at the door, and I ran down the stairs with some ridiculous plan of interfering between two raging men. I was just in time to see Darius punch a red-faced, blustering blond man in the jaw who staggered back from the doorway. James fell onto his backside and jumped up quickly, rubbing his jaw. His eyes widened, and he stared beyond Darius—to me.

"Molly Hamilton," he spewed. "You witch. I knew it. You didn't die after all." He wiped at his mouth where spittle gathered. "You let them hang my brother," he said as he spat in my direction. Darius jumped in front of me and hid me behind him as he had earlier from Mrs. White.

James looked up at him.

"She's going to prison for this, Ferguson. If they don't hang her first," he raged. "Murderer!" he screamed. "She murdered my brother as sure as she killed him herself."

"This is not Molly, James," Darius ground out between his teeth. "Molly is dead." I trembled at his words and he pressed me tighter against him. I didn't know what nightmare I had awakened in, but I was absolutely certain I wasn't going to go to prison. Was I?

"I don't think so, Ferguson," James blustered. "Just wait till the sheriff and the town hear about this. I hope they get a lynch mob together."

"James! Wait!"

James disappeared from view, and I heard the sound of his footsteps running off the porch. Darius released me and ran after him. I heard James bellowing what sounded like obscenities, but I didn't recognize any nineteenth century curses. I peered around the corner to see James mount a brown horse and race away down the drive, turning right when he reached the road.

Darius chased him to the road and stared after him as he galloped away. Then Darius turned and ran back toward the house, bypassing the porch to run toward the back.

I ran out the door and around the side of the house just in time to see Darius run into the shed, although it was in much better shape than the one I was familiar with. I chased him inside just in time to see him step into a stall, grab the halter of a large, black horse, pull himself onto its unsaddled back and urge it forward.

"Darius!" I yelled. "What's going on? Where are you going?"

"Stay here!" he shouted. "Get back inside and lock yourself in. I will return."

I dug my heels in. He was leaving me? In the wrong century?

"Please, Molly, go inside," he yelled. He spurred the horse forward, and they flew out of the back yard kicking up dirt and sod. I ran around the corner of the house to see Darius thunder down the drive and turn right. If I hadn't been so confused and terrified, I could have admired how absolutely wonderful he looked astride a horse.

I ran back inside the house and toward the front door to peer out the windows, but Darius had disappeared from view. I slumped to the floor and hugged myself, fighting an overwhelming sense of anxiety, and wondering what to do. My shoulder ached, and I couldn't breathe.

Darius was heading to town—I didn't doubt that for a moment. I didn't know whether he was going to try to stop James from telling everyone about me—about Molly, that is—but something awful was going to happen. Darius seemed to have murder in his eyes, and I couldn't just sit here and cower if I could do something to help.

Surely, I could do something to stop what seemed to be an impending disaster. Coming from the twenty-first century, I had to know something that would be useful in the nineteenth century. Couldn't I convince them that I wasn't Molly? That I really had come from somewhere else? I was sure I couldn't even try to convince the authorities that I had actually come from another time.

I pulled myself up and peered out the window. No one was in sight. I pulled open the door and peeked outside. All seemed quiet, save for a few birds chirping nearby and the small trees rustling in the wind. I ran out onto the porch and down the steps, jogging toward the road. I pulled up short at the end of the drive and peered down the road to the right—where Darius had gone. I knew the road was not long, only about three miles back to town. Surely, I could jog that distance in good time. I had no plan once I got there, but it seemed likely I would see Darius's horse somewhere.

And Darius had made it onto the road without disappearing. Could I? Of course, the implications for my pending return to the twenty-first century were at stake if I didn't disappear, but I couldn't worry about that now. I needed to stop whatever was going to happen.

With moisture on my upper lip and a knot in my stomach, I stepped out onto the road...and I had my answer. A kaleidoscope of images featuring Sara, the cats, the bright blue and pink Victorian house and a cemetery dotted with white tombstones sent me into a dizzying vortex, and I couldn't see anything. I thrust my hands out blindly ahead of me but felt nothing. My knees buckled and I felt faint. Which way back to the drive?

A pair of strong arms lifted me up into the air and I landed on my stomach over a hard surface...a surface that bounced. Still blinded by the myriad of rotating and colorful patterns reminiscent of a speeding photographic presentation, I kept my eyes closed for a moment. The distinctive smell of horsehair tickled my nose, and I opened my eyes.

"I told you to stay in the house. Yet somehow, I knew you would not, so I returned."

I looked over my shoulder at Darius, astride the horse and holding me as I lay on my stomach draped over the horse's back. We were back in the grassy driveway. Darius brought the horse to a standstill, slid down and pulled me with him.

"Forgive me for throwing you over the horse like a saddle bag, but I saw you disappearing, and I knew there was no time for the niceties. I thank my lucky stars that I returned in time." Darius's voice was husky. "It seems you cannot go beyond the property line—just as it was for me."

I hung my head, still shaken and light headed.

"I thought...I thought I could help. I thought I could try to explain."

Darius pulled me to him and bent to whisper in my ear.

"There is no explanation that will satisfy James, my love. No one will believe that you have come from another time. I could not bear to lose you, Molly. Please do not attempt to leave without me again. We must go together when we go, or we will be parted forever. It is my greatest fear."

"Where were you going? What were you going to do? Why does this James think I'm your Molly?" I recalled bits of the words I'd heard. I clutched at his shirt. "Someone killed her, Darius, didn't they? And he hanged for it?"

Darius sighed and covered my cold hands with his warm ones.

"Let me take you back into the house, Molly. I must go after him, before he—" He didn't finish. "I will return as soon as possible.

Then...we can talk."

I allowed him to lead me back into the house. He bent to kiss the tip of my nose.

"I will return," he murmured. "Please stay here. It is not safe for you out there."

He strode out the door, and I followed his progress from the window, my heart cold in my chest. Once again, he pulled himself onto the horse's back and galloped out of the driveway in a cloud of dust. I could do nothing to protect him because I could not follow him, and I could do nothing to protect myself because I wasn't quite sure where the danger lay. Running into the road to return to the future—if that's where I traveled to—without him, wasn't an option. I might lose him forever, and I might lose the house.

I hugged myself and turned away to face the house that I loved almost as much as I loved the owner. The sense of the surreal continued as I studied the details of the living room—the bright red of the bricks on the fireplace unsullied with no evidence of prior smoke, the bright white paint on the walls, the unmarred sheen of the highly varnished floor. I wanted to commit it all to memory, so that I could re-create the house in its original image...the house that Darius built and loved.

I crossed the living room and dragged myself up the stairs to the bedroom, ever alert for the sound of hooves signaling Darius's return. I wondered what Darius would do to try to resolve the situation. It certainly didn't sound like James was going to listen to reason...not that there was any "reason" to offer.

Restlessly, I entered the bedroom and sank down onto the window seat. Sara would be so worried. I didn't want to imagine Sara's terror when she saw us disappear, especially since I had disappeared with a man she didn't trust.

I tried to steady my nerves with several deep breaths, my ears alert for the sound of a horse's hooves. As my gaze roamed around the room, a wooden trunk at the foot of the bed caught my eye, and I rose to open it. Though the style of the trunk appeared old-fashioned, the brass latches seemed to be quite new, and they opened easily. I lifted the lid and peered inside.

The smell of cedar and some other scent, something sweet like lavender, drifted up from the inside of the trunk. Of course, I was snooping, but anxiety made me forget good manners. I wanted to know as much about Darius as I could before I left the nineteenth century.

The trunk seemed to hold mostly paper, not the blankets one would expect from a bedroom trunk. I picked up a stack of envelopes tied together with a blue satin ribbon. The handwriting was exquisite, much like Darius's copperplate but smaller, more petite, more compact. The letters were addressed to Mr. Darius Ferguson, Lilium, Iowa, and the return address read Miss Molly Hamilton, Lilium, Iowa.

My hand shook as I looked at the return address. *Hamilton?* Her name was Hamilton? Like mine? My knees buckled, and I dropped down to the thick oriental carpet in front of the trunk. I hung onto to the side of the trunk, resting my head against the rim as I struggled for air. I felt like I was suffocating—as if my lungs would not even try to drag in air. My pulses pounded in my ears, and I looked down at the packet of letters in my hand again. This was no coincidence. It wasn't possible. A thousand thoughts ran through my mind, not the least of which were—was I adopted? Had *I* somehow traveled through time to the twenty-first century? None of these seemed likely. Sara and I looked alike, and I had very strong memories of playing in the backyard in Seattle with Sara when I was of preschool age.

I settled for some form of odd panting—one might call it rapid, shallow breathing—as I pulled open the ribbon on the letters. Was it okay to read Darius's letters? No, but I really didn't care at the moment. I ignored the guilt and opened the top letter.

The paper was thick, like the old logs and records I'd seen in my genealogical explorations. A date was penned at the top right hand: 1 June 1879. So, the letter had been written last year...in Darius's time.

My dearest Darius,

I so enjoyed our picnic together yesterday. I miss you every moment that we are apart, and I cannot wait to marry you so that we may be together every day and every night for the rest of our lives. You and I have talked at length about our future marriage and how best we can approach my family with our good tidings.

Jack is a difficult situation to resolve, and I do not know yet how it can be done. My father and his father combined their farmlands many years ago, and they have always been set on seeing Jack and I wed. I never knew of these plans when I played with Jack and James as a child. But I am very certain that I would not have married him, even had I not met you! Marriage without love would never have been possible for me, though my own parents seem content with their arrangement. My mother once confessed to me that she did not even know my father when she came west to marry him. I cannot imagine living such a loveless life.

But that does not matter. I do not live a loveless life, but one filled with joy and the hope of a bright new day when you and I will be together forever. We will overcome these difficulties, and I believe with all my heart that you and I will live happily ever after. I am as certain of this as I am in your love.

Until tomorrow, my love, Your Molly

Tears flowed freely down my face, and I ran a tender fingertip along her signature. That she had loved Darius was unquestionable. I swallowed down a lump in my throat. And that I loved him was unquestionable. What woman would not have fallen in love with a man like Darius? Handsome, kind, intelligent, full of life, funny, affectionate, passionate, and straight out of the nineteenth century. It was only natural that I would fall instantly under his spell.

I put the packet down, unwilling to intrude any more on their relationship. I peered in the trunk once again. Several photographs caught my eye, and I picked up the top one. It was the portrait photograph of Darius—the one Cynthia and Laura had let me have. He had his mustache in this one. With it or without it, he was devastatingly attractive. I kissed the photograph and laid it aside. The next few photographs appeared to be of a couple—the man sitting, the woman standing next to his chair. I turned it over. Someone had written in black ink on the back. Mother and Father, 1879.

I turned it over again to study it. A handsome couple. The pose was typical for the portrait studios of the time. Yet the photograph looked new...for a sepia-toned picture, that is. Darius shared his father's thick wavy hair and apparent height. The lean length of his father's legs were apparent even when he sat. He seemed to have his mother's generous mouth. Though she was not smiling, as was the custom in photographs at the time, I thought I could still detect a light in her eyes. I suspected he had inherited her sense of humor. I gave them a kiss for raising Darius and put that photograph aside.

The next photograph was a portrait of a young woman, and it was this picture that I supposed I'd been looking for. Before I looked at it closely, I turned it over, and was not surprised when I saw "Molly Hamilton, 1879" written on the back in the same script I recognized on the letter.

Lightheaded from holding my breath, I released it and dragged in some air as I turned the photograph over. Her face was in a partial profile. Dark hair was pulled away from her face and piled into some kind of bun high on her crown. Soft curls seemed to escape to hang down the side of her neck. Curly bangs adorned her forehead, making her dark eyes sparkle as she looked at the camera. Her full mouth showed no expression, and yet it appeared soft and given to easy smiles. The face was set off by a high-collared dark dress with a hint of lace just under her firm chin.

I supposed I noted all of this in a split second, because I stared in shock as I realized the face that looked up from the photograph was the face of the woman of my dream the other night—and that face was mine.

Chapter Fourteen

The sound of hooves caught my attention, and I pulled myself up with one hand by bracing myself on the trunk while I held the picture in the other. I ran from the room and paused at the top of the stairs. I crouched down on my knees so I could see the door. What if it was this James character back again? And for all I knew, I either was Molly or I looked a lot like her, and his brother had hung for her death.

I was debating on what to do, on the vague assumption that I would know if it was James by the yelling, when Darius strode through the door, still wearing his blue jeans and denim shirt, his hair appearing windblown. His gaze went immediately to the stairs, and he crossed over to look up at me. His grim expression told me things had not gone well, but he seemed unhurt, and that was all I needed to see.

"Molly, my love. Thank goodness you did not try anything foolish while I was gon—" He stopped when his gaze dropped to my hand. He stared at the photograph with an indecipherable expression on his face.

I held the photograph up with a shaking hand. "I can't pretend to understand what this is, Darius, or how it happened, but I do believe that your Molly and I look alike." I tried a grin, though my chin shook.

Darius moved to speak, but I rattled on.

"And this James thinks that I am your Molly. He thinks that I'm responsible for his brother's death, is that right?"

Darius took a step up the stairs, and I put out a hand to stop him.

"I should leave, Darius! My presence here is endangering you. For all I know, they think you've been hiding me...Molly, that is."

Darius's shoulders sagged.

"He has already begun spreading the rumor that you are here—that *Molly* is alive—and that his brother died in vain. I saw the sheriff and denied everything. I said that you were a cousin come to visit from back East. I am not sure he believed me, but he has promised to watch for James and apprehend him if he makes any further threats." He raised his gaze to my face with a grimace. "We are fortunate that Jack was not well liked in town, and his death was not unwelcome. But James has vowed to—" He bit his lip and stopped.

"He said he was going to kill me, Darius. I heard him."

I turned cold and shivered, and Darius grabbed me and pulled me against him.

"I will not let him harm one hair of your head, Molly. If necessary, I will deal with James myself, as I did with his brother. They will not take you from me again," he whispered. "But you are right. You must to return to your time...I cannot go with you yet. I have not had a chance to see to an attorney."

"I'm not going without you, Darius!" A wave of nausea overtook me as I contemplated life without Darius. "Forget about James. Forget about the attorney. Come with me now!" I pulled his head toward mine and pressed my forehead against his. "Please come with me."

"I am torn, my love," he said with a shaky laugh. "I want to go with you now, but we will lose the house, the land, everything I built—for us—if I do not do the necessary paperwork to leave the house to my brother."

"We'll find other land," I argued. "You'll build another house." I looked around wildly. "It's just a house," I surprised myself by saying.

He raised his head and kissed the top of my forehead.

"You may be right, Molly, but if I do not leave a will, my brother will not come and a chain of events may be set in motion that could alter the future. Cynthia and Laura are born here in this house. If this house is not in the family, and they are not born here, will they fail to exist?"

I gaped at him.

"Are you serious? I can't even figure out where you and I will be tomorrow. How can I possibly try to guess the outcome of our actions on future generations?" My shoulders slumped. He was right, of course.

"I know your face too well, Molly. You realize there is truth in what I say," he said as he leaned in to kiss the corner of my mouth.

He hesitated, and I raised my gaze, waiting for further bad news.

"My attorney was away on an errand to Council Bluffs and due to return in the morning. I cannot complete the necessary paperwork until he returns."

"You're a lawyer," I muttered. "Why can't you do your own will and leave it on the kitchen counter?"

He chuckled and cupped my face in his hands.

"I am not licensed to practice in Iowa, my dear, an omission I should have rectified had I known I would be in dire need of an emergency will."

I refused to laugh with him.

"I'm not leaving without you," I repeated firmly. "I'll stay here until you do what you need to do."

He sighed and kissed the tip of my nose again.

"I am selfish enough to be pleased to hear it, Molly. I was trying to be noble and self-sacrificing when I suggested you should return at once—without me, but I do not want you to go. I do not know the mechanics of how I came to you in the beginning, and I fear that I will not be able to get back to you if we are not together when we travel."

I buried my face against his chest.

"I know," I said in a muffled voice. "It seems like I can leave your time, and you can leave my time just by stepping into the road, but if we're separated—we will not be able to get to each other."

"I cannot bear the thought," Darius whispered against the top of my head.

I raised my face to look at him. His eyes were dark, and his face somber.

"How do you think you came to my time in the first place?"

He frowned in concentration.

"I do not know, my love. I was in the cemetery..." His voice trailed off. He turned to look out the window next to the front door.

"You said you were standing over a grave..." I prompted. I hadn't forgotten that piece.

His gaze flickered in my direction and returned to his contemplation of the scenery in the front yard.

"Yes," he said quietly.

"Whose grave, Darius? Can I ask?"

He returned his gaze to mine, the gold flecks seemingly gone from his dark blue eyes. He picked my hand up gently and brought it to his lips. I slid my fingers to his cheek, and he covered my hand with his own.

"Molly's," he said briefly.

Of course, I had known. I knew Darius.

"You had her buried on the hill," I said quietly. "Is that why you turned it into a cemetery?"

He pulled my hand to his mouth and kissed it again before lowering it to his lap. He did not let go but held it firmly. He turned to me and nodded, his eyes less dark than a moment ago.

"As you love that hill, so did she. Like you, she would raise her arms at the windiest point and imagine she was a bird. The first time I saw you, you were doing that. I knew you were Molly then."

I laid my head against his broad shoulder, and he put an arm around me as we continued to sit on the stairs, both of us looking out the window toward the front yard.

"We have the same name," I murmured.

"I cannot explain it." His voice was quiet, thoughtful.

"We look alike," I added.

He tightened his embrace and ran the tip of his index finger lightly across my nose.

"Exactly alike," he murmured. "The only differences between you and Molly are time and customs."

I looked up at him again with a half smile.

"Oh, yes, the customs. Like these shorts?"

He surveyed my legs, his face bronzing slightly as it always did when he was embarrassed, and he nodded silently with a broad smile.

"I'd like to go to the cemetery. I'd like to see her."

Darius stiffened and hesitated as he met my gaze.

"Is that wise?" he asked with a worried frown.

"Do you mean am I afraid to see her grave, the answer is no. It seems obvious that she and I are connected somehow. Maybe we're the same person, I don't know. But, yes, I want to see her."

I stood, and he rose with me.

"Shall we?" he asked as he took my hand. "We will go out the kitchen door. Until I hear that James is no longer a threat to you, I am using all precautions."

I followed him, my hand in his, as we crossed the lawn and climbed the path. The trees on the side of the hill had not yet grown to their full size, and marveled at how large they would become by the twenty-first century.

We arrived at the top of the hill, with me winded, and I came to a stop. Darius turned to look at me with a question on his face, but I shook my head while I caught my breath.

"This is what you must have felt when you first saw the cemetery full of stones...in my time."

"Confused?" he volunteered.

"To say the least," I answered.

The cemetery wasn't really a cemetery at all. It was just a beautiful meadow on a hillside with several small oak trees adorning it. The wind blew as I remembered it.

"It's beautiful up here," I whispered.

"It is, isn't it?"

"Where is she?" I asked.

"I think you already know," he said quietly.

I turned to stare at him, as memories flooded in—the bright stone that first caught my eye, Darius avoiding questions about the stone, seeing the stone from the house as it caught the sunlight on the hill.

I turned toward the top of the hill, and there she was, basking in the golden rays of the late afternoon sun.

"I should have known," I said with a smile. I pulled at him, and we walked across the meadow, which as yet had no paths. As I neared the top of the hill, I noted several more stones scattered throughout.

"Anybody you know?" I asked with a playful grin. I realized that my quip had been in poor taste though when I remembered that these were Darius's contemporaries, possibly people he knew. They were not just tombstones of people long dead as they would be in my time.

"I'm sorry, Darius. That was thoughtless."

He looked down at me, his eyes light with affection, and I was relieved.

"It is likely that I do know who they are, so I will not look at the names today. This time traveling business is confusing enough as it is," he said with a rueful smile.

I squeezed his hand in empathy.

We came to a stop in front of Molly's stone. The wind blew in earnest up here. She had no nearby neighbors...at least not yet. I kneeled down in front of the bright white sandstone to read her inscription.

Molly Hamilton
28 years 2 mos 4 dys
Born 1 April 1851 Died 5 June 1879
Beloved Daughter

"I was born on April 1st," I whispered as I ran my fingers along the crisp lettering. "We're April Fool's Day babies."

"I always played a joke on her for her birthday," Darius murmured behind me. He continued to stand.

I looked up at him.

"What date is it now...in your time?"

"It is the 8th of June 1880."

I turned back to look at the stone.

"So, it has been a year," I murmured. Even though I was looking at Molly's tombstone, I really didn't want to use the term "since her death." I knew Darius grieved, the tension in his body was evident, and I didn't want to push him any further.

"Yes, a year ago." He was silent for a moment. "I should have bought marble. I did not realize the sandstone would erode as much as it does."

I wanted to lay my face against his knee as he stood so close, but I hesitated to touch him in his sorrow. It seemed somehow intrusive—especially coming from me.

"We'll get a new one when we get back...if you like," I offered.

Darius leaned down and smoothed my hair.

"That would be nice. She would like that."

I gave the stone a quick sisterly pat and rose to gaze down on it. Darius wrapped an arm around my waist, and I hoped Molly didn't mind—if she could see us.

"What day was it when you came to the cemetery... before you traveled?"

"The 5th of June 1880, the anniversary of her death." He gave me a curious look, obviously wondering what I was getting at.

I turned to him.

"But Darius! That doesn't make sense. If you left here on the 5th, and today is only the 8th, then you've only been gone three days. You've been in my time for almost three weeks."

He nodded.

"Yes, I have thought of that...discrepancy. It would seem that time does not necessarily run simultaneously in both centuries." He shook his head with a puzzled expression—very similar to the one on my face. "That is to say, the length of time during the traveling does not correlate." He sighed. "See how I struggle even to attempt to articulate the situation."

I looked back down at Molly's stone.

"I wonder how long we've been gone from my time. Sara must be so frantic. What if it's been days?" I whispered, almost to myself.

The sun lowered in the sky, and dusk stole the light from Molly's stone.

"Let us hope not," Darius murmured as he tightened his arm around me and kissed the top of my head again. "We will return to your time tomorrow—as soon as I have seen the lawyer and settled my affairs."

I nodded and pushed my hair back as it swirled around my face. The wind seemed to have picked up with the departure of the sun.

"Come, the night grows cool, and you are still not properly dressed. We should return to the house." He surveyed my bare legs once again. He was right. It had grown cooler.

"I don't think I planned on cemetery hopping when I put these shorts on this morning...a hundred and thirty some odd years in the future," I noted dryly as we moved away and re-crossed the meadow.

Darius chuckled.

"No, I imagine not," he murmured. "Perhaps Mrs. White has left some food in the ice box, though if I have been gone several days, she might well not have done so."

He kept his arm around my shoulder and squeezed me against him as we walked in the direction of the house. We reached the house in the usual ten minutes and entered through the front door.

Darius closed the door behind him, and I stood in the living room, uncertain of what to do.

"Are you cold, my love? I will light the fire and make some of that hot chocolate that you like...if Mrs. White has kept some milk in the ice box."

I nodded. Hot chocolate by the fire with a handsome man whom I loved. Such a romantic notion.

"Yes, that would be great." I tried to keep my voice normal.

Darius opened a drawer of a side table next to one of the couches and struck a match to light a white glass oil lamp on the table.

"Sit and rest," he murmured as he moved to the fireplace. I sat down on the velvet sofa, noting its surprising comfort, as I watched him handle the kindling and wood with expertise. A small flame flickered and grew stronger within seconds. Darius leaned on one knee, staring at the flames—as I stared at him. The fire highlighted the waves of his hair and accented his high cheekbones.

As if he knew I stared at him, he turned and looked at me over his shoulder. His eyes seemed to sparkle...or maybe it was the reflection of the fire.

"Are you still feeling cold? Can I get a blanket for you from upstairs?"

I shook my head. I could definitely feel no chill at the moment—not when he looked at me like that.

"No, I'm fine, thank you," I said without telling him how much I loved him.

But I wondered if he could read my mind anyway. He rose and came over to the couch, placing one knee on it while he bent to press his lips against mine. I reached for him to pull him to me, and he captured my hands against his chest, lifting his head with a shaky laugh.

"Hot chocolate, I think. Are you hungry?" He smiled down at me as he ran a finger along my jaw. I wanted to grab his hand and hang on, but I held back. I sensed that Darius wasn't quite ready for the passion he incited in me...for the physical expression of my love. He was definitely old-fashioned, as they say.

"No, I'm not hungry, Darius. Are you?"

He shook his head.

"I will return shortly. I do not have your microwave machine, so I must heat the milk on the stove." He grinned and bent to kiss the corner of my mouth. He straightened, turned away, and walked into the darkened kitchen. I heard him strike another match and a glow came from the kitchen as he must have lit another lamp, a much larger one from the brightness of the light.

I wanted to follow him into the kitchen and hang around while he made the hot chocolate—just as I had only a few days ago—in my time, but I held back. I wanted to hang onto him, to wrap my arms around his waist and never let go. The image of me clinging to him while he attempted to make the hot drinks was ludicrous. It was best I stay in the living room and luxuriate in the plush, comfortable sofa that I would never again sit in as a new piece of furniture.

I slipped off my shoes, pulled my legs onto the sofa and leaned my head back to watch the flames, wondering if Darius had ever been intimate with a woman. I hesitated to wonder about Molly and him because it seemed too invasive. She was dead, and it felt wrong somehow to acknowledge that I was curious about the extent of their relationship. I was, but I didn't want to admit it even to myself.

I was a 28-year-old woman in the twenty-first century with all that implied. I was not inexperienced, nor naïve, although I expected Sara might disagree about the latter. I longed to be with Darius, but his values were not the same as mine. While he was passionate, he pulled back before our kisses went too far. He was flirtatious, but to use modern day vernacular, I suspected that was all hot air. I grinned and closed my eyes. My old-fashioned gentleman, I thought with affection. Someday, I would know the truth.

"Molly. Molly, wake up..." Darius sat next to me and shook me gently.

I opened my eyes to the continuing glow of the fire, and straightened up.

"Oh, goodness, I'm sorry. I must have dozed."

"I can imagine that you did. I hated to wake you, and perhaps I should not have." He handed me a teacup on a saucer. "Drink your chocolate. It will help warm you. Then, I think you must retire to bed."

I took the cup from him and sipped the chocolate. It was the same delicious chocolate he'd made only days before. I could almost believe that we were back in the twenty-first century, but my microfiber orange sofa couldn't compare to the luxury of the velvet sofa.

"So, I suppose there's no chance we can take the furniture with us." I grinned as I ran my free hand along the sensuous material.

"I much prefer that orange affair you have," he murmured with a bright smile. "It is very comfortable."

We chuckled simultaneously and sat together in companionable silence as we watched the fire and drank hot chocolate. I leaned against Darius's strong shoulder and kept at bay all my worries about Sara, our pending return, the wild man named James, and what the future would bring for us

I finished my cup and set the saucer down on the side table. He put his down as well and rose, holding out his hands to me.

"Shall I see you to your room?"

I looked up at him.

"Which room is mine?" I quipped, though I knew he would put me in the master bedroom. I wished he would not. It would be difficult to be in the room with Molly's letters. I remembered with a sigh that her picture was probably still on the stairs.

I knew that I would sleep alone this night. There was no chance—no chance at all that Darius would volunteer to spend the night with me. Not one single, solitary, nineteenth century chance. Not with my old-fashioned conservative lover.

"I'll take the spare room, if you don't mind, Darius."

"As you wish," he said with a puzzled smile. He led me up the stairs, stopping to pick up Molly's picture along the way. He opened the door to the spare room and stood aside as I entered. He followed me in and, as he had downstairs, he reached into a side table and struck a match to light the oil lamp by the bed.

"Just blow it out when you are ready for sleep. You know where the washroom is." He bent to kiss me lightly on the lips and then turned away. I wanted to beg him to stay with me, but I couldn't. He couldn't.

He closed the door softly behind him, and I sat down on the bed feeling lonelier than I'd ever felt in my life. And why shouldn't I, I wondered? I was lost by over a century. I missed Sara, I missed my mother and father, I missed Sassy, I even missed Marmaduke. And I would have let both Sassy and Marmaduke sleep with me in the bed if I could have had them with me.

I kicked off my shoes and lay back on the bed, listening to the sounds of the house in the night. I heard the wind blowing outside as it did even in my time. I couldn't hear Darius in the next room at all...if he was even in there.

I tossed and turned, sleep eluding me. I needed Darius. I needed to be with him. I slipped off the bed to go to his room when I heard a light tap on the door.

"Molly," he called in a low voice.

"Come in," I said eagerly. I waited by the bed as he opened the door and stepped in. He wore a satin robe over some dark trousers.

"You are lonely and feeling a little lost, aren't you?" He came to me and paused. "Somehow, I can feel it—even in the room next door."

I nodded mutely.

He took me in his arms and buried his face in my hair, whispering in my ear.

"Come to bed. I will hold you, and you will sleep in my arms."

He propped up a pillow for himself and half reclined on the bed as he opened his arms to me. I wasn't sure if I would ever be able to get to sleep in his arms, but I climbed back onto the bed and nestled into his embrace. He held me to his chest, and I listened to the sound of his heart, steady for the most part, although it sped up occasionally. I was fairly sure my own heart was doing exactly the same thing.

"Sleep, my love," he whispered.

I thought I'd lie awake all night, but I soon found myself drifting off to sleep with images of the dark curls and long skirts of a woman fluttering in the wind as she stood with her arms outspread like a bird's near the oak trees on the hill that would soon become a cemetery.

****

My eyelids flew open to the sun streaming in through the window, and I jerked awake. I was alone. Darius was gone. Apparently, he had pulled the quilt over me in the night, though I didn't remember it. I pushed the cover back and crawled from the bed. I didn't have my watch with me, so I had no idea what time it was.

What I did know was that this was the day that Darius would come back to my time with me, and we would begin our new life. If the house was still there, if we didn't travel to another time, if Sara hadn't somehow buried an empty coffin for me on the hill, if...I swallowed hard and gave myself a shake. So many ifs...

I tiptoed to the door and listened. I could hear vague sounds in the house, but I wasn't quite sure where they were coming from. The kitchen? Had Mrs. White returned?

I eased open the door and rushed across the hallway to the bathroom. It looked remarkably the same although I couldn't find any faucets. A jug of warm water had been set by some kind soul on a table near the pedestal sink, and I assumed this was for me to wash with. I cleaned my face and looked at my expression in the oval mirror. Dark shadows made me look as tired as I felt. I spotted a hairbrush and ran it through my hair before using the facility. It seemed to work in much the same way, though I had to look for a pull string on the wall to make it work.

I stepped out of the bathroom, having given up on any hope of sneaking downstairs. The water running through the pipes had given me away.

"Molly?" Darius called from downstairs. His warm voice still sent shivers of excitement up my spine. "Are you finally awake?"

"Yes," I answered quietly. Was Mrs. White down there, I wondered? I still hadn't found any "proper" clothing to wear. What would she think?

He came around the corner and looked up at me. I saw that he no longer wore the denim shirt and jeans but wore a white shirt like I'd seen him in before, a gray vest and matching trousers. He looked stunning. No matter what he wore.

"Good morning, Molly." He tilted his head boyishly as he grinned at me.

"Good morning," I whispered shyly. We had, after all, spent the night together.

"Would you like some hot chocolate this morning? Mrs. White is cooking breakfast."

"You're back in your clothes," I commented.

He looked down at his trousers with a rueful smile. "Yes, I am afraid my new clothing needs to be washed, so I donned some of my usual attire. I think it best I wear normal clothing when I go into town this morning."

He pulled his pocket watch from his vest and looked at it.

"I must go now, but Mrs. White is here and she is anxious to meet you. Will you come into the kitchen and have some breakfast?"

"Yes," I continued to speak quietly. "But what is she going to think about *my* clothing? We were supposed to put me in something." I descended the stairs and met him at the foot. I longed to reach up on tiptoe and kiss him but dared not. I saw the same longing in his eyes.

He cleared his throat.

"I will think of something to say."

"Does she know about James? Did she ever meet Molly?"

"Yes, she has heard the rumors. And yes, she knew Molly. They were extraordinarily fond of each other."

I turned to look up at him with widened eyes.

"What am I supposed to say? Won't she think I'm Molly risen from the dead?" How coarse that sounded. I winced.

Darius blinked, but his lips twisted in a smile.

"You and I will improvise. Just as we have done in your time," he whispered.

"Okay," I muttered. "Let's do this," I said, in the tone of a member of a military rescue operation. I sailed toward the kitchen, leaving Darius in my wake.

Mrs. White busied herself at the stove with what appeared to be pancakes, and despite my anxiety, my mouth watered. I couldn't remember the last time I'd eaten. Certainly not in this century.

Out of bravado and steam, I paused at the doorway uncertainly, and Darius came up behind me. He touched my shoulder quickly and lightly. He cleared his throat.

"Mrs. White, may I present Miss Sara Hamilton, Molly's sister?"

At that, I turned to look at him in astonishment, but only for a second as Mrs. White turned from the stove and bustled up to me. She put out a plump hand, and I shook it.

"Well, Miss Sara, it's so nice to meet you. I am so sorry to hear about your sister. Mr. Ferguson tells me that you are up here from one of the Southern states to visit her grave?" She dropped her gaze to my bare legs before pulling them back to my face with an effort.

I dared not look at Darius. What a concoction of convoluted lies! What a great imagination! I could never have come up with a story for my appearance...and my shorts.

"Yes, I did, thank you, Mrs. White." I didn't know how far to push it, but I tried. "It's very nice to meet you."

"I knew Miss Molly had a sister, but I didn't know that you lived in the South. What state are you from exactly?"

"Ummm...Florida," I said quickly. Was Florida already a state in the 1880s? I should have paid more attention in American history, I thought.

"Oh, that *is* a long way from here, isn't it? Did you travel by train?"

I looked up at Darius over my shoulder, cursing him with loving affection. He managed to keep a straight face, but seemed in no way inclined to help.

"Yes, by train."

"All the way to Lilium. Imagine that," Mrs. White said in wonder. "How many days did you have to travel?"

I really needed Darius's help at the moment. I had no idea how long travel took in the nineteenth century.

"I think she said approximately a week, didn't you, Sara?"

I nodded mutely.

Darius coughed.

"Well, ladies, I must go into town. I have promised Sara some of your special flapjacks, Mrs. White. I know she'll enjoy them." He ran a discreet finger along my back out of Mrs. White's sight, and I longed to turn to him and beg him to stay, but I knew he had to go.

"See you later," I mumbled toward his retreating back. To my embarrassment, a tear of anxiety and exhaustion slid down my face. I was hoping Mrs. White would miss it.

She didn't.

"There, there, Miss Sara. Come sit down, and I'll pour some of Mr. Ferguson's hot chocolate for you. He says you like it. I know your sister did."

Mrs. White led me to a well-polished round oak table nestled where my glass kitchen table sat. Five high-backed oak chairs were pushed up to the table, and Mrs. White pulled one back. She went to pour a cup of the chocolate, and I wondered how long Darius would be gone.

"Will you have some pancakes, dear?"

I nodded with enthusiasm. Mrs. White brought a lovely white and blue porcelain plate over to the table with several pancakes stacked in the middle. She poured a glass of obviously freshly squeezed orange juice and set it on the table along with silverware and a white linen napkin.

I stared at the food with admiration. The woman really could cook, I thought. I'd never imagined Darius as a porcelain plate kind of guy, which only served to remind me that there was a great deal I didn't know about him yet.

"And here is some lovely syrup direct from the New England states. It's wonderful." She set down a small glass pitcher no bigger than a creamer.

"Won't you sit and have some breakfast, Mrs. White?"

I probably sounded as pathetic as I felt, because I saw her hesitate.

"Well, Miss Sara, I've already eaten, but certainly I will sit with you."

She poured herself a glass of orange juice and sat down on the other side of the table. I gave her a small smile of gratitude and poured syrup on the pancakes.

"I understand your husband and children work here as well?" I prompted as an opening. I was sure she had questions for me, and I wasn't sure I could come up with any credible answers, so I went on the offensive...so to speak.

She beamed. "Yes, they do. My daughter does some cleaning and laundry. And my husband and son take care of the yard, the farm and the animals. They've all done their chores and gone home for the day." She looked out of the window. "Mr. Ferguson works with them during planting and harvesting season, but in between times, he works around the house."

I scooped my first forkful of pancakes into my mouth and stilled for a moment as I savored their delicious light texture.

"Mrs. White! These are delicious. So light and fluffy."

"Thank you, dear," she beamed. "It's an old family recipe. Mr. Ferguson loves them, so I made them special for him today." Her face sobered and she shook her head. "He's not been himself this last year. It was such a pleasure to see him smiling this morning and preparing his special hot chocolate." She smiled at me brightly.

I supposed I should ask.

"You know that a man named James was here yesterday."

She bit her lip and looked down at her lap.

"Yes, I know. The whole town knows by now. He's told them that you are Molly, that she didn't die after all, and that his brother was wrongly hanged down in Council Bluffs for her murder."

I stopped eating. Chills ran down my arms.

"Mr. Ferguson has gone to talk to the sheriff again, hoping to pass the word along that the woman James saw yesterday was you, Molly's sister." She looked at me with a kindly expression, but I thought I saw a note of skepticism in her eyes.

"We look almost exactly alike," I murmured as I stuffed some pancake in my mouth.

"Yes, the resemblance is remarkable."

"People used to mistake us for twins," I added.

"I certainly would think so," she agreed.

"How are your parents, Miss Sara? We haven't heard from them since they left after the funeral."

"Ahh...well, I believe my parents have traveled west," I murmured. Shouldn't I know that? "At least, they wrote to me and told me that's where they wanted to go."

"I wished they had left earlier and taken Miss Molly with them." Her face almost seemed to crumple, and I could see that she was very attached to Molly.

"Things were very difficult for her around here, Miss Sara, with that Jack threatening her and Darius." She leaned forward conspiratorially. "I heard that even your father decided Jack would be a dreadful husband for her, and he told James's father that any plans they had in the past were over."

"Really?" I mumbled, trying to tread lightly in case I made a mistake. "I'm pleased to hear my father came to his senses finally." I took a final bite of pancake and gave up. My heart ached for Darius and for poor Molly.

I rose from my chair, and Mrs. White stood.

"Thank you so much for breakfast, Mrs. White. I think I'll take a walk now."

"You're welcome, dear. I'm glad you liked the pancakes." She picked up the plate and glasses and shooed me away when I tried to help. "Take your walk now. You look so pale. The sun will do you good."

I nodded and turned toward the kitchen door.

"Miss Sara."

I turned back to Mrs. White, whose cheeks took on a rosy hue.

"I think perhaps the clothing in the South is a bit more...brief...than we are used to here in the north." Her gaze flickered to my shorts. "I think it might be best if you didn't try to go into town or anything until Mr. Ferguson finds your luggage. He said it was lost on the journey here?" she said with a lift of her eyebrows.

"Yes, that's right, Mrs. White. I lost it." How true those words were in modern day vernacular. I nodded with an effort at a grin. "I'll stay out of sight."

"I won't see you when you get back, Miss Sara...not until tomorrow. Mr. Ferguson said he won't need me any more today, so I'm just going to tidy up the kitchen dishes and go home," Mrs. White said.

I had my hand on the door when she spoke, and I turned to look at her. Little did Mrs. White know, but I would never see her again. Never. I bit my lip at the thought that someone would live and die in the time it took me to travel back to the twenty-first century.

I moved to where she stood by the sink and gave her an impulsive hug. I could feel her body stiffen for a moment before she wrapped her arms around me and patted my back soothingly.

"There, there, now, dear. What's this all about?" Mrs. White murmured. "You're upset about your sister, I know." She made consoling clucking noises as she returned my embrace.

I pulled away from her and dipped my head in some embarrassment at the unwarranted display of warmth for a virtual stranger. Although she would never know I was saying goodbye for a lifetime, I knew it was the last time I would see her. I wasn't quite sure whether Mrs. White would stay and take care of the house for Darius's brother, but I was sorry she could not return with us.

"I'm sorry, Mrs. White." I blushed. "I think I am a little bit...distraught. Thank you for letting me hang on you." I managed a slight grin.

"Oh, pooh! 'Hang on me' indeed. What an expression!" She chuckled. "There's no reason why we can't offer each other a little comfort in our times of need." She patted me on the shoulder. "Now, go for your walk. It will do you a world of good."

I smiled once again and went out the door with a backward glance over my shoulder to see that she was washing dishes. I stood on the porch for a moment, wondering what to do. I supposed I could walk up to the cemetery. I crossed the lawn and started up the path. The climb didn't take long, and I came through the trees and emerged into the meadow on top of the hill.

Even though I had seen it only a few hours before, albeit at dusk, the unfettered expanse of the field with only a few tombstones caught me by surprise. Long feathery grass drifted lazily in the wind while the small oak saplings rustled with just a promise of the majestic shade trees they would become.

I strolled along to my favorite spot on the far edge of the meadow, giving Molly's stone a pat and a good morning, as I passed. I faced the wind coming off the valley and raised my arms—as I had done only days before—truly wishing I could fly away.

The wind—blowing as strongly as it did in the twenty-first century—buffeted me, and I braced myself against it. My hair flew behind me, and I smiled, letting the stiff breeze carry my worries away.

"Molly."

I heard a voice behind me, and I swung around, thinking it was Darius.

And I saw her.

Chapter Fifteen

She came forward with her hands outstretched.

"Molly... You are here."

I stared at her aghast. This was definitely a ghost. I was certain of it. My shoulder burned, and I clutched at it.

She had the same hair as I, though hers was caught up in a bun at the back of her head. Tendrils escaped at the back of her neck and blew in the wind, as did the folds of her dark gray skirt. A white shirtwaist blouse with a high-necked lace collar set off her lovely pink cheeks. She smiled with full, generous lips. Dark eyes sparkled as they regarded me.

"I don't understand," I murmured. I dropped my hand and allowed her to take both of mine in hers.

"I know you are confused and frightened, Molly," she murmured. "I wish I could understand what is happening as well." She shook her head. "But I do not. I only know that as I lay dying, I seemed"—she paused and scrunched her face as if searching for the right word—"unable to go beyond the light. As if I could not leave. I saw images—Darius...and you. Though you looked different, I knew you and I were the same. If I did not believe it was impossible, I would say that Darius willed me—and you—not to die." She grinned. I recognized the grin as my own.

I loved looking at her. She was just so beautiful—much more attractive than I. I was certain I didn't have that sparkle in my eyes—or if I did, it had been some time since I'd seen it.

As if she read my thoughts, she tilted her head and smiled.

"You look just like me, Molly. We are the same person...but centuries apart. He loves you...us. I am not the *other* woman. I am you."

She ran her gaze down my legs—as did everyone in the nineteenth century, it seemed.

"And you are not bound by the demure, voluminous skirts as I was in my time!" Her eyes sparkled with delight.

I matched her chuckle. We sounded like an echo as we giggled.

She sobered up and cocked her head for a moment, as if listening to something I could not hear.

"I must go, Molly. Darius returns to the house. He is looking for you."

My face fell, and she seemed to read my mind again.

"Molly, he loves both of us. I am you in the nineteenth century, and you are me in the twenty-first century. We do not exist separately."

"I don't understand," I mumbled as I shook my head.

"I am afraid I do not understand either, my other self. But it is true. I have been waiting for you." She looked around and raised a graceful hand. "I cannot leave this place, it seems."

"It does. How did you die, Molly? Exactly."

"I think you have probably heard much of it. Jack shot me...in the shoulder. He could not understand that I did not wish to marry him, and he came to my home one day. No one could have predicted that he would go to such great lengths to keep Darius and I apart."

I clutched my shoulder again, the ache springing up once more.

Molly looked at me and put her hand on my shoulder as Darius had done. The pain eased immediately.

"I am so sorry it still hurts. Perhaps when all is resolved, the pain will disappear. You should not carry this burden for me." She frowned and looked over my shoulder into some distant place. "I knew how volatile Jack could be. Darius wanted to take me away, but I would not leave my parents. And I waited too long."

My throat ached from holding back tears.

"I'm so sorry, Molly. I'm so sorry that you were not able to live out your life. Darius misses you so much."

She returned her gaze to me.

"There is no one to miss, Molly. I have never gone away. I am reborn in you."

I shook my head without understanding.

Her eyes sparkled again, and she grinned as she grabbed my hand.

"Come! Let us fly. I used to do this often, and I know I still do it through you. I have seen you."

She whisked me away to the edge of the hill.

"Together!" she called to me as the wind almost drowned out her voice. I watched her raise her arms, and—like my dream—she held them aloft as the wind grabbed at her hair and gray skirt. I grinned and raised my arms as well. The wind felt wonderful, invigorating, soothing, and I relished the companionship of my other self.

We let our fingertips touch as the wind blew around us and through us.

Molly dropped her hand with regret.

"You must go. Darius is at the house. He is searching for you." She took my hands in hers and whispered in my ear. "Take care of him for me...for us. I will not send you empty handed." She laid her warm cheek against mine...and myriad pictures flashed through my mind. Scenes of Molly and Darius laughing together, walking hand in hand, the picnic they had in this meadow, their first kiss—which was exactly like our first kiss, or what I thought had been our first kiss.

Molly had given me the gift of her memories with Darius.

She released my hands and straightened, seeming to move away although I didn't actually see her take a step backward. She grinned, and—in an unexpected gesture—blew me a kiss. Something I myself might have done.

"Goodbye, Molly."

"Wait!" I shrieked as I realized that her image was disappearing. "Wait! Don't go. Darius will want to see you."

And she was gone. I couldn't see her any longer.

"He has you now, Molly—and you are me." I heard her voice on the wind. And then she was gone.

I scanned the cemetery for her, but couldn't see her anywhere. With a sigh, I turned to face the valley once more. I raised my arms, wishing I could take flight for a little while as I recaptured the memories she had shared with me.

With a sigh, I turned to walk back across the cemetery—uncertain if I would tell Darius about meeting Molly. It seemed so far fetched. Would he believe me?

I'd been staring at the ground as I walked, and I looked up. Dark smoke billowed up over the tree line ahead of me, and I smelled burning wood. Something was on fire, and it came from the direction of the house. I broke into a run and flew into the trees, slipping and falling as I scrambled down the slope. I felt the heat before I came out of the trees, and when I emerged onto the lawn of the house, I recoiled for an instant from the onslaught of the scorching blaze. The house was on fire. Flames billowed out of the kitchen window, and I screamed as I rushed forward.

"Mrs. White! Mrs. White!"

I couldn't get very close to the house because the flames shot out of every window and enveloped the porch.

"Miss Sara! Miss Sara! Over here."

Over the roar of the fire, I thought I heard her voice across the lawn.

She stood at the end of the driveway near the road. I ran across the lawn, giving the house a wide berth because of the flying embers and falling debris. The heat was intense.

"Oh, Miss Sara! There you are!" Mrs. White grabbed me in an embrace, and I hugged her back with relief.

"Look what that James has done," she cried. "I was half a mile down the road when I saw him galloping away from the house and dark smoke behind him. I screamed at him, but he didn't pay any attention, and I ran back to the house." She sobbed as she struggled to stay upright. I kept an arm around her while I turned to watch the wonderful house burn. There were no sirens. No fire trucks would come rushing to put this fire out.

"I'm so glad to see you safe," I gasped. "I thought you were in the house."

She turned to me with a wild-eyed stare.

"Mr. Ferguson ran into the house. He rode in on his horse as soon as I arrived. He was looking for you. He asked where you were, and I didn't know if you had returned from your walk."

I barely heard her last words before I wrenched myself out of her arms and ran for the house. She grabbed me by my arm and pulled me back.

"Let me go," I screamed. "Let me go. I have to find him. I'm not in the house," I screamed even louder, hoping Darius would be able to hear me above the thunder of crashing debris.

"Sam, George, thank goodness you've come," Mrs. White kept a vice grip on my arm while I fought her. I barely noticed an older gray-haired man and a younger twenty-something man who'd arrived, panting and out of breath. "Help me with her. She's trying to get into the house. Mr. Ferguson went into the house to look for her."

"Darius! Darius!" I screamed over and over, almost completely immobilized as the two men took over holding me by every means possible including by my shoulders, my waist, and my arms. I couldn't breathe. Desperation robbed me of oxygen as did the smoke from the fire.

"He hasn't come out yet, George. I'm afraid..." Mrs. White didn't finish. And I kept screaming, and choking and gasping.

"Take her away, George. She can't breathe from the smoke. Take her out onto the road. There is nothing we can do. The house is gone, and I don't see Mr. Ferguson anywhere." Mrs. White started sobbing herself.

George and Sam pulled me backward, trying the best they could not to hurt me, but I fought against them with every ounce of my being to try to get back to the house. Darius could not be dead. He just couldn't be dead!

They pulled me off the driveway and out into the road. Out of the corner of my eye, I saw more people running toward the house, just before the kaleidoscope began.

"Don't," I tried to scream. "I'm going to disappear. Don't take me out to the road," I shouted, though my voice sounded far away, even to me. "Take me back. Darius!"

I felt myself slipping out of George and Sam's hands. Their faces took on similar horrified expressions. The last thing I saw was Mrs. White's shocked face silhouetted against the backdrop of the burning house.

****

I must have fainted this time, because my first impression was of lying curled in the fetal position in an unpaved road—the road that ran in front of the house. My second impression was of the bitter smell of burning wood. My throat ached, and I coughed, wondering if the smell was in my clothes.

The fire! I scrambled to my knees and jerked my head in the direction of the house.

It stood! It still stood—and it looked exactly the same! The same faded pastel colors of turquoise and salmon pink begged the onlooker to take notice of its more festive days. The same peeling weathered and dingy white paint adorned the wraparound porch.

And Sara came running out the front door, shouting at me, although all I could hear at the moment was the pounding in my heart and the roar of a fire from over one hundred years ago.

I stood on shaky knees as I watched her trot down the driveway. Darius was gone. He was gone—dead in the fire. But the house still stood. Had there been a fire? Had Darius been real? I felt so confused, and I sank to my knees in the road, sobs shaking my body.

Darius... Darius, I moaned silently.

"Molly! Where have you been? What happened to you?" Sara reached me and tried to pull me up, but I must have been dead weight, because she gave up trying and came down on her knees beside me.

"Molly!" she cried as she pulled my hair back from my face to look at me. "What's wrong, honey? What happened?"

I hugged myself and rocked back and forth, moaning.

"Darius," I sobbed. "Darius." I had no other words. Darius was dead...or he was a figment of my crazed imagination. Either way, he was not with me. He had not traveled with me, and I had no way to get back to him.

"Molly, honey, let me take you to the house. At least, let me get you off the road."

I resisted when Sara tried to pull me up—as if by leaving the road, I left my last best chance to get back to Darius. What if I left the road, and the "window" to travel in time closed?

"I can't leave the road. I have to stay here," I muttered feverishly. "If he comes back, I have to be here."

"Are you talking about Darren, Molly?"

I pushed my tangled hair back off my wet face and grabbed her arms as I stared at her.

"His name is Darius, Sara. Darius. Do you remember him? Do you remember Darius?" I whispered hoarsely.

Sara frowned. "What's happened, Molly? Where is he? Did something happen?"

"What do you remember?" I gave her a slight shake. "What do you remember about him?"

"Molly, stop it. You're hurting me." She loosened my grip. I barely registered that Marmaduke paced back and forth at the entrance of the drive. "What are you talking about? What shouldn't I remember?"

"I'm sorry," I choked out. "I'm sorry, Sara. Everything is so mixed up right now. I feel like I'm in a nightmare."

She rose to a standing position and managed to pull me to my feet as well.

"Well, so do I! You've been gone for five days. Just like that!" She wrapped one arm around my waist and held my elbow with the other while she pulled me out of the road. "I didn't know what to do when I saw you disappear!"

"Did you see Darius disappear with me?" I could only focus on him. I let her propel me forward toward the porch. Marmaduke ran back and forth around our legs as we moved.

"Yes, I did. Both of you."

We reached the porch and I made my way to the love seat where I dropped onto it. I didn't think I could face going inside.

Sara sat down next to me and took my shaking hands in hers.

"What happened to you? I didn't dare call the police. I didn't know what to do. What would I have told them?" she asked with a lift of her shoulders.

I shook my head and gave her hands a squeeze, grateful for small favors.

"I'm so glad you didn't. I knew you'd be upset and worried, and I tried to get back here as fast as I could, but Darius..." I bit my lip in an effort to stop the shaking in my jaw. "I can't believe I was gone five days though. It was only overnight."

Sara frowned and pressed her lips together. She peered into my face as if to divine an answer.

"Where is Darius, Molly? What happened to you guys?"

I swallowed hard. My throat ached so bad...maybe from holding back tears...maybe from the fire. If there *had* been a fire. I turned to look at the peeling porch railing where Marmaduke perched watching us with interest. It certainly didn't look as if it had been burnt and repainted. The ferocious fire I remembered would have left nothing standing. Had it only been moments ago?

"Molly?" Sara gave my hand a tug.

I shook my head and looked down at our hands.

"Well, you saw us disappear. Where do you think we went?" It would have been so much easier if she guessed. I didn't know how to explain it.

"I have no idea. I've never seen anything like it," Sara said in a strained voice. "That's why I couldn't call the police. But I was going to in the morning if you hadn't come back today."

"I'm so sorry, Sara," I muttered as I clutched her hand. "I would have never disappeared without telling you first if I'd had a choice."

"So?" she prompted, her impatience at my hesitation evident.

"Do you remember talking to me about time travel?" I said quietly. I kept my gaze downcast, sounding crazy even to myself.

Sara nodded. "The book I'm reading."

I stared at her, willing her to guess. She watched my face carefully, and within seconds, her eyes widened.

"What?" she said incredulously.

I could only nod.

"Are you trying to tell me that you traveled..." she couldn't finish. I didn't blame her. She pulled her hand from mine and wrapped her arms around her chest.

"Are you nuts?" she whispered.

"Well, you saw us disappear? You tell me," I muttered.

She turned to look at the end of the drive, and I followed suit

"Where is he?"

I gave her a quick look and shook my head, desperately trying to keep the ever ready burning tears in check. I looked back at the road, wondering how I could have taken my eyes off the drive for even the last few minutes. What if Darius came? Wouldn't he need me to help him? Was he alive? Was he dead? Pain carved such a deep hole in my chest that I wondered if it would ever stop hurting. I suspected not. This was not fixable.

"Where did you go?" she asked in a voice tinged with awe.

I gave my head another befuddled shake. "To his time. To 1880."

"Are you telling me that Darius was from the past?" Her raised brows suggested I was out of my mind, and I was fairly sure she was right.

"If he even existed at all," I gave her a quick look before returning my gaze to the road.

"Oh, he was real all right. No wonder you guys made no sense," she muttered with a shake of her head.

"What do you mean?"

"Nothing about him seemed quite normal, and nothing about his story seemed plausible." She nudged me in the arm. "You lied to me," she said accusingly.

I nodded, too depressed to feel guilty.

"Yes, I had to. I couldn't just say, "Oh, guess what, here's this strange guy I met in the cemetery, and he has come to live with me."

Sara leaned forward to get in my field of vision.

"You met him at the cemetery?" She gave a short mirthless laugh and sat back in the loveseat. "I suppose I shouldn't be surprised by now. But I am. What possessed you to bring home some man you met in a cemetery?"

I opened my mouth but had no answer to give her. I still couldn't understand anything myself.

"Oh, wait! Is that why you were asking me about ghosts? Did you think he was a ghost—because of the cemetery?"

"We both thought he might be." I wanted to smile at the memory, but the pain in my chest forced me to concentrate on breathing shallowly. Smiling just didn't seem possible right now. I kept my eye on the road.

"I don't think I can talk about this anymore right now, Sara. I don't feel very well," I mumbled. "I just can't..."

Sara nodded. "I understand. I just have one quick question, and then I'll leave you alone for a while."

I nodded wearily.

"Is he coming back?"

I broke down in sobs, and with a mumbled curse at herself for insensitivity or some such thing, Sara wrapped an arm around my shoulders and rocked me while I cried for what seemed like hours but must have been fifteen minutes or so. When I ran out of tears, though the ache in my chest continued to burn, I told her everything I could remember.

"And now I don't know if I'll ever see him again," I murmured in a broken voice. I lay my aching head against the back of the love seat and closed my burning eyes...for just an instant. I had to maintain my vigil on the road.

"I-I don't know what to say, Molly. This sounds so...fantastical." She paused. "And to top it all off, you think you saw...what?...your ghost?"

I opened one swollen eye and looked at her briefly before I scanned the road. She held her hands to her temples.

"I know," I sighed. "I know." Although I'd told her about Molly, I wished I had kept that part to myself, though I was in no intellectual shape to think about future implications if I managed to edit the story. I wanted to keep Molly to myself. After all, she was...my other self, and I wanted to honor her memory. The word "ghost" simply did not do justice to Molly's vitality. I had fallen in love with her in an instant...and I found myself missing her. She had truly understood everything I was feeling. And why not? She was me.

"Time travelers and ghosts," Sara murmured in a bemused tone. "You sure have had a busy week."

"I'm sorry to have put you through all this, Sara. You were supposed to fly back today, weren't you?" I held my breath. I didn't want her to go.

"Yes, but I rescheduled the flight for tomorrow. It's summer, and there's no school. I've got meetings next week though. And Brad will be all right on his own without me."

She gave me a quick impulsive hug.

"I'm so glad you're alive."

I gritted my teeth to stem the scream threatening to erupt at the word "alive." Was Darius alive? Even if the house had not burned down, and I didn't know how that was possible, he would not really be alive—not in the twenty-first century. I couldn't bear the thought. I simply couldn't bear it. I hugged myself tightly.

"Cynthia and Laura came by yesterday," Sara said on a quiet note. "I told them that you and—"

She paused, and I waited anxiously. Me and Darius?

"I told them that you had gone to Council Bluffs. They're almost ready to head off to Florida."

I tried to focus on the faces of the sisters, but everything seemed fairly blurry at the moment. I wondered if I was in shock.

Darius's great-great nieces...or was it another great? I couldn't figure it out. They lived. We had not changed the future. Darius must have been successful in settling his estate, and it seemed likely the house might not have burned down after all. Who wills a burnt-down house to his family? Had I dreamed the whole thing? How had I gotten to the road?

Had I asked the sisters everything I could about Darius and his family? What had they said about him? That he'd "disappeared mysteriously?" What did that mean? Had he died in the fire then? But the house still stood!

"Wouldn't Cynthia and Laura have mentioned that the house burned down...if it had?" I asked aloud. I'm not certain I really expected Sara to answer, but she was game.

"We could ask them," she said in a tentative voice. "We could call them."

The road was empty. No one walked up the drive.

I turned to look at Sara. "Yes, I think I need to talk to them." At the look of alarm on Sara's face, I almost chuckled. Almost.

"No, no. I'm not going to tell them my bizarre story. But they might know if the house burned down. And they might remember hearing anything about how..." I meant to say how Darius died, but I couldn't voice the words.

"We'll call them," Sara said quickly. She seemed to know when I couldn't talk further.

The picture! Darius's picture! Was it real? Did it exist? I jumped up without a word and ran into the house, ignoring Sara's startled exclamation.

"Where are you going?"

Sassy jumped down from the couch and followed me up the stairs to the master bedroom.

"Molly!" I heard Sara's voice down below and then on the stairs. "What is it?" she called out.

I pulled open the nightstand drawer and fell back against the edge of the bed with weak knees. There it was, lying on top of an assortment of paper, pens and the rest of the house photos the sisters had given me. Darius's picture!

I straightened and reached for it slowly, reverently—as if it were the last thing I would ever have of him.

Sara ran into the room.

"What the—" She stopped when she saw me. I didn't take my eyes off the photograph as I passed her to leave the room.

"I just had to get this. I have to run back downstairs. I need to keep an eye on the road," I murmured. I cradled the photograph against my chest as I hurried down the stairs. Both Sassy and Sara followed me.

"I didn't know you had a picture of him," Sara said. She took her seat beside me again as I scanned the road before lowering myself to the loveseat.

I knew she wanted to look at the photograph, but I couldn't seem to make myself pull it away from its place near my racing heart.

"Laura and Cynthia gave it to me. It was in a box of old family photographs they'd left here. I wanted it, and they let me have it." I took a steadying breath as I stared at the road. "They said he didn't have any descendents to leave it to."

"Oh, Molly," she almost crooned. "I'm so sorry. I can't imagine what you're going through right now."

I turned to look at her then, and with a tight smile, I pulled the photograph away from my chest and let her look at it. She probably knew better than to ask if she could actually hold it at that moment. She leaned forward and peered at it.

"Look at his mustache!"

I looked down and ran a tender finger over the length of his mustache.

"He shaved it off," I said quietly. "For me, I think."

"Well, he looks handsome with it or without it, either way, although it is easier to see his smile when he's clean shaven." She leaned forward again. "What year was the photo taken?"

I turned it over. "1880 Sometime this year...or the other year, I guess."

"Molly..." I knew she hesitated, and I tensed. "Why do you think he's not coming back? What if the fire wasn't real?" She turned to look over her shoulder at the picture window where Sassy sat watching us intently. "How can the house still be here if that really happened?"

I shrugged. "I don't know. Even if the fire wasn't real—and I couldn't have imagined anything that ferocious—I don't know why he would come here."

"Because he loves you. Even I could see that. Victorian house restoration specialist, my foot." She chuckled, and even I felt a corner of my mouth lift momentarily. "Well, I imagine he probably did—does know more about Victorian construction than most men."

I didn't miss her use of past tense, and I winced.

Sara rose. "Let me get you something to drink. When did you last eat?"

I shook my head and shrugged. "I don't know. This morning? An hour ago? Over a hundred years ago?"

"Why don't you come inside," she asked as she headed for the door, "while I get something for us to eat?"

I threw her a desperate look. "I can't. I need to wait here...just in case."

She turned to look at the road and then brought her gaze back to mine. I didn't want to see the pity in her eyes. Her sympathy seemed somehow to make Darius's absence an unalterable future reality. I couldn't give up hope so easily. I wasn't sure how I would go on if I didn't have some small spark to cling to—even if it seemed almost an impossibility.

"Okay," she shrugged lightly. "I'll bring it out here, along with the phone...so you can call Cynthia and Laura."

****

Laura pulled the car up the driveway about an hour later, and I stood to go help Cynthia alight.

"Molly, dear! I'm so glad you called. We wanted to see you before we leave for Florida."

Sara came out of the house and down the porch steps.

"And here's Sara. How are you, dear?"

I wasn't sure to whom she was talking at the moment, so I let Sara be "dear." I nodded at Laura as she came around the front of the car.

"Let's go sit on the porch. The late afternoon breeze is so nice," I said, just in case anyone had an idea that I was going to give up my vigil. Sara hadn't said anything further as we ate—or as I picked at my food and she ate—but I knew she was wondering how long I was going to stand guard watching the road. As far as I was concerned, I was sleeping on the porch.

"Yes, it is wonderful, isn't it?" Laura agreed. "It's days like these that make me forget why we're moving to Florida." She settled into one of the single chairs while I lowered Cynthia onto the loveseat.

"Not me," Cynthia chirped. "I'm not likely to forget the winters here." She shivered delicately. "Brutal."

"Can I get you some lemonade?" Sara asked.

"No, thank you, dear, not for me," Cynthia murmured. "Laura?"

Laura declined, and I shook my head, impatient to ask the sisters about the house. Sara read my face and took a seat.

"I'm so glad you were able to come by," I rushed in. "I was wondering. It's the strangest thing really," I chuckled nervously, "but I was wondering if you had remembered any more details about the history of the house...or the builder?" I ended on a bit of a squeak. "I mean...is this the original house? Or did it...burn down at one point?" I saw Sara's cautionary look as I finished on a stilted note.

The sisters looked at me with puzzled brows for a moment and then at each other.

"Oh, goodness, Laura! Do you know, I think it did," Cynthia murmured thoughtfully. "Do you remember mother saying something about that? A fire? Part of the house burning?"

Laura pursed her lips and nodded. "Now that you mention it, I do." She leaned forward in my direction. "Molly. We would have told you if we had remembered. Is this a problem?"

"Oh, dear, Molly! Is there a problem with the house?" Cynthia asked with worry lining her frail brow. "Is that something we should have disclosed in the sale? I don't even know much about it...just what Mother mentioned." She looked at Laura for confirmation.

I watched them as if in a stupor, barely aware that Sara leaned forward in her seat and stared hard at me.

"I know almost nothing about it. I think most of the house burned. The basement survived. At least, I think that's what Mother said. And then it was rebuilt."

"Who rebuilt it?" I whispered, hoping my voice didn't reflect my despair. Through the haze over my eyes, I saw Sara's face drop in dismay.

Cynthia looked at Laura with a question on her face, and Laura shrugged.

"I don't know. We didn't ask. It was long, long before we were born."

I nodded and forced my lips into a semblance of a smile.

"Did you happen to remember anything more about your great-great uncle, Darius?" Even saying his name seemed to tear me in two, and I raised my hand to my face to cover my struggle for air. Darius was dead. I couldn't breathe.

"No, nothing more than what we said. He disappeared, I think. Well, no one knew where he was buried, so my family guessed he disappeared. They couldn't remember." Laura swung her gaze to Cynthia. Neither one of them seemed to notice that I was about to faint. I couldn't breathe.

"That's right, Laura. I think you might have had quite the crush on him as well to remember so much more than I do." Cynthia grinned and shook her head. "Nope, no one knows where he's buried."

I wanted to stand up and scream, "He's buried in the ashes of this house, that's where he's buried. He's buried here...dead...burned."

Sara stood swiftly and came over to my chair to put a soothing hand on my shoulder. I clutched at her hand, noting with faint surprise that my shoulder no longer hurt—not since Molly laid her hand on me.

Darius died looking for me, and I wanted to die as well. I really did not want to go on. The pain of losing him was horrific, but the guilt was so much worse. And I couldn't fix it. I couldn't make it right. Despite my best efforts, a hot tear slid down my face.

"Molly, are you all right? You look so distraught!" Cynthia asked. "Is it about the house? What can we do? Do you want to cancel the sale?" She swung a quick look at Laura. "We will do that, Molly. We should have remembered to tell you about it."

"No," I moaned as I clutched my stomach and bent over. "No, no, the house is mine. It's mine. I want the house."

"I think Molly is ill, ladies. I should take her inside."

Laura stood and put a competent hand on my forehead.

"She does have a bit of a fever. You should put her to bed, Sara."

Sara pulled my unresisting body up. There was no one to wait for...no need to watch the road any longer. Darius was not coming. He was dead.

Laura helped Cynthia up, and they said goodbye as Sara held my limp body to her side while we watched them go. Sara watched them go. I fought against overwhelming nausea.

"We'll come back to see you before we go," Cynthia called in a strained voice as Laura walked her across the porch and to the car. "Maybe we'll see that nice man who's doing your remodel when we come back. Get better soon," she sung out as Laura put her in the car.

I put a hand to my face and moaned.

"Bye now," Sara called as she sprang into action and dragged me into the house. She pulled my dead weight up the stairs and half carried me to the bed.

"Oh, Molly, I'm so, so sorry. I just can't imagine—"

She must have stopped talking—or I couldn't hear her anymore after I rolled over, buried my face in my pillow and started screaming.

Chapter Sixteen

My memories of that night were chaotic and few. I screamed, I cried, I pled with Sara to change the facts, I struggled to rise and return to my vigil only to remember that Darius would not come. At some point, I may have actually fainted and awakened again to begin sobbing anew.

Sara did her best throughout the long night to keep me safe and sane, and it was to her credit that I survived to see daylight.

When I awoke from a short fitful doze to see the lightening of dawn in the window, I realized that Sara had fallen asleep on top of the bed. She must have covered me with a blanket in the night, and I reached over to drape some of it over her still form.

I lay on my back and looked out of the window, wondering about the days to come. Sara had to leave today. She had preparatory meetings for school in the coming week. I suspected she would ask me to return with her for a while, but I couldn't seem to visualize myself away from the house. With Sassy in tow—and Marmaduke—I would have to take the car, and I didn't relish driving all the way back to Washington State...alone. Not at the moment.

I looked over at Sara. Her breathing was even. I slipped out of bed, found my shoes and made my way out of the bedroom. As I wandered down the stairs with no specific goal in mind, I started to look for changes—changes between this rebuilt house and the house in 1880. Nothing seemed different, other than the awful paint job. All the materials seemed to be the same. Whoever had rebuilt the house must have had Darius's blueprints because it looked exactly the same.

I stood on the last stair and gritted my teeth. If I could just avoid even thinking his name, I thought I might be able to breathe without pain...and guilt.

Sassy looked up from the couch with a yawn but made no move to rise. Marmaduke came around the corner from the kitchen licking his lips.

I wondered if the cats realized he was gone.

I stepped down and crossed over to the door, pulling it open to step outside onto the porch. The eternal breeze shook the leaves of the oak trees in the front yard. The road was empty.

My heart skipped a beat, and then another. What if I...? Even my thoughts stuttered. What if I walked out into the road? Could I return to his time—to before the fire? Could I save his life—as he had tried to save mine?

My heart began to race as I flew off the porch and ran down the path. Marmaduke scrambled and jogged along beside me. I ran out into the road and came to a halt, thrusting my hands out in front of my face...waiting. I waited for the kaleidoscope of colors, the dizziness, the vortex. Nothing happened. I looked to Marmaduke who paced back and forth at the entrance of the drive.

"It's not going to happen, is it, Marmaduke?" I dropped my arms and my shoulders sagged with exhaustion. I really hadn't expected anything. The wind kicked up some dust from the road, and I looked up to trace its path. A small dust devil swirled to the left—in the direction of the cemetery. I turned and followed it, keeping my eye on the wispy thing as it darted here and there across the unpaved road.

I followed it to the top of the hill where it dissipated at the entrance to the cemetery. I could have wondered what I was doing there, but I knew. Since my return to the present time the day before, I'd had every intention of revisiting the cemetery as soon as possible. I wanted to see Molly's stone again, and I wanted to see if Darius was buried there as well. Although, a fire...there wouldn't be much left. I gave myself a shake.

I stepped under the black iron arches, instantly aware that the breeze had strengthened to the strong wind I'd come to love.

My hair flew about my face as I walked slowly up the short drive and turned left onto the gravel path. I neared the general vicinity of the white stone that had caught my attention when I first came to the cemetery—only a few short weeks ago, although it seemed more like a lifetime.

I saw it—the brightness seeming to outshine every other marker around it, but something was distinctly different about it. As I had before, I approached the stone and knelt down on my knees before it to trace the letters with my fingers.

The stone was cool to my touch...and marble—a bright white gleaming marble. And the writing was as clearly etched as if it had been engraved yesterday.

Molly Hamilton
28 years 2 mos 4 dys
Born 1 April 1851 Died 5 June 1879
Beloved Daughter
Across the Winds of Time
You Will Always Live On

I shook my head in disbelief. Was it possible? Had someone replaced her stone? I wondered if her family had returned to the area to arrange for a sturdier marker for her. Although she had shared her memories with me, I still could not think of her parents as anything other than strangers. I had my own memories of my own parents.

The addition of the last line was new. *You will always live on* had not been on her original stone. It seemed a lovely touch. She did live on in me. I had all her memories.

I laid my forehead against the cool stone and closed my eyes. I missed her. I'd only met her for a few short moments, but I missed her—my other self. It seemed likely that she had already been dead when I "met" her, but I wished I'd gotten the chance to know her. Would the world have been big enough for two of us? Would the laws of physics or time travel or whatever it was that governed that sort of thing allow for two Mollys?

We both had our memories of Darius—and she had shared hers with me. I knew that when I died, I wanted to be buried next to her. My other self. Two Molly Hamiltons lying next to each other. I smiled to myself. Wouldn't that give future genealogists something to mull over?

I raised my head and looked at either side of her grave. Was there room for me? There seemed to be some space just to the right of the stone. I made a mental note to check with the town clerk to see if that spot was available. Because I knew that I would be staying in my Victorian house down the hill for the rest of my life—rebuilt as it was—for better or worse.

I rose to a standing position, and with a knot in the pit of my stomach, scanned the nearby stones looking for Darius's name. Nothing remotely resembling his name was visible, and I knew it would take me days to cover every stone in the cemetery. I took a steadying breath of air as I reminded myself that Darius had died in the fire—and that most likely, there had been no body to bury. My stomach rolled over at the thought, and I staggered for a moment, putting my hand on Molly's stone to steady myself.

Touching her tombstone somehow gave me strength, and I swallowed hard and straightened. I tilted my head to hear the loud rustling of the oak trees overhead. I loved the sound. I moved toward the peak of the hill, and when I reached the spot overlooking the valley, I lifted my arms in the strong current—willing myself to fly. I wriggled my hands as if I were touching Molly's fingers as I had the day before. She was not there.

"Molly." I heard a woman's voice from behind. I turned around, half expecting to see my other half, Molly, once again.

And as if I were experiencing déjà vu, a movement underneath one of the massive oak trees caught my eye. It was just like the second time I'd returned to the cemetery. A figure stood there, beneath the canopy of the tree—although there was no shadow this time because of the early morning hour. Darius moved away from the tree with a tentative step. His clothing was formal as it had been the last time I saw him.

"Molly." Despite the wind, I heard him repeat my name in a husky voice.

Cold sweat broke out on my forehead, and I put my hand to my mouth as if to hold back the morning's breakfast—if I'd had any. For here—in the flesh—was the man of my dreams. And my déjà vu ended there.

"Are you a ghost now, Darius?" I called in a bemused tone with a loving smile. "I believe in ghosts now, you know." I watched him walk toward me, and I rambled on. "I met Molly. Did she tell you? Did you see her? She's so much fun. I really liked her."

His handsome face wore a puzzled frown as if he was trying to hear me...or understand me. He continued to move toward me, his pace deliberate.

"I'm so glad to see you, Darius. I never thought I would see you again. I wasn't in the house, you know," I said conversationally. He came to a halt in front of me, as tall and vibrant as he had ever looked. Sudden tears slipped down my face, and I looked up at him. "I'm so sorry, Darius. It's all my fault that you're dead. I wasn't in the house."

He pulled me into his arms and buried his face in my hair. I heard his beloved voice speaking into my ear—husky, determined, warm.

"Molly, my love, I live. I am alive. No fire could come between us. Neither can a century of time."

I turned my face toward his, and he kissed me—as passionately as he had the first time—as passionately as he had the last time he kissed Molly at their picnic more than a hundred years ago. A tremor ran through his arms as he held me against him tightly—kissing me one moment and whispering into my ear the next. The wind seemed to swirl around us, wrapping us in a cocoon as we clung together.

I had questions—many, many questions—but they could wait. I reveled in the feel of Darius's arms around me, and I didn't want to let go. What if he slipped away again? What if I couldn't hang on to him? What if he was just a ghost? I couldn't stop Molly from *leaving*. How could I stop Darius from leaving me?

I held onto him with all my might, pressing against the length of his body, desperately trying to mold myself to him as if, in some way, that would ensure we stayed together.

Darius finally lifted his head to look into my eyes. The glints of gold in his blue irises sparkled, and I held his gaze though my mouth trembled and I found I couldn't breathe in the intimacy of his gaze.

He raised one hand to my face, holding me tightly with the other and traced the line of my cheekbone with his fingers.

"I thought I had lost you," he murmured in a rough voice. "When I saw the house burning and Mrs. White told me she thought you were inside—" He broke off. I saw a muscle working in his jaw, and a hint of moisture made his eyes glitter. He swallowed. "I lost you once, and I wanted to die. I could not lose you again," he whispered as he bent his head to kiss my lips again. His lips traveled across my face to my cheek before he raised his head. He swallowed hard and he gritted his teeth.

"I'm so sorry," I whispered. "I was here at the cemetery. When I got back to the house, Mrs. White said you'd gone inside to find me. She said you didn't come out..." I reached up to cradle his face—to reassure myself that he was unharmed. "I tried to find you, but Mr. White and his son, they held me back—they carried me into the road, and..." I fought against the tears of frustration and grief that erupted at the memory. "I ended up here...and I couldn't get back to you."

His face broke, and he bent to kiss the outer corners of my eyelids where the tears had begun sliding out despite my best efforts to keep them in check.

"Hush, my love. It is over now. Hush, do not cry. We are together."

I clutched at his arms, perhaps to see if he was solid.

"But how can you be here? How did you get here? What happened? I thought you die—" I bit my lip and stared up into his face in wonder. "Are you a ghost, Darius?" I pressed my face against his chest, where his heart beat loudly if somewhat rapidly. "I don't care," I mumbled. "I'm not going to let you go. I can live with a ghost."

I heard a rumbling in his chest, and I looked up to see him chuckling. With his free hand, he brushed the hair from my face as it blew in the wind.

"I am no ghost, my love. I was able to search the entire house for you. I was in the basement when it collapsed but was somehow protected down there until I was rescued."

"So, your beautiful house did burn down after all," I said with regret.

He nodded and pulled me tight against his lean body.

"Yes, it did."

"But it has been rebuilt. Did you know that?"

"I do know that," he murmured with a chuckle. "Come, let us go back to the rebuilt house, and we will discuss all." He wrapped an arm around my shoulder and guided me down the path.

I stopped when we came near Molly's grave. Darius seemed to know what I was looking at.

"She has a new stone, Darius," I said in wonder. "Did you see that?"

"Yes," he said in a husky voice. "I know." He cleared his throat and tightened his grip on me. "Knowing the sandstone would not last, I ordered a new one for her."

I swung to look up at him.

"Did you do that when you went into town that morning? Yesterday morning?"

Darius leaned down to brush his fingers against her stone, and then straightened to put his arm around me again.

"There is much to explain, I think, though I am not certain I understand everything myself," he said with a bemused smile. "We will talk at the house. You look exhausted. I want to get you home before I have to carry you." He chuckled and guided me down the path toward the house.

We were halfway down the hill when I remembered that Sara was still at the house.

"Sara is here. She is leaving today. She knows everything, Darius." I heard the note of warning in my voice, but I really wasn't certain why I needed it. Having Sara know about Darius and where he came from would make life easier—not harder.

Below me on the path with his hand on mine as he helped me down the hill, he paused and turned to me with a wide grin. I hadn't seen that grin in so long.

"Good. I am pleased to hear it. Now, perhaps she will stop throwing daggers at me with her eyes."

I returned his bright smile. "And you can stop sleeping on the couch."

He tilted his head and eyed me appraisingly. "Did you purchase a bed for the spare room in my absence?"

My face burned. How long was this man going to do the old-fashioned thing?

"No?"

"Then until you do, I am consigned to the couch, I fear. The cats will keep me company."

He pulled me to him, and because I was higher on the hill, we met at eye level. I resisted, needing to hear the truth. How did one ask? His eyes softened as he gazed at me, and he pressed his lips against mine. The passion of his kiss and the movement of his body left me in little doubt of his reactions to me.

As if he knew what I was thinking, he whispered against my ear.

"Not until we are properly married, my dear. I can wait for you." At the moment he spoke the words, I realized that he and Molly had waited as well. Molly had indeed shared all of her memories with me.

I kissed him back with abandon.

"Okay, if you insist on being old-fashioned," I whispered against his lips. "Then we'd better get married pretty soon, because I don't know if I can wait!"

Darius threw back his head and laughed, but I caught the bronzing of his cheeks—no less red than mine must have been.

"I love that you say the most extraordinary things, Molly. I do not think I will ever tire of being surprised by you."

We moved on and arrived at the house a few minutes later. Marmaduke, pacing at the drive, saw us and ran across the lawn to greet Darius who held me by one hand as he bent down to pet him.

Sara came running out the kitchen door.

"There you are," she cried as she came toward us. "Do you have any idea what I thought when I couldn't find you this morning?" She stopped in front of me with her hands on her hips. I was unrepentant.

"I'm sorry, Sara. I thought you'd still be sleeping."

"And where have you been, I'd like to know?" she muttered at Darius who beamed at her. "1880, my foot." She linked her arm in mine and pulled me toward the house, in turn pulling Darius because I wasn't about to let go of him.

"You need to have something to drink and eat. You look awful," she said as she pulled open the door. Marmaduke ran into the kitchen in front of her. She stood aside and watched us enter much like a schoolteacher inspecting her charges after recess.

"You've got some explaining to do," she said to Darius as she closed the door. "I've just finished making some of your toaster waffles, but I haven't got the faintest idea how to make that hot chocolate of yours, Darren..." she made a face, "Darius, that is. Do you mind?" She pointed to a chair at the table for me and sent Darius a pointed look toward the kitchen with her eyes.

"I am pleased to do so. It is nice to be missed," he said with a flash of bright teeth. "Sit, Molly. You do look tired. And you too, Sara. I will prepare the hot chocolate and serve the meal."

I leaned my elbows on the table and rested my chin on my hands as I watched Darius's every movement. He turned to look at me often, his smile widening more each time. Sara watched us both for a few minutes—her head turning side to side as if she watched a tennis match. I knew she had to be bursting with questions, but she restrained herself much better than I might have.

"Look, you two. There's a lot I want to know. I have a bunch of questions for you—like where you found him,"—she gave me a pointed look—"but I want Molly to eat first...and you too, Darius, if you haven't eaten in almost 24 hours like Molly here."

"I think that is wise, Sara. I am worried about Molly's health as well. She did not have a chance to eat while she was with me." He looked at me. "Did you?"

I nodded. "Mrs. White fed me pancakes."

"Ah!" he nodded. "Yes, I ate some before I left that morning," he shook his head, "that is—back then."

"Was she well when you last saw her?" I couldn't keep a note of sadness from my voice.

"Yes, Molly. She was well." He smiled faintly. "Confused, but well."

He brought the hot chocolate to the table, and Sara jumped up to get the waffles and syrup. They put the food in front of me and stared at me until, self-consciously, I took a bite of the waffle.

"Okay, I'm eating now, you guys. Join in anytime," I encouraged with an affectionate roll of my eyes.

Darius and Sara smiled at each other in the spirit of team work and ate their own food. I probably picked at my food more than ate it, but I was with two people I loved and all seemed right with the world at last.

Darius and I would marry, although that presented some logistical problems such as a birth certificate for him and having to bring someone to the house for the wedding because he couldn't leave. Having children—and I sincerely hoped we would have children—might be a lonely process in that Darius would not be able to be at the hospital with me. I didn't think I would want to have the children at home—not even for Darius. I could see small problems that might crop up, but nothing insurmountable. All in all, I was a happy woman. I sipped my hot chocolate and smiled serenely.

Though I had many, many questions, I held them until Darius and Sara had eaten. They both deserved a small measure of peace. We finished the meal and picked up our hot chocolate mugs to take them outside to the porch. Sara settled into a single easy chair and I sat on the loveseat next to Darius. Marmaduke, who had followed us out, took up a position on the porch railing and draped himself over it. Sassy frowned from inside the window.

"I can see Molly has a bunch of questions for you, Darius," Sara grinned. "But I think I'll get mine in first. Where did she find you this morning?"

"In the cemetery," he answered, "where she found me the first time. That is where I seem to *appear*."

"Are you a ghost? Or did you travel through time?" Her face reddened as if she doubted her sanity in asking the questions. I knew just how she felt.

"It would appear I have traveled through time. I was not dead last I checked." He pretended to make a cursory survey of his chest, arms and legs.

"How do you travel through time?" she asked in her interrogation.

Darius looked at me and gave a slight shrug.

"I do not know. That last time I traveled—that is, the last time *we* traveled—it happened when we stepped into the road. Molly clung to me, and I believe that is why she traveled with me. It would seem that I cannot leave this property, or I will travel back in time again." His face took on that look I hoped never to see again—an expression of despair. I grabbed his hand and clung to it. He turned to me and searched my face.

"It's going to be all right," I whispered.

He smiled, seeming to clear his troubled brow with effort. He brought my hand to his lips and kissed my palm, keeping it tucked safe within his own when he lowered it.

"Yes, it is," he said quietly. "I lost you and I have learned my lesson."

I looked back at Sara who stared at us. I could see her brain was working out the logistics as I had done.

"That will present some problems, I can see, but you two will work it out," she announced. Darius sent her a grateful smile, and I nodded optimistically.

"Yes, we will."

"Your turn, Molly. My flight doesn't leave for four hours," Sara said as she settled back in her chair and sipped the chocolate she brought outside with her.

I looked at them both, wondering where to start. I guessed I ought to start at the beginning, as they say. I turned to Darius.

"Where did you go yesterday morning...when you left?"

"Yesterday morning?" he hesitated. "Do you mean the morning of the fire?"

"Yes, yesterday morning," I said with a knit between my eyebrows. He seemed a bit confused. I suspected he might have been disoriented from all the traveling back and forth in time. I know I was.

He stared out to the yard and his eyes took on a distant look for a moment.

"I met with the lawyer and prepared a will, leaving the estate to my brother. I made sure to leave Mrs. White and her family provided for. And I secured some funds for myself so that I do not come to you destitute," he said with a smile. His face sobered.

"When I returned," he said in a husky voice, "and Mrs. White told me she thought you might be in the burning house..." He couldn't seem to finish.

I squeezed his hand.

"I felt the same way."

He looked at me with soft eyes and nodded. I bit my lip and looked to Sara and back at Darius, hoping they would bear with my otherworldly experiences and not think about institutionalizing me. I took a deep breath.

"I met Molly in the cemetery yesterday, Darius—in your time."

Darius tilted his head and regarded me with a puzzled expression. I waited for his questions. I still had many of my own. He studied my face for a minute before he smiled gently and nodded.

"I believe you."

"Tell me about her stone," I asked softly. Sara looked at me curiously but held her tongue.

Darius looked down at our hands and laced his fingers through mine before he answered.

"I had the stone replaced before I returned."

"I don't understand how you found time to order a new stone. Do you mean between yesterday and this morning?" I looked at the sun, still early in the day.

"Time has passed since you left, Molly. You do not think I was rescued from the basement looking as clean as this, do you?" He surveyed his suit—similar to the one I'd first seen him in. "I had many things I needed to do before I could come to you."

"What things?" I whispered.

He looked over his shoulder at Sassy who sat in the large picture window behind us. He chuckled.

"Well, I had to rebuild the house, for one."

I gasped and threw a look at Sara who stared at Darius with wide eyes.

"I could not have you return to a burnt shell," he murmured with a self-satisfied smile.

"How-how long did it take you to rebuild the house?" I stammered.

"One year," he said quietly. "I lost you one year ago."

I shook my dazed head.

"How is that possible? How can you have lived a year when I've only lived a day?"

"A better question might be how can he travel in time at all?" Sara muttered as she pulled her feet onto her chair and rested her chin on her knees.

He shrugged his shoulders.

"I still do not know. Given that I was terrified to leave the property—for fear that I might accidentally travel before the house was finished, it took considerably longer than I thought. I avoided entering the road and had everything delivered, and I did not return to the cemetery until just this morning...in my time."

I turned a confused face to Darius.

"So, you went to the cemetery this morning? Did you see Molly?"

Darius shook his head with a faint smile. "No, I have not seen her since she died—at least, not until I saw you a year ago."

"And what happened to James?" Sara asked in an even voice.

"He is in prison," Darius said quietly.

"Good," she said with a smile.

"I agree," Darius returned her grin.

Although I was relieved I would never have to see James again, I was more curious about Darius and his apparent ability to travel through time—at least this time.

"What happened this morning? How did you travel?" I asked.

He gave me a sheepish look and glanced at Sara before dropping his gaze to our entwined hands.

"This is difficult to say. I finished the house yesterday, and I returned to the cemetery for the first time in a year this morning—in my time. I knelt at Molly's gravestone, and I prayed. I prayed to return to you. And the colors began."

At that moment, Darius's heirs pulled up into the driveway in their large town car. Cynthia waved from the passenger side but made no move to get out of the car. Laura climbed out and came up to the porch carrying a packet. Marmaduke jumped down to inspect the car as he always did.

"Hello there. We won't stay. We're just on the way to the cemetery for our last visit before we leave in the morning. I found these extra photographs, and I wanted to drop them off for you."

"Laura! It's so nice to see you," I said as I stood up to take the pictures. "Are you sure you can't stay?"

"No, we have so much to do. We're nowhere near being ready to go," she muttered with a brief smile. She turned to greet Sara and looked at Darius, who had risen at her arrival.

"Darren, it's nice to see you again. Take care of this house now." She tilted her head and gave him a frank appraising stare. "And take care of our Molly here. I can see that you'll still be here when we return in a year for a visit."

I colored and began to stammer with a sideways glance at Darius, who smiled serenely.

"I will take care of her, Laura. You have my word."

"Okay then. We've got to run. Maybe we can stop by tomorrow morning before we leave."

"That would be great," I murmured. I gave her a final hug and watched as she got into the car. Cynthia waved with glee, and we waved back to her.

Marmaduke had given up inspecting the car and had taken up his position alternately standing or pacing across the front of the driveway. Laura turned on her engine, and I called to Marmaduke.

"Kitty. Come here. Get out of the road."

Laura began to back up, and Darius ran off the porch and toward the cat. I ran after him, shouting at Laura to stop. She couldn't hear me with her windows up, and she couldn't see me waving with her head turned over her shoulder. For some reason, she didn't see Marmaduke in the road.

Like a streak, Darius flew down the driveway shouting for Marmaduke. Marmaduke, suddenly frightened, ran into the road, and Darius ran after him.

I screamed then.

"Darius, don't! Don't go into the road," I screamed. "Darius, come back."

Darius snatched up the cat, who looked confused once he'd crossed his invisible barrier. Laura brought her car to a jerking halt, and I ran out into the street to grab Darius.

If he was traveling, I was going with him. I clung to him and looked back at Sara who stood next to the car. I waved to her, and she stared at me in horror.

I closed my eyes and waited for the kaleidoscope, but nothing happened. I felt nothing except Marmaduke's sharp claws as he squirmed in Darius's arms.

I opened my eyes and looked at Darius.

He looked and felt solid, as if he weren't going anywhere. I looked down at our feet. We were definitely in the road. I could see both ways—toward the cemetery and toward town.

Darius looked down at me, and his wide smile seemed brighter than any sun I'd ever seen.

I heard Laura ask us if we were all right, but at that moment, I only had eyes and ears for Darius.

"It is over. I have found you. I do not need to search any longer," he whispered. "I am here to stay with you, Molly, my love."

I reached up and hugged him as tightly as I could, making Marmaduke bellow with rage. Darius put him down, and the cat ran back into the yard to lick his mussed up fur.

Darius put his arms around me, uncaring of who was watching. Out of the corner of my eye, I saw Sara and Laura talking.

"I came forward in time to find you, Molly, and I do not need to travel again. Everything that I love is right here in my arms."

"She's with us, Darius. She shared her memories with me."

"Yes, she would do that," he whispered against my hair. "And you would do that for her. Because you are the same woman. I do not know how this happened, but you came back to me—more clever, more lovely, more intoxicating than ever."

"I love you, Darius." I remembered Molly's sparkling eyes—my eyes—and I knew that they sparkled now. "I have always loved you."

A gentle gust of wind came from the direction of the cemetery and lifted my hair to blow it around my face.

Darius laughed and smoothed it back with tender hands.

"The wind seems to love you as much as I," he chuckled. He put his arm around me, and we turned toward the house that he had built for me.

About the Author

I began my first fiction-writing attempt when I was fourteen. I shut myself up in my bedroom one summer and obsessively worked on a time-travel/pirate novel set in the beloved Caribbean of my youth. Unfortunately, I wasn't able to hammer it out on a manual typewriter (oh yeah, I'm that old) before it was time to go back to school. The draft of that novel has long since disappeared, but the story still simmers within, and I will finish it one day soon.

I was born in Aruba to American parents and lived in Venezuela until my family returned to the United States when I was twelve. I couldn't fight the global travel bug, and I joined the US Air Force at eighteen to "see the world." After twenty-one wonderful and fulfilling years traveling the world and the birth of one beautiful daughter, I pursued my dream of finally getting a college education. With a license in mental health therapy, I worked with veterans and continue to work on behalf of veterans. I continue to travel, my first love, and almost all of my books involve travel.

I write time-travel romances, light paranormal/fantasy romances (lovelorn ghosty stuff), contemporary romances, and romantic suspense. Visit my website at http://www.bessmcbride.com

Made in the USA
San Bernardino, CA
20 February 2015